LIVING

Henry Green was the pen name of Henry Vincent Yorke. Born in 1905 near Tewkesbury in Gloucestershire, he was educated at Eton and Oxford and went on to become managing director of an engineering business, writing novels in his spare time. His first novel, *Blindness* (1926), was written whilst he was still at school and published whilst he was at Oxford. He married in 1929 and had one son, and during the Second World War served in the London Fire Brigade. Between 1926 and 1952 he wrote nine novels, *Blindness*, *Living*, *Party Going*, *Caught*, *Loving*, *Back*, *Concluding*, *Nothing* and *Doting*, and a memoir, *Pack My Bag*. Henry Green died in 1973.

ALSO BY HENRY GREEN

Henry Green

LIVING

*With an introduction
by Paul Bailey*

VINTAGE

Published by Vintage 2000

2 4 6 8 10 9 7 5 3 1

First published in Great Britain by The Hogarth Press 1929

Vintage
Random House, 20 Vauxhall Bridge Road, London SW1V 2SA

Random House Australia (Pty) Limited
20 Alfred Street, Milsons Point, Sydney
New South Wales 2061, Australia

Random House New Zealand Limited
18 Poland Road, Glenfield,
Auckland 10, New Zealand

Random House (Pty) Limited
Endulini, 5A Jubilee Road, Parktown 2193, South Africa

The Random House Group Limited Reg. No. 954009
www.randomhouse.co.uk

A CIP catalogue record for this book is available from the British Library

ISBN 0099285126

Papers used by Random House are natural,
recyclable products made from wood grown in
sustainable forests. The manufacturing processes
conform to the environmental regulations of the
country of origin

Typeset in 10½/12 Sabon by
MATS, Southend-on-Sea, Essex
Printed and bound in Great Britain by
The Guernsey Press Co. Ltd., Guernsey Channel Islands

For Dig

'As these birds would go
where so where would this child go?'

INTRODUCTION

AFTER LEAVING MAGDALEN COLLEGE, Oxford, without a degree, Henry Vincent Yorke worked for some months on the shop floor of his father's engineering works in Birmingham. The firm, H. Pontifex and Sons, had been moved from London to save costs, and many of its Cockney employees had found it necessary to leave their East End homes and settle in the Midlands. The prospect of losing their jobs was too dismal to contemplate. This was in the 1920s, when even factory work was relatively scarce.

Yorke had written one novel, *Blindness*, which was published when he was eighteen. He had chosen the pseudonym Henry Green, after toying with the duller-sounding Brown. The book had won the admiration of Edward Garnett, the champion of Joseph Conrad and D.H. Lawrence, and was favourably reviewed. Green was, by general consent, a promising novelist. What kind of novelist he might have become if he hadn't gone to Birmingham is a matter for speculation, since the work of fiction that came out of the experience changed the course of his writing life. *Living* appeared in 1929 – just to look at the date makes me rub my eyes in disbelief – and has lost none of its originality and its bracing freedom from the tyranny of plot. It captures the inconsequentiality of day-to-day experience, its unanticipated delights as well as its sudden disappointments.

In Birmingham, Green listened – he was a considerable listener – to an English that would not have been tolerated, let alone heard, at Eton and Oxford. It was, bizarrely, the language of the London streets – sharp, spontaneous, coarse, inventive and, he discovered, poetic. It opened his ears. He confessed later that listening to the men in the foundry, their girlfriends and wives, was a constant pleasure. He stayed in working-class lodgings (Vincent, his father, was a skinflint) where he wrote *Living* at night, and joined his mates for a beer in the pub. (In an interview with Nigel Dennis in the 1950s, Green said that some of the best lines in his novels had been overheard in pubs.) His imagination was released by their chatter, which often seemed unstoppable. In *Living*, he is their recording angel. He neither mocks nor judges them. He lets them, quite literally, speak for themselves.

Working-class people in conventional English fiction tend to come in two distinct types. There are the ennobled, battling against the wicked capitalist system that has brought them low, and then there are the comic cautions, touching their forelocks and uttering contrived malapropisms. Angela Carter once remarked that whenever she came across a comic charwoman in a novel, she invariably threw the book against the nearest wall. She must have thrown a lot of them, for that particular character crops up, a regular fixture, in the novels of good, bad and even a few distinguished writers. Those politically committed novelists who enjoyed a vogue in the 1930s, and then again in the 1950s, did not understand that to ennoble is to belittle. Their brave heroes and heroines, for such they are undoubtedly intended to be, have been robbed of an essential humanity. And to create men and women as objects of fun, or perhaps derision, on the basis of their lack of a formal education is to exhibit a certain literary meanness, a lack of honest observation.

Over seventy years ago, Henry Green created real, vibrant human beings in the pages of *Living*. There isn't a trace of condescension when he lets us know that young Lily Gates, who is like a daughter to old Mr Craigan, dreams of going to the Far East after seeing a film set on a tea plantation. She tries to persuade her boyfriend, Bert Jones, who is thinking of emigrating to Canada, that the East would offer him and her better opportunities:

'. . . Anyway what's the hours and wages in a tea plantation.'

'I don't know for sure, but it'll be more than in factories.'

'Yes, but I don't know the trade.'

'They'd learn you. You see Bert there's not so many white men out there, here there's too many, that's what keeps wages low. I say go out to where a working chap's wanted, not where there's too many already.'

'Well and if we did go out, what about the 'eat. Could you stand the 'eat. It's the tropics where tea grows you know.'

'Oh yes I could stand it, yes I like it where it's warm.'

'Ah, but it's hot out there. How'd you know you could?'

'H.O.T. – warm,' she said and rubbed arm between palms of her hand.

'I know I could dear,' and he kissed her while she laughed at him.

'Crazyhead' he kept on saying to her then.

There is a discreet authorial tenderness in the conception of Lily, but then Henry Green is one of the rare male novelists who positively likes women. He affords Lily a natural, if limited, intelligence, and a bright hopefulness when her life takes an unexpected turn for the worse. The ever-pregnant Mrs Eames, happy to be bringing another child into the world, is similarly treated with the kind of disinterest that allows her to be herself. Green never tells the reader what to think about the people in *Living* – a fact that in itself makes the novel revolutionary.

Someone resembling the young Henry Yorke appears in the book as Dick Dupret, the son of the factory's owner, Mr Dupret, who is mortally ill. Dick, in the closing scenes, is shown to be a tough businessman, which – in reality – Henry Yorke wasn't. The real Mr Dupret, as it were, lived to a great age, unlike his fictional counterpart. Vincent York, who barely tolerated his youngest son's second career as a novelist, must have been bemused, at the very least, to find himself being killed off in a strange novel. Vincent, in common with so many of his class, read the popular fiction of the day – John Buchan, say, or Sapper; books with exciting stories. *Living* does not tell an exciting story. Vincent Yorke had no patience with it.

*

What makes Henry Green unique, lastingly so, is his interest in people lesser novelists would consider dull. He writes beautifully about states of boredom and nullity. The monotony of working in a factory, hour upon hour, has seldom been given the attention it receives in this, the first of Green's masterpieces. The men and women in *Living*, as its title suggests, are doing just that. Their inner lives consist of flights of ordinary fancy, unexpressed longings, credible dreams. There is little indication of an intellectual life, especially among the upper-class characters, who are either concerned with money or protocol. Mr Craigan, who is seen with *Little Dorrit* on his lap, is the only person who has read a book of any substance. It is Green's brilliant gift to hint at the secret lives of people generally deemed average by the startling things he makes them say.

My copy of *Living* is scored with a hundred or more underlinings, such is the delight it continues to give me. 'Yes there was a feller opposite my bed that had lengths cut out of his belly', which is said by the storekeeper Albert Milligan on page five is the first of these. Later on, Mr Bridges, the works manager who is known by the men as 'Tis 'im, remarks 'Worry, I've 'ad enough of that washing about in my head to drown a dolphin.' Mr Bridges, too, seems to have a distant knowledge of the now defunct practice of suttee: 'like an Indian widder woman that is burned beside 'er dead husband.'

The reader coming to *Living* for the first time may be disconcerted by the eccentric absence of articles, nouns and, occasionally, verbs. There are, perhaps, too many dropped 'h's. But these are minor irritations. The vivid speech, the contrast between the Dupret family in London and the men and women in Birmingham, the sense that being poor does not exclude a rich way of living – these are qualities to treasure. *Living* remains fresh. It's filled with the kind of stories you can still overhear on buses and trains and in those pubs that don't insist on a dress code. Green understood 'the overtones and undertones' of common speech, as his great admirer V.S. Pritchett noted. The dialogue in *Living* is appropriately, lively.

Here, to end with, is an entire sequence I marked when I read the book in my late twenties. I still love it, missing articles and all. It's at the lyrical heart of this extraordinary, and extraordinarily beautiful, novel:

Miss Gates went out in afternoon to buy food in shops and now was last sunshine of winter on the streets. She came into high road and trams went by her rocking, roaring sound came from them and sound of their bell like metals. Along line of shops which were on each side of this road women in dark clothes went in and out of them.

She passed by and black man passed by her. She had in mind to turn back and look at him. But she saw chest of tea in shop window. She stopped by it. She thought of film she had seen which was advertisement of tea firm, she had seen in it black women that gathered the tea, and how delicate she had thought them and she remembered now, how delicate their arms and hands which did not seem touched by the hard labouring.

Were tins of pineapple in shop window and she wondered and languor fell on her like in a mist as when the warm air comes down on cold earth; in images she saw in her heart sun countries, sun, and the infinite ease of warmth.

Paul Bailey

Bridesley, Birmingham.

Two o'clock. Thousands came back from dinner along streets.

'What we want is go, push,' said works manager to son of Mr Dupret. 'What I say to them is – let's get on with it, let's get the stuff out.'

Thousands came back to factories they worked in from their dinners.

'I'm always at them but they know me. They know I'm a father and mother to them. If they're in trouble they've but to come to me. And they turn out beautiful work, beautiful work. I'd do anything for 'em and they know it.'

Noise of lathes working began again in this factory. Hundreds went along road outside, men and girls. Some turned in to Dupret factory.

Some had stayed in iron foundry shop in this factory for dinner. They sat round brazier in a circle.

'And I was standing by the stores in the doorway with me back to the door into the pipe shop with a false nose on and green whiskers. Albert inside was laughin' and laughin' again when 'Tis 'im comes in through the pipe shop and I sees Albert draw up but I didn't take much notice till I heard, 'Ain't you got nothin' better to do Gates but to make a fool of yourself?' And 'e says to Albert, 'What would you be standin' there for Milligan?' And I was too surprised to take the nose off, it was so sudden. I shan't ever forget that.'

'And that was all that 'e said to you Joe?'

'Not by a mile and a bit. 'E went on about my being as old

as he was, and 'ow 'e'd given up that sort of thing when 'e was a kid, and he told on me to Joe Brown that was foreman in this shop at that time, but 'e didn't take much notice I reckon. Yer know I couldn't take that nose off, I was kinder paralysed. And it was just the same when I see old Tupe fall at me feet this morning, I was that glad I couldn't move one way or t'other to pick 'im up.'

'What does 'e want to go fallin' about for at his age?'

'That's what I told him. I said "You'll go hurtin' yourself falling about one of these days" I said, "and when you do it won't only be but your deserts. It's a judgment on you" I said "to be tumbling at my feet, you dirty old man" I said "for all the things you've said about me and my mate." There were several there. They heard it. Then he started cussin'. I laughed! It 'urt the cheeks in me face.'

'I can't see 'em.'

'You silly bleeder and 'ow does your little bit like it when you come 'ome and lay yer head up against hers on the pillow and her 'as only been married to you three months and as can't be used to the dirt.'

'All right with yer has 'as's, all right.'

'But I'd like to see that Tupe dead and I don't mind who knows it. So 'e will be if 'e goes on fallin' about. Every bloody thing that 'appens straightaway 'e goes and tells 'Tis 'im. I shouldn't wonder if 'e hadn't fetched him when I 'ad the green whiskers on me face. And that was six years ago now. Dirty sod.'

'Ah. He's not like the one you work with Joe. 'E tells too much, Tupe does, always nosing into other people's doings.'

'Tis 'im, who was works manager, and Mr Dupret's son were going about this factory. They went through engineer's shop. Sparrows flew by belts that ran from lathes on floor up to shafting above by skylights. The men had thrown crumbs for them on floor. Works manager said they were in the way, it made him mad, he said, to see them about, 'the men watch them Mr Dupret while God knows what may be up with the job on the lathe. I say to them – don't throw crumbs to sparrows on the floor, one of these days you'll get hurt from not watching your job. We pay them while they bet on these sparrows. And you can't stop it. You can't keep the sparrows out. I've had a man on the roof three weeks now patching holes they come in by. But they find a way.'

Works manager and Mr Dupret's son went through sliding doors and works manager said this was the iron foundry. Black sand made the floor. Men knelt in it. Young man passed by Mr Dupret and works manager.

'What a beautiful face.'

'What? Eh? Well I don't know. He works for that moulder over in the corner. He's getting an old man now but there's no one can beat him for his work. The best moulder in Birmingham Mr Dupret. And he's a worry. That's his labourer there by him now. That man gets on my nerves. I'd have sacked him years ago but I didn't dare. Joe Gates 'is name is. I've seen that man make paper aeroplanes and float them about the shop and I couldn't do anything for fear I might put Craigan in a rage. He won't work with no one else Mr Dupret and he's the best moulder in Birmingham. But then the best engineer I ever met couldn't see you to talk business with you but he 'ad his pet spaniel on a chair by him. There's no accounting for it, none.'

Foreman came up and works manager asked him about stamping frames he would be casting that evening and they talked and Mr Dupret looked at the foundry. He walked over nearer to where Craigan worked. This man scooped gently at great shape cut down in black sand in great iron box. He was grimed with the black sand.

Mr Gates was talking to storekeeper, Albert Milligan. 'And the old man fell at me toes and I wasn't goin' to stretch out me 'and, "lie there" I said to him, "and serve you right you dirty old man" I said, "that has no right to be falling about at your age. Ye'll fall once too often," I said.'

'Ah, he'll kill himself one o' these days. It'll be a judgment on 'im. Everything that goes on 'Tis 'im hears of it through him. But as to falling it ain't healthy for 'im, there was an old chap in 'ospital that had done just the same.'

'That's what I said to 'im. But 'ow would you be feelin' now Albert?'

'Middlin' Joe. I 'ad it bad again yesterday. I said to myself if you sit yourself down you'll grow morbid. So I kept on. It worked off in the end. Yes there was a feller opposite my bed that had lengths cut out of his belly and when they brought 'im in again, an' he come to after the operation, they told him 'e could eat anything that took 'is fancy. So he said a poached egg on toast would suit 'im for a start but when they took it to 'im 'e brought it up. Black it was. And everything they took him after he brought it up just the same till they were givin' 'im port, then brandy and champagne at the end.'

'Ah.'

'And one day I couldn't stick it no longer and I said to the sister, 'I want to go 'ome.' And she said "but you can't." And I said "I want to go 'ome" and she said "but it would kill you Mr Milligan." And I said I didn't mind, "I want to go 'ome" I said. So at last they sent the matron to me. She came and sat by the bed. She could do anything with you, and she said "What's the trouble Mr Milligan?" and I said "I want to go 'ome, I want to sleep in my own bed." And she said "but it'll kill you" and I asked if there weren't an ambulance as could take me. "I can't stick it with that poor feller over there" I said, "what's the matter with 'im that 'e can't keep nothing down. He'll die soon, won't 'e?" And she said "we can't keep them 'ere as God wants to take to himself Mr Milligan." I reckon that was a fine woman. Well I stayed and I seemed to do better after that. And the next day the chap next me said, "What was the matter with you yesterday Albert that you got jumpy like you did? Stick it, you'll be out soon." And I said "yes, I'll stick it," and we shook 'ands on that. But I wouldn't go back.'

'Well you can't expect to get right in a day not after anythin' like what you 'ad. Any road yer looking as fat as an egg now, old sow pig.'

'Out yer go. I got more to do than stand talking to foundry rats. Gor glomey ain't 'Tis 'im about with the governor's son. Come out now, go on back to yer old man. 'E'll be 'owling for yer. But 'ere. Joe, you might've given the old bleeder a 'and up, there was one or two came in here this morning that didn't like your standin' by Tupey and not doin' nothing. And there was no one else but you about for a few moments. Though I'm not saying I shouldn't've done the same.'

''Elp 'im, I'd be dead before. Look what 'e's done to others, what 'e's said along o' their private lives. Give 'im a hand, might as well 'elp the devil shovel coals.'

'Ah. Well so long Joe.'

''Elp that carcase. It was as much as I could do not to wipe me boots on 'is lying mouth. I'll be — before I 'elp 'is kind.'

'And that'll come to you one of these days.'

Mr Gates went back to foundry with chaplets he had fetched from stores shouting against storekeeper's dirty mind, and laughing, but noise of lathes working made it so what he said could not be heard.

(Standing in foundry shop son of Mr Dupret thought in mind and it seemed to him that these iron castings were beautiful and he reached out fingers to them, he touched them; he thought and only in machinery it seemed to him was savagery left now for in the country, in summer, trees were like sheep while here men created what you could touch, wild shapes, soft like silk, which would last and would be working in great factories, they made them with their hands. He felt more certain and he said to himself it was wild incidental beauty in these things where engineers had thought only of the use put to them. He thought, he declaimed to himself this was the life to lead, making useful things which were beautiful, and the gladness to make them, which you could touch; but when he was most sure he remembered, he remembered it had been said before and he said to himself, 'Ruskin built a road which went nowhere with the help of undergraduates and in so doing said the last word on that.' And then what had been so plain, stiff and bursting inside him like soda fountains, this died as a small wind goes out, and he felt embarrassed standing as he did in fine clothes.

Works manager gave up talking to foreman of iron foundry shop and said Mr Dupret must be tired of seeing iron foundry now and they must get on. 'It's all beautiful work we do Mr Dupret, beautiful work. And we turn it out' he said.)

*

5

As Mr Dupret and Bridges walked through the shops Mr Tarver followed them. This man was chief designer in Birmingham factory. He was very clever man at his work.

As they went round he followed, like a poacher, for he had no business to be following them. But above all things he wanted to speak to young Mr Dupret because he was afraid he was being forgotten.

Mr Dupret and works manager came to outside assembling shop. Old man stopped them there, it was Tupe, and told Mr Bridges how he fell that morning. As they talked Mr Dupret began to notice man signalling from behind a big cylinder which had been machined. This man beckoned and waved arm at him, it was Tarver. Mr Dupret turned to works manager but Tupe had got hold of that one's coat and was passionately saying, '– and there was one there as dain't make no move to 'elp me.'

But Mr Dupret interrupted them.

'Mr Bridges I think there's someone wants to see you,' he said, 'that man behind that thing over there.'

'Where?' said Mr Bridges. Tarver had disappeared. Then he saw Mr Tarver walking off behind. 'Oh that's Tarver,' he said, ''e can see me any time.' But Bridges took Mr Dupret away at once, and young Mr Dupret wondered why Bridges seemed displeased.

Afterwards Mr Tarver saw his opportunity. Bridges was called away to look at something and then he came up. He brought it all out in a rush: 'Mr Dupret sir,' he said. 'could I trouble you for a few words with me sir. I figured it out in my own mind that it was my duty and I'll put it to you in this way sir – would you think it right that any works manager, I don't mean especially Mr Bridges there, but any works manager in any factory would let you see none but 'im. Look here Mr Dupret,' he said and went on about how all of them were old men in this firm except Dupret and he, was no punch in what they did, 'no shoulder behind it sir,' he said. Luckily he took strong line with Mr Dupret who at first was surprised, then was beginning to be impressed when works manager came back again.

'That's all right John' said Mr Bridges, 'you get along now.

This way Mr Dupret. Don't you listen to 'im, your dad knows 'im. I keep 'em from you, those like 'im. Ah they're a worry to me. He's a good man mind you, your dad's got a great opinion of 'im and there it is. But 'e's a worry to me' said Mr Bridges and led young Mr Dupret away.

Mr Alf Smith and Mr Jones worked on bench. They were vice hands in the tool room. Both were young men.

Mr Jones said what was the time. Mr Smith went out to where by bending down he could see clock on the wall in shop next to them.

'It wants a ¼ to 4 Bert.'

'Then I'll go and have a sit down,' said Mr Jones.

He went out of their shop but at the door he knocked against Tupe who was struggling with a trolley.

'Look out' he said, 'you nearly 'ad me over then.'

'Over,' cried Tupe, 'over, ah an' I wish you was over an' all. Ah. and talkin' of that, why this morning I tripped over meself. Bang on me 'ead I went and there was Craigan's nose-wiper by me, Joe Gates, but 'e dain't stir, no, 'e watched me lie. But then he's tired, 'e is. Soon as 'e gets 'ome – on with 'is pinney an' 'e does the 'ousework for 'is daughter, her makes 'im. 'Is gaffer's slops an' 'ers. 'E don't get much rest in the night time neither as 'e's reading fairy stories for the old gaffer to get to sleep by. 'E's a wretched poor sort of a man. 'E ain't no more'n my age. Where'll I pull this 'igh speed stuff Bert?'

'You'll go hurtin' yourself one of these days, you know, falling about at your age. Blimey,' said Mr Jones, 'if we picked you up every time one of you old chaps fell down we'd be wore out, regular wore out.'

'Ssh!' said Mr Tupe, 'I ain't a young wench. In course you wouldn't pick 'er up where she'd laid 'erself down. An' that reminds me I seen you out with 'is daughter, only I was forgetting just now. But she ain't destinated your road. Craigan 'as picked 'is young mate for 'er, Jim Dale.'

'So he may pick for all I'm bothering. Come on now, put them rods in 'ere and get out of my road.'

'Where would you be off to then, hurry?' said Mr Tupe. 'Ain't any tarts in this factory, you know, the more's the pity' he said. 'But you ain't a bad young feller so you did ought to look 'igher than Lily Gates. Fly 'igh' he said, 'and you'll see the birds circling up to yer, the darling little tarts. Then you can pick the 'ighest as comes to yer fancy.'

Evening. In their house works manager sat with his wife. He said a hard day it had been, with the young fellow down. It wasn't that he did not mean well young Mr Dupret, 'but they live different to you and me' he said. 'I've worked over forty years. I 'ave been fifteen years manager for Mr Dupret. Then 'e sends his son down, presumably. I say to myself "where am I?" He's good intentioned but 'e's soft. He never took much notice of the works but then he wouldn't do, not having been through the shops. Work with the men, do what they have to do or you'll never be a salesman, I look at it that way. All he wanted was to let our men know the profits. What'd that help them but unsettle them. They wouldn't understand. They'd not draw more money than it. I've worked for 'is father fifteen years. Ten with the O.K. gas plant before. What's he send his son for throwing educated stuff at me? He didn't interfere before. And all through today them others, like crows after sheep's eyes, trying to get 'old of 'im and tell lies. I'm tired. Tired. Takes the use out of you.'

Evening. Was spring. Heavy blue clouds stayed over above. In small back garden of villa small tree was with yellow buds. On table in back room daffodils, faded, were between ferns in a vase. Later she spoke of these saying she must buy new ones and how nice were first spring flowers.

2

MR BERT JONES with Mr Herbert Tomson, who smoked cigarette, walked along street. They did not speak. Then blowing ash from cigarette end he said:

'I'm going off.'

'Where to? Down the road?'

'I'm going off. I'm fed up. In this country it's nothin' doin' all the time. I'm going to Orstrylia.'

'What d'you want to go there for?'

'You can't get on in this country. You'll never get out of that tool room an'll be lucky if you stay there, just the same as I shan't never get off the bench in the engineers but be there all my life. I'm goin' to get off while there's nothin' keepin' me. You can get somewhere out in Orstrylia.'

'And what'll you do when you get there?'

'I got an aunt out there.'

'I got you fixed in me mind's eye tucking away lamb with mint sauce.'

'I wouldn't go ranching not me but in the shops out there where you've got a chance not like 'ere where you're lucky if you keep the job.'

'Well they say there's a lot of unemployment out there.'

'It's those that don't want a day's work I'm for getting on.'

'There won't be no job for you 'Erbert. Take my tip, don't you go, not for nothing. They'll only ship you back again and where'll you be then?'

'I'll 'ave 'ad the trip any road.'

'No but honest are you going?'

'Honest.'

*

Craigan sat at head of table in his house. His mate Mr Gates sat with him to supper and his mate's daughter brought over shepherd's pie from range and the young fellow also was at table who worked with him also in the foundry, Jim Dale.

She laid dish on the table. She wiped red, wet hands on dishcloth. She said:

'Mr Craigan Mrs Eames that's next door, her sister says a job's going with the packers at Waley's.'

'None o' the womenfolk go to work from the house I inhabit' he said.

'Don't get thinking crazy Lily' her father said to her and she wiped fingers white. She carried dirty plates to the sink then.

She came back to table and ate of the shepherd's pie. She took big helping. Her father swallowed mouthful and said:

'You got a appetite' he said. 'You didn't ought to eat that much. Yer mother was sparin'.'

Craigan said: 'Who'd think anybody was the worser off for eatin' a stomach-full at her age.'

Weather was hot. They lived back of a street and kitchen which they ate in was on to their garden. Range made kitchen hotter. A man next door to them kept racing pigeon and these were in slow air. They ate in shirt sleeves. Plump she was. They did not say much.

Baby howled till mother there lifted him from bed to breast and sighed most parts asleep in darkness. Gluttonously baby sucked. Then he choked for a moment. Then he slept. Mrs Eames held baby and slept again.

Later woke Mr Eames. Sun shone in room and Mrs woke.

'Oh dear' he cried. He sneezed.

'What makes you always sneeze at the sun I don't know' she said most parts asleep and he said 'another day.' She now was not quite woke up and said you wouldn't believe, she was so happy now.

'Dear me' he murmured sliding back into sleep.

They slept.

Later alarm clock sounded next door. They woke. She began to get out of bed and he put on his spectacles. 'Another day' he said after he sneezed. She said was one thing to these

10

houses with narrow walls it saved buying alarm clocks; 'they're ten and six now if they're a tanner and it's wonderful to me old Craigan let his folk buy one.' Rod of iron he ruled with in that house she said, pulling on stockings, 'or more likely a huge great poker. That poor girl' she said, 'and not even his daughter but 'e won't let 'er go out to work, nor out of the House Hardly'; and he said, quite awake, 'Oho, listen to your haitches.'

Lily Gates and Jim Dale, who was Mr Craigan's young mate in iron foundry, stood in queue outside cinema on Friday night. They said nothing to each other. Later they got in and found seats. Light rain had been falling, so when these two acting on screen walked by summer night down leafy lane, hair over her ears left wet on his cheek as she leant head, when they on screen stopped and looked at each other. Boys at school had been singing outside schoolroom on screen, had been singing at stars, and these two heard them and kissed in boskage deep low in this lane and band played softly, women in audience crooning. Lily Gates sank lower over arm of her seat. Mr Dale did not move.

Play on screen went on and this girl who was acting had married another man now. She had children now. But her husband thought she still loved other man because when they had first started on the honeymoon this other man had taken his new wife away in the motor car. They had spent night together leaving husband alone in America. But she had gone back to him. They had children now. Still he wasn't sure.

Lily Gates was sitting up now and she told Jim Dale to take arm off arm of her chair; 'you might give me room to move myself in' she said, and he said 'sorry.'

Then this play ended and Lily Gates thought this girl on screen still loved both men though it was meant she should love only her husband. 'She loves the first one still in her heart and then she loves the father of 'er children' she said to herself. Mr Dale spoke and mumbling said band had not played so well tonight and she said he mumbled so you could not tell what he said. Before he could speak again she said he was kill-joy taking the pleasant out of the evening, not that it was not a bad film she said, by saying he thought band had played badly when they had played better than she had known for three months. Then she said she could not understand what he came to cinemas for, to listen to the band and not watch the picture, she liked the stories.

Later her head was leaning on his shoulder again, like hanging clouds against hills every head in this theatre tumbled without hats against another, leaning everywhere.

Eight o'clock of morning. Thousands came up the road to work and few turned in to Mr Dupret's factory. Sirens were sounded, very sad.

Then road was empty, only one or two were running and bicyclist, bent over handle bars, drove his legs fast as he could.

Later office people began to come up road. And man, Mr Tarver, who had spoken to Mr Dupret's son outside brass foundry came along with a man in drawing office, Mr Bumpus, and talked to him. 'Tis 'im, he said, could be decent at times almost or it wasn't decent rather but the pretence and that did not take him in. He and the wife had gone with 'Tis 'im and the wife 'Tis 'er out on motor ride to a ruined abbey 'and you know the style 'e throws himself about in a tea-room well 'e put the napkin under 'is chin which is what the wife won't stand for and while I was talking to his wife there was the wife snatching 'is napkin down each time 'e put it up. It wasn't fair on 'er to behave that way before everyone. You know what womenfolk are. I 'ad a time with 'er that night for taking her but as I put it to 'er I said: "How could I tell 'e was going to indulge himself in what 'e learned in Wales."' They stood now by works office doors and Mr Bridges came in and said:

'How are you, John?'

And he said, speaking refinedly, 'Top hole. What about you Colonel?'

'I'm fine. Come in John. Take a cigar.'

'I'm sure I don't mind, sir.'

'Eh it's a fine leaf, a great smoke. John, I don't know what's the matter with me but I feel like someone had given me a cut

12

over the brow with a five-eighth spanner. Worry, I've 'ad enough of that washing about in my head to drown a dolphin. If another bit comes along it'll displace the brains. Yes there won't be room, something'll have to go. Anyone else'd be dead now in my place. Ah, so it goes on, every day, and then one day it breaks, the blood comes running out of your nose as you might be a fish has got a knock on the snout. Till you drop dead. I'll have to get right away, go right away for a bit.'

They talked. John and Mr Bridges' faces grew red with companionship and Bridges waved cigar and John got smoke once in lungs and coughed; – they shouted together and held each other by the arm.

This girl Lily Gates went shopping with basket and by fruiterer's she met Mrs Eames who stood to watch potatoes on trestle table there. Mrs Eames carried her baby. Lily Gates said why Mrs Eames and oh the lovely baby the little lump. She said she saw prices was going up again. She put finger into baby's hand and sang goo-goo. Then she said to Mrs Eames who had not said much up till then how the old man would not let her try for job at Waley's though she knew her father would not think twice about that if it was for him to decide, who thought only of money. Mrs Eames said to listen at her, talking like that of her own dad. But Lily Gates said it was so lonely doing house all day with the food and everything that it put her all wrong, and Mrs Eames said she would be in rooms of her own not so very long now. Most likely with a husband.

'Well I don't know much about that.'

'That's what you all say. And when you 'ave children's when you'll find your hands full my girl.'

Baby in her arms lay mass of flesh, no bones, eyes open to the sky. Lily Gates sang goo-goo at baby.

Craigan household was at supper. Mr Craigan, Dale his young mate, Joe Gates and his daughter Lily, sat eating rhubarb tart there. Mr Gates asked Mr Craigan if he had ever taken rhubarb wine and that it was very strong, he had had it once. Mr Craigan did not speak. Mr Gates said but after all was nothing to touch good old beer and they could say who liked that water was what lions drank. His daughter Lily broke in saying would he get the beer tonight for she was going to the movies, and he said didn't he fetch it every night and work to buy food for her stomach all day and every. She answered him that she could just change and only be in time for second performance now. He said he'd never go. This time was once too many he said. But Craigan told him to go and fetching down the jug from dresser he stood by mantelpiece. Then why didn't they both go off now both of them he said if they were in so much hurry; but Dale said he was not going. Lily Gates opened door and went out quickly then. Mr Craigan asked slowly who was she going to pictures with; Dale said she had told him it was Bert Jones, who would be the one working with Alf Smith on the bench in tool room. Mr Craigan said nothing and Joe Gates thought Mr Craigan did not mind Lily going out with Bert Jones so he said how when he was young chap his dad would never have let his girls go, but that now things were different. Mr Craigan said nothing so he went out with the jug.

Soon after Lily Gates came quickly out of house and went quickly up the street.

Then when Joe Gates came back with the beer and he and Mr Craigan sat on kitchen chairs and Dale on a box, at back of house before garden, he said he met a man in the public who had told him one or two good tales. Then for some time then Joe Gates told dirty stories. He spoke of tarts and birds. 'An' speakin' of birds' he said, 'look there's a bird caught in the window.' (Window was open and a sparrow was caught between upper and lower window frames.) He went over and began to push up upper frame to free this bird. But it fluttered and seemed as though it would be crushed Mr Dale said, 'don't push 'er up so Joe, you'll crush it,' and he went over to the window. Mr Dale said he would put his hand in between the two frames, which he did, but bird fluttered more and pecked at his finger. 'Don't go 'urting it Jim don't be so rough with the little bleeder' Joe Gates said and Dale answered him 'ain't they got sharp beaks to 'em.' Joe Gates now took over and raised upper frame again, and gently. This bird only fluttered the more. At this time Mr Craigan came over and took fork and said to leave it to him. Very gently he pushed up upper frame and put fork under the bird and very gently tried to force the bird up but the bird got away from this fork and fluttered. Then all three together moithered round the window and then they all drew back and watched and the bird was still. Then Craigan said to fetch Mrs Eames and Dale went. Mr Craigan and Joe Gates stood and said nothing, watching, and now still the bird was quiet.

Mrs Eames came and she lowered upper frame and put hand in and gathered this bird up and gently carefully lifted it out and opened hand and it flew away and was gone. Mr Gates asked to strike him dead. Mr Dale said it looked easy the way she done it, and Mr Craigan, dignified and courtly, said they had to thank Mrs Eames for what three men could not do. She said, 'Where's Lily then?' and Mr Dale said she had gone out. Mrs Eames said what a fine evening it was to be sure but Craigan was saying no more though Mr Gates began talking at once to Mrs Eames; this happening of the bird put him in mind of some stories, he said, and not long after Mrs Eames had gone, offended. Dale said she did not like Joe's stories and Joe Gates answered that anyone could see it and he knew it before but he wanted to wake her up he said. Mr Craigan did not speak and looked to be troubled in his mind. He sat outside in the last light of sun which had shone all day.

In the evening Gates went to public house. He went alone, which he did not do often. Every Monday night Mr Craigan and he went together to their public house but this was Friday so he went further up Coventry Road to house he did not often visit. Tupe was there. At first they did not speak. Mr Gates looked at tiled lower part of wall (pattern on the tiles was like beetles with backs open and three white lilies in each of these) and he looked at rows of bottles on shelves against mirror glass which was above these tiles and at paper doylies which now again regularly were under bottles there and hung down in triangles from the shelves. (Orange coloured roses with a few curly green leaves were round corner of these which hung down.) Then Tupe shouted across saying was no

15

use in saying nothing and what would he have and Mr Gates said another half of mild and he was obliged he said. Soon they were sitting next each other and they told dirty stories one after the other to each other and Gates laughed and drank and got a little drunk.

Soon then Mr Tupe made him begin laughing at old Craigan. Mr Gates never used to laugh about that man. Soon he told Tupe Lily had gone out with Bert Jones and left Dale at home. Tupe said didn't the old man mean Lily to marry Jim Dale and Mr Gates said Craigan was mad at her going. Tupe said wasn't Joe Gates her father and wasn't a father's word enough in arranging for his daughter and Gates said but Craigan hadn't dared speak to her about having gone out like that. He had said you put a girl wrong with you nowadays and like too independent minded if you talk to her straight away. Tupe said wasn't Joe Gates her father and wasn't what a father said and thought enough for his girl without another interfering. And soon Mr Gates was saying it was and never again would he let himself be bossed in his family, not ever again, no, not he, said he.

Joe Gates stood by tap in factory, drinking water, and Mr Tupe came by wheeling barrow of coke. 'What'll you 'ave' Tupe cried and Mr Gates answered him 'a pint of mild.' 'It's strange to see you drinkin' water' and Gates said he could hardly believe it of himself but they had been casting in their shop and running metal made their shop warm in such weather. Maybe Aaron Connolly had the only cool job, he said, up on travelling crane in the machine shop among draughts; but it was cold up there in winter. Tupe said perhaps that was why he was so mingy, not a penny coming from his pocket without his making a groan. But he had been paid out for it. Had Joe Gates heard, he asked, about the other night, and reason for Aaron Connolly's black eye next morning. He had told his son it wasn't right him paying so little in at end of the week at home, 'not as if Aaron drew more'n labourer's wages though he be on the crane,' Tupe said. 'But 'is son up and knocked him spark out, and he done a good job that night.' Mr Gates laughed and said that would

16

teach him. 'Ah and his missus' said Tupe 'dropped the chamber pot on his head not so long ago when 'e was at her for buying a 'aporth of salt, her being on the landing as he were coming upstairs.' They walked through machine shop, Joe Gates laughing with Mr Tupe when five-eighth spanner fell from above close to them. They looked up and saw the crane but they could see no one on the crane. 'Hi Aaron' bawled Mr Tupe and Mr Connolly's face came out over side of it, 'Hi Aaron you'll be killin' people next dropping things, bein' like palsied from 'oldin' too tight on to yer money.' 'In 'ell they will stoke the coke on your tongue babble baby' he answered and several men laughing at Tupe, Gates also, he went off with his barrow load. Mr Gates went to the stores.

Just then in iron foundry shop Craigan look up from big cylinder he was making and beckoned to boy who was one of the boys making cores. This one came up. Craigan said how would he like piece of cake and while boy ate piece of cake he said it was easier for boys in foundries now than when he started. Boy said it may have been but all the same wouldn't have been a misery like Craigan in any iron foundry, not to touch him, not since they started. Mr Craigan said in his young days you could never have said that to a moulder when you were core boy. 'You would say worse' boy said and Craigan said this one would never make a moulder. 'And your mate' boy said ''as been laughin' with old Tupey this last 'alf 'our, I seen 'em' boy said earnestly. Craigan answered him 'Clear off my lad and don't tell tales.'

Mr Milligan who was storekeeper told Joe Gates about his health. But soon he came back to iron foundry and Dale told him to look out against Mr Craigan.

3

'WHAT WILL WE do with him? Beauty, when you grow to be a man, eh, what will we do with you?'

Waking, Mr Eames turned over. Rain came down outside.

'When you grows to be a man, a man.' She put her face up against his. 'Maybe like your dad you'll be a turner when you're a man. Beauty!' She sighed. She fed him. She felt cold, and he was warm.

His father said: 'a turner like his dad?' and she answered for him saying: 'Yes and so long as 'is lathe goes round he'll be there, earning 'is money like 'is dad.'

Mr Eames said it always did rain in this town though garden would benefit.

'When you're grown you'll be a turner, lovely, when you're grown up. We shan't be up to much work not when you've been a man for long so you'll look to our comfort when we'll have worked to see you come to strength. Beauty, ma's cold but if she draws up the clothes you'll stifle seeing you're still at me.'

Mr Eames sneezed again.

'And when you're grown you'll marry and we shall lose you and you'll 'ave kiddies of your own and a 'ouse of your own, love, we'll be out in the cold. (Ain't it chill this morning?) Why do we bring kids into the world, they leave you so soon as they're grown, eh? But you don't know one of these things yet. But sure as anything you'll leave us when you're a man, and who'll we 'ave then, eh cruel? Sons and daughters why do we bring them into the world?' She was laughing. 'Because, because' she said laughing and then lay smiling and then yawned.

*

18

'"Yes I'm goin' to Orstrylia" 'e said' said Aaron Connolly to Mr Eames, '"I'm goin' to Orstrylia, don't care what no one says but I'm goin'," 'e said. And I told 'im not to be 'asty but to bide 'is time, that's what I told 'im – "it am a grand country for one that 'as some money," I said, "but it am a 'ard bleeder for one that ain't."'

'That's right,' said Mr Eames.

'It am right' said Mr Connolly. 'I told 'im right but 'e wouldn't listen. "It am a grand country" 'e said to me, "this be a poor sodding place for a poor bleeder," 'e said. "I'm for going'." I said "don't be a fool 'erbert, sure as your name's Tomson you'll be back within the year without you go Christmas time and where'll you be then?" I said. 'E laughed and made out 'e'd 'ave this trip any road and I told 'im 'e'd be laffing tother side of 'is mug when 'e got back, "for what d'you get for nothin' not since the war?" I said. "Time was they'd give pint and a 'alf measure when you asked for the usual, but now they put publicans in jug if so 'appen they give yer a smell over the pint."'

These two were in lavatory. Mr Eames went so soon as he was done but Connolly waited there. He smoked pipe against the rules. Mr Bert Jones came in.

Aaron told him how Mr Tomson said he was going to Australia and Bert Jones said he had been the one to tell Aaron himself. 'Well now' said Aaron Connolly 'but 'e told me I'll be positive.' It seemed crazy notion anyway you looked at it said Mr Jones, why not go to Canada he said, though it was fool's game to go at all. Tupe looked in then. At once he went away. After Aaron Connolly said how he was glad always to see backside of that man's head he said Eames was poor sort of a chap, most likely ginger pop was all he could stomach, and Bert Jones lit cigarette. They gossiped. Mr Bridges came in then. He caught them smoking, both of them. He was very angry. 'Discipline,' he shouted, 'keep the shops going, I got to do it. When I come in, here I find you smoking. It's our bread burning away. I got to stop smoking. I don't come in 'ere once but I find someone miking. Firm'll be ruined. Debtor prison. Siam. Bankrupt.' He gave each fortnight's holiday after shouting much more.

When he was gone Bert Jones said Father had not been in for over twelve month. Aaron Connolly spat and said, 'It am Tupe done it. It am Tupe. Nor it won't be spanners I'll drop next time.'

They were in cinema. Band played, tune tum tum did dee dee. She hugged Dale's arm. She jumped her knees to the time.

Couple on screen danced in ballroom there. She did not see them. Dee dee did da.

Tum tum tum tum tum. Dale did not budge. Dee dee de did dee. She hummed now. She rolled his arm between her palms. Da da did dee – did dee dee tum, ta.

'I do love this tune' she said.

'Ah' he said.

Did dee dee tum ta. Tune was over. She clapped hands and clapped. Applause was general. But film did not stop oh no heroine's knickers slipped down slinky legs in full floor.

eeeee Lily Gates screamed.

OOEEE the audience.

And band took encore then. Tum tum ti tumpy turn.

Lily arranged her hair. Dum dum di dumpy dum.

She hummed then. She moved her knees in time. Heroine's father struggled with policeman now in full ballroom. She did not watch but jumped her knees now. Da da did DEE – (what a pause!) – did dee dee tum ta. Great clapping of hands. Attendant moved up gangway and shouted 'Order please.' He moved down. Lily Gates said to young Mr Dale he didn't take much interest in nothing did he? 'Why not take a bit of fun Jim when it comes your way?' she softly said. He said 'I can't enjoy the music when I'm not in the mood.' 'Why you funny' she said ''ave a mood then.' He said 'Don't call me your names Lil when there's so many can 'ear you.'

'Why they're all listenin' to the music.' She was whispering 'Jim!'

She hummed tune band was now playing whey widdle o.

'It's 'ot in 'ere' he said.

'H.O.T. warm' she said.

'Why they're playin' it again' she said. She looked at screen.

She saw heroine's knickers again were coming down, now in young man's bedroom.

ooeee she screamed.

EEEEE the audience.

The band played that tune. Tum tum ti tumpy tum. Dum dum di dumpy dum. She jumped her knees to time. Da da DID DEE – (it wasn't her knickers after all) – did dee dee tum ta.

In Dupret factory man had now been put on guard over the lavatory door. He had to clock men in and out.

'Seein' we're animals 'e's got to treat us as animals' Mr Bentley cried very much excited. 'Put a man on at the lavatory door, it ain't decent, seven minutes every day ain't long enough for a man to do what nature demands of 'is time, stop 'im a quarter 'our of 'is pay if 'e's a minute over why 'e ain't allowed to do it by law, I'm raisin' the question in the Club tonight, and if I was out o' work for three years I wouldn't take on a job of that description. It's plum against the laws of this land, checking men in and out o' lavatories and only seven minutes for each man. Why in kennels even they don't do it.'

'You go and see Tupe about it, Bob, 'e brought it on.'

'I know nowt against Tupe. There's no proof 'e went to Bridges when 'e saw Aaron here and Bert smoking. It ain't justice 'im sending Bert off for a fortnight and having Aaron stay back – no offence to you mate.'

'It am a bleeder. "Aaron" 'e says to me "Aaron I got no one but you to work that crane in your shop. But man" 'e said, "the next time and you're sacked and out you go." It am a bleeder.'

Joe Gates was saying as much to Mr Craigan in iron foundry shop. And Dale asked him why he went round with Tupe then and Mr Gates said me never and Dale said he seen him and Joe Gates answered it might have been once. (They were ramming.) Gates said Tupe should have tongue cut and why didn't some of the shop go and dig his grave in his back garden to show him. When he smiled it rained, Mr Gates said of him, and he'd be glad when he was dead: 'glad, more'n glad, I'll go straight into the boozer and 'ave one.'

'Think you'll live to see 'is 'earse?' Dale asked him.

'Me' cried Mr Gates 'with my clean life and 'is dirty living, me?' cried Mr Gates.

4

MRS DUPRET AND her son, (who had walked round factory with Mr Bridges) these two were in drawing-room of the London house; each had engagement book, hers she had laid on her knees, he held his up close to his nose, so she would not see him picking his nose.

She said: 'Tuesday fortnight then is the first evening I've got free.'

Slowly he turned pages.

'No I can't manage Tuesday fortnight I'm dining with the Masons for their dance.'

Mr Tarver came home.

'The old man's been at it again' he said to wife. 'Been and sacked my best fitter.' 'Jim!' said Mrs Tarver. 'Yes sacked 'im, said 'e was faking his time on the outdoor jobs but it's spite, that's it go and sack the only man who can put up my work and then expect me to carry on.' 'It's low' said Mrs Tarver. 'Low' said Mr Tarver, 'low' he said 'but when Walters comes down Wednesday from the London office I'll speak straight out to him, but it's crazy, 'ow can you do your work conscientiously and be 'eld up like this and a pistol put to your heart. It is a firm. It's a policy of obstruction. Do you know what 'e did today on top of that, 'e caught two men lounging about and gave one a fortnight's holiday and let the other johnny off. Well you can't do things like that. You can't run a factory on those lines, one rule for one and none for the other. I'll go raving mad. Then my fitter.' 'It's downright low' said Mrs Tarver. 'Whitacre was the only man I could trust,' he said, 'the others would put a spanner into the job and

23

wreck it to please 'im, or they didn't know the difference between a nut and a washer. It's no wonder we're the laughing stock of every firm in Brummagen. If I 'ad a better chance I'd go this minute. But I got nothing to show for it, 'e's seen to that, 'olding my stuff up in the shops and in the end, after you've 'owled to get it, turning out a job a dog wouldn't sniff. Then 'e says it's the design, while 'e can't read a drawing. Why if you asked 'im the principle underlying the simple bolt and nut 'e couldn't tell you. It's sickening. I'm wearing away the best years of my life. Walters's in league with him, 'e's backed 'im up all along. There's only Archer on my side. I'll write to Mr Dupret, that's what I'll do. I saw 'is son but 'e's a schoolboy, 'e didn't take it in. That's what I'll do. I'll write to Mr Dupret.'

'You write to Mr Dupret, John and act by what your conscience tells you and he'll see you're a honest man.'

'That's right, I'll do it. What is there for supper? I'll write after I've 'ad a feed. I'll put it to 'im this way, I'll say . . .'

He wrote to Mr Archer, chief accountant in London office, instead.

Mr Bridges picked up letter in his office.

'Ah these cylinders, they're a worry' he said to Miss Alexander, typist. 'In business there's always something wrong, I've had my share of it. These big cylinders, you never can depend on them. And 'ere's Simson howling for delivery and Walters been shouting for 'em from London. I said to 'im on the telephone, "What can I do?" Can never depend on a foundry, same job same men and perhaps they'll go three months without a waster and then they'll get a run of seven that are scrap and a loss to the firm. It's enough to drive you crazy, eh?'

'Yes Mr Bridges.'

'Tarver sent those drawings down?'

'Not yet Mr Bridges.'

'Then why the devil not eh? Here I am, been waiting for 'em six weeks now. What's up with the man?'

'He's been very excited lately ay think.'

'I can't understand Tarver. What's the matter with him

24

anyway. I can't live with that fellow about, my life's no pleasure to me. And I take him with his wife out in the car, there's nothing I don't do, keeping everyone happy.'

'Yes and grateful you'd hardly believe' said Miss Alexander, 'ay don't think he knows the meaning of a long word layke that, why he said you were crazy only yesterday Mr Bridges.'

'What? Eh? What d'you mean? How do you know about that any way?'

'He said it to my face.'

'Did 'e? In front of you. It's a comedy ain't it? What's 'e mean. Crazy am I? You see who'll be in Siam first, him or me. That's what it is, you work with a man, you make things difficult for yourself to be pleasant and easy, and then 'e rounds on you. Spits in your face. It's dis'eartening. Walters knows how things are and 'e can't abide the man no more than me. I'll see him. I'm through. Done up. Who's manager here, perhaps 'e can tell me, Mr lord Tarver? Yes, who's boss here? Said it to your face? I'll wait till tomorrow though. I might raise my 'ands to 'im if I saw 'im now. Yes there's no knowing what I might do to him, so his mammy wouldn't know 'im.'

Four o'clock. And now men in iron foundry in Mr Dupret's factory straightened their backs for the fan had been started which gave draught in cupola in which the iron was melted. They stood by, two by two, holding ladles, or waiting. Craigan and Joe Gates and Dale stood by their box ready weighted for pouring and in which was mould of one of those cylinders. They said nothing. They had worked all day. The foreman stood near by. They waited. Gates was tired. Foreman stood near by. Mr Craigan threw spade to ground then which had been in his hand. He went up to foreman.

'I know there's been three wasters off this job better'n nobody. But man I'll tell you this'ns a good un.'

'Right you are Phil' foreman said and moved away. 'I can't sleep at night for those cylinders' he told himself again, 'I can't sleep at night. I took tablets last night' he told himself 'but did I sleep, no I did not. No I didn't sleep,' he said to himself, moving away.

'Dirty bleeder, what call 'as 'e to stand waiting for?' said Mr Gates muttering.

'You talk more'n is natural in a man' Mr Craigan said and then no word was said between them not while their eight ton of metal was carried them in a ladle by the crane or after when they fed their casting, lifting their rods up in the risers and letting them down, and again and again.

Later moulder going home, his boxes cast, called to Gates saying: 'is it a good one this time Joeie?' and Mr Gates answered him it would be if his sweat was what it used to be.

In the foundry was now sharp smell of burnt sand. Steam rose from the boxes round about. On these, in the running gates and risers, metal shone out red where it set. On Mr Craigan's huge box in which was his casting Mr Craigan and Jim Dale stood. They raised and lowered long rods into metal in the risers so as to keep the metal molten. Steam rose up round them so their legs were wet and heat from the molten metal under them made balls of sweat roll down them. Arc lamps above threw their shadows out sprawling along over the floor and as they worked rhythmically their rods up and down so their shadows worked. Mr Craigan called to Gates to take his place. He got down off the box. He sat himself on a sieve and wiped his face. And all this time as the metal set and contracted down in casting so metal which they kept molten by disturbing it with their rods, sank in the risers down to the casting. So their strength ebbed after the hard day. Mr Craigan's face was striped with black dust which had stuck to his face and which the sweat, in running down his face, had made in stripes. He put hands up over his face and laid weight of his head on them, resting elbows on his knees.

Continuing conversation Mrs Dupret said to her son well she was sorry it could not be then, she had so wanted they should have one quiet evening together, well it would have to be another time. He said some other time. Immediately he thought: 'When I am with her I echo as a landscape by Claude echoes.' She yawned. She said it was so boring discussing engagements and he answered he thought planning the

26

evenings most important part of the day. Immediately, as was his custom, he analysed this and thought very clever what he had said, and correct.

She yawned and said she was tired, season was so busy.

He said he was tired, last night had been late.

'Whose dance dear?'

'The Whites'. I was back at four. And tonight it will be late again,' he said. 'I take Mary on to Prince's after Mrs James' dance.'

They went in to dinner, Mrs Dupret and her son. Butler and footman brought soup to them.

'James' said Mrs Dupret after searching 'I left my handkerchief upstairs' and footman went to get this.

'Now this is very unexpected' she said to son, 'Emily threw me over and here you are when I thought we were never going to have our quiet evening together.'

'Dolly chucked me. I'm tired. It's so tiring in the train.'

'Yes trains are very uncomfortable now. You went to the works at Birmingham today didn't you? Tell me about it.'

'Well there's nothing to tell really. I'd never been before you know. It was all grimy and tiring. It was so dirty there that I had to have a bath as soon as I was back before going out to tea somewhere. Where did I go for tea now? But no matter, yes, the works, yes you know there's a kind of romance about it or perhaps it's only romantic. In the iron foundry the castings, they call them, were very moving. And there was a fellow there who had a beautiful face, really beautiful, he was about my age . . .'

(He went on talking and she thought how true when she had told Grizel he was really so appreciative.)

'. . . . but it was pretty boring on the whole.'

'Tell me' she said with fish before her, 'are you still happy in the London office?'

'It's all right, but of course I can't do anything. You can't shift Father, he's set in his ways and the others are like him, you've no idea of it, they've had no fresh blood in the show for years. Look at Bridges the manager at Birmingham, he's an old man, so's Walters our head man in London, they all

27

are. A man came up to me in the works just now and said as much, he'd be Tarver I expect, he's about the only coming younger chap in the place. You see Father's all right in his way only he's slow, but he hasn't the time with all his other business.' And while he talked she thought what a success it had turned out, putting him into business.

'What we want in the place is some go and push' he said 'but it's what none of them seem to realize.'

She smiled and had occasion to sniff. 'Where can James have got to' she cried, breaking into his argument. 'I sent him for a handkerchief while we were at the soup, and here we are in the middle of the fish.'

She pushed button of bell; this was in onyx. She laid hand by it on table and diamonds on her rings glittered together with white metal round onyx button under the electric light. Electric light was like stone. He was cut short by her. He was hurt at it. He kept silence then.

'Pringle,' she said to butler 'would you mind going up to see what has become of James?'

Mr Walters was saying in Mr Bridges' office at Birmingham factory if you took average profits of all engineering firms in the country you found it was but three per cent. Mr Bridges said 'that's right, that's right.' Mr Walters went on saying were no profits anywhere, why look if they quoted for one of their big cylinders their price was double what those Belgians asked. 'It is' said Mr Bridges.

'It's wonderful isn't it?' said Mr Walters.

'You've got it' said Mr Bridges. 'Not as if' he said 'there isn't worry every minute either, it wasn't as if we sat still and did nothing. And you can't keep your men' he shouted. 'Whitacre now, one of the best fitters I've taught, what's he do? He goes and fakes his time. He's on a job outside and takes three days off and charges it on the firm. Says he was working. But I've got the letter here, from their manager, complaining 'e wouldn't stay on the job. I sacked him, had to. What can you do? Then I go into the latrines, what do I run into, more trouble two robbers sitting on the seat, without even their trousers off, smoking. I said to them "You might as well go straight to the chief's back pocket and take the money from it." That's right isn't it? I'm going to put a honest man on at the door to clock 'em in and out, seven minutes each man. And one of them was the crane driver in the machine shop, a key man. Then when I sack that Whitacre Tarver comes to me and says I did it to spite 'imself. To spite him! Said he was the only one could do his work. But I never get his work, that's where it is, I never get it down from the drawing office, I've been standing my thumbs tied for a drawing seven weeks now. What can you do, eh? 'E's no good.'

'I don't know Arthur, we've got to be careful. Young Mr Dupret thinks well of him, and his father does.'

'What's the young chap know of it?'

'I know but don't you forget he's the one the old man sees most often. If he was in his pram I'd still treat him like a lord. What do you know he tells the old man about us, the old man don't come into the office often now. He's getting shaky, he might be run into by a bus, with this circular traffic you're lucky if you get away with it crossing the street. He'll leave it all to his son soon.'

'And I've served 'im faithfully for fifteen years. It's a nightmare. Where am I, eh? Where do I stand then, tell me that.'

Mrs Eames put cold new potato into her mouth.

'Ain't they good' said she.

'They are' he said.

'Better'n what you could get up the road or if you took a tram up into town.'

'There's none like your own.'

So for a time they ate supper. She sat on then looking out of window. When she turned and put hands on table to get up and clear away supper she noticed those flowers.

'Why look' said she 'you brought 'em back from the garden only yesterday and I put them in that pot, and now all their faces've turned to the sun.'

5

WATER DRIPPED FROM tap on wall into basin and into water there. Sun. Water drops made rings in clear coloured water. Sun in there shook on the walls and ceiling. As rings went out round trembling over the water shadows of light from sun in these trembled on walls. On the ceiling.

They came back from work. Mr Joe Gates was speaking.

'Ah and didn't I tell that foreman only a month or two back it would go, silly cow keeping on using it till it went. "It's dangerous" I said to 'im "it's dangerous it'll go one of these days" I said "you see, it's all wore away that wire rope is and the block too, look at it, being lopsided like that, it ain't safe." And he said "What business is it of yourn?" and I said "Ain't my life my business with a daughter to keep at 'ome" and 'e said one of these days 'e'd get on a line about me so I sheered off then, it doesn't serve no purpose to lose a job through just talking, might as well lose it for something better'n that, knock 'is bloody 'ead off.'

Mr Craigan washed first in basin. Lily Gates came in then.

'D'you know what nearly came to pass Lily, it were nearly all up with 'im, ah, the wire rope parted when they were pulling out the trolley with it from the core stove. Ah and it dain't miss 'im but by inches.'

Lily Gates went to basin and stood there by Mr Craigan.

'Why grandad!' she said.

'Ah and when I sees 'im standin' there I thought to meself it ain't safe standin' there, now if it went now it would get anyone as was standin' there as 'e was. Then it parted. It dain't miss 'im but by inches.'

30

Mr Craigan dried face and hands. Joe Gates put head under the water in basin.

'It weren't far off' Mr Dale said.

'You mightn't have come back?' Lily Gates picked piece of cotton off his sleeve.

'Don't do that my wench' Mr Craigan said 'I can still do that for meself.'

'It didn't ought to be' said Mr Gates, drying face.

'They did ought to look to them things and not wait till you complain to 'em about it and then do nothing. With that trolley gear and with the boxes you've got to wait for 'em to go before they change them and when a box breaks when the crane's carrying it the feller underneath, why think of it, flat, when I was working at Grey's I seen a feller catch a six by four box on top of 'im and when they lifted it it was just like they'd mangled 'im, 'orrible, like as if they'd mangled 'im, like they'd put a steam roller on to 'im. It's a funny thing to get a living by ain't it?'

Once she had said to Mrs Eames she had said it made you ridiculous she had said walking with Jim, yes she had said that to Mrs Eames, when he looked odd like that, daft you might say, she had gone far as that even, dafty with his eyes yes, she had said, yes and with the girls tittering behind him it made you feel awkward to be with him and Mrs Eames had said she shouldn't be so touchy, not she meant you shouldn't be particular so she said, but touchy it only brought you trouble in this world so your life wasn't your own, that's how she thought so she had said. Now walking with Dale Lily thought that. Girls tittering behind not that he was posh. Not as if they would like to be with him, but for his being strange.

She wasn't the giggling sort. No.

So it wasn't hardly respectable going up the street with him, drawing so much notice.

(He had on bowler hat, high, high crown. Thousands walked along broad pavements of this big street in bowler hats with high, high crowns, in sun, in evening.)

He didn't ever speak either.

(She walked with him, arm round his arm. Party in front,

four girls four young men, the girls on one pavement men on the other side, two parties but one at same time, these did Charleston dance along pavements.)

'What d'you think of that?' she said.

'Ah' said he.

'It mightn't be a public place where they can see you for all they take notice of' she said 'be'aving as if they was in their favourite dance 'all; it's funny what people are coming to these days' she said.

They walked on, said no more. He was pale. Many were laughing, screeching, not at him really, perhaps partly, but it was Friday night.

She then had to sneeze. As she sneezed Mr Dale called out: ''Ello.'

She said: 'Yes it's me sneezing, I know that thank you.'

''Ello' he said to Mr Bert Jones who had come up.

'Oh' she said.

''Ow do Jim, I hear your old man very near 'ad a nasty accident last night.'

'Ah and it was a near go and all. 'Ow d'you come to 'ear?'

'Oh someone round at the club. So you 'eard about my being suspended for a fortnight.'

'It's the talk of the shops. By the way you know Miss Gates would you? This is Bert Jones from our place.' Lily Gates shook hands, holding limply out hand, looking down her nose.

'I believe we've met before' said Mr Jones. He had on plum coloured suit, trousers were cone-shaped.

'And it was Jim here introduced us' said Miss Gates furiously.

'Now I come to think on it it would be' Mr Dale said.

'I remembered right enough' said Mr Jones.

'Did you?'

'It's the talk of the shops' Mr Dale said. 'Giving you a fortnight's 'oliday and not doing the same by Aaron.'

'Ah it's a firm ain't it. Twisting, twisting all the time. And by all I 'ear what nearly made your old man a goner was the fault of their never getting new equipment. It's the same old tale, in our shop anyway.'

'You're right. I don't know if you knows your way about a foundry but we 'as to dry some moulds before the metal can be poured into 'em. They're put on a trolley, see, and the crane pulls it into the stove with a wire rope. Well the wire rope give. Ah, it parted right at the top, mate, right by the eye and whipped out not above a foot away from our old man. It's wicked I reckon.'

'No, they don't give you a square deal. If you work for them they ought to see you can do it with a decent amount of safety.'

'Yes' said Lily Gates. 'I think it's a shame, yes, I do.'

'That's right. And you can't get a job outside, that's where it is. So we've got to put up with it and there it is. But you know 'erbert Tomson, well 'e's going to Australia,' but Mr Dale was not listening.

''E's a feller that works in the fitters. I don't know. They tell me there's not a great many jobs going there.'

''Ere you don't mind' Dale said suddenly. 'See you in the park' he said pointing across road and quickly went off.

'Well that's a bit sudden.'

'It's his digestion you see' said Miss Gates.

'Ah.'

'It comes over him all of a sudden, yes, no matter where 'e may be' she said furiously.

'But that's a bad bit of news about your old man.'

'Yes' she said. 'There'd still've been breadwinners in the house,' she said, 'but where we'd've been without 'im I don't know at all. We all live by Mr Craigan.'

'All the men in the place respect 'im.'

''E's been like a father to me. And now I shan't' lie quiet in my bed at night for thinking harm'll come to 'im.'

'Ah.'

They stood silent.

'Look 'ere' he said 'shall we go across the road into the park' he said 'and wait for Jim there?'

'Oh! I shouldn't like to.'

'Go on. I got nothing on tonight.'

'I don't like to bother you like that. You go on, I'll wait here.'

'Get out. It's a pleasure.'

'Oh well it's nicer in the park isn't it?'

They crossed the road.

'We went to the Lickeys Sunday' she said.

'It's nice there isn't it.'

'Yes, and don't they keep the roads beautiful with the grass in between them and the trams going one road and cars t'other. Yes it's a pleasure to be there of a Sunday afternoon. I'd say I saw quite seven from our street up there. And only a 6d bus ride.'

'Ah, it's worth a tanner every time.'

'Yes it is. Yes we all went there last Sunday. Mr Craigan said 'e'd like a bit of fresh air after all the hot weather we've been 'aving so we packed up and went. I cut steps of bread and cheese that we took with us, oh we did 'ave a time.'

'I reckon it was a good thing when the Corporation took it over, giving the people somewhere to go on a Sunday.'

'Yes because you can get right out into the country and get the fresh air. You know where we live there's a factory where they make phosphor bronze they call it, I don't mean they make only that but when they're making it the fumes come down into our 'ouse when the winds is one way and the fumes is awful. I wonder the poor fellows can stick it inside.'

'It's terrible stuff by all accounts.'

'Yes. Of course we could live in a better part than we do now but Mr Craigan won't live in another man's house, yes that's what he says isn't it funny, and 'e bought this one years back and he wouldn't change now for love nor money. I keep 'ouse for them. Of course it's very lonely sometimes, there being no one much to talk to while they're all out at work. Yes sometimes I wish I could go outside into a factory but Mr Craigan won't hear of it, yes, isn't it funny. He won't 'ear of it. Still I get along I suppose like we all do.'

'It must be lonely at times.'

'It isn't as if you don't soon get used to that though, don't you.'

'I'm glad that accident didn't turn out any worse for 'im. Did 'e seem at all affected by it.'

'No but 'e'd never show you you know. But isn't it a shame

34

about your being suspended, well I never.'

'I thought I'd lose you' Mr Dale said coming up 'seeing it's dark in this park. Lil' he said 'we ought to be going 'ome or the old man won't like it.'

'I'd better be getting along' said Mr Jones and they said goodnight then and went their ways.

'Where'd you go?' she said. 'There ain't no public lavatory for miles round 'ere.'

'In the Horse and Lion.'

'Well what about it?'

'What about what?'

'Work.'

'How's that?'

So began Mr Bridges to Tarver, so Tarver answered him. That's how he answers me thought Bridges. Then Mr Bridges said he didn't see Tarver got through anything, couldn't go on like that, here he'd been six weeks for those drawings, and Tarver said what about Bumpus was it his fault he'd gone to bed and not got up since. Mr Bridges said couldn't he do work without Bumpus and Tarver said what did he mean.

'I mean what I speak.'

'What's that?'

Bridges said Tarver not to be gay with him, he was general manager, people could think they were fine, fine, but he was general manager, was no one disputed that, and what he said was what went through in this firm. Mr Tarver said what he had meant was he hadn't heard. Bridges went on not listening that he'd soon see who stuck himself up against him, whatever friends that one had in London office, he and his friends he'd see who was general manager, while Tarver speaking at same time said what he'd meant saying was pardon me, I could not hear you, girls in office make such noise giggling.

Later Mr Tarver was saying 'Yes sir' and Father said 'my boy' often then.

Bentley came up to where Mr Eames worked on his allotment garden.

'That's a fine crop of apples you'll pick off that tree of yours' he said and said was no tree in all the gardens like it there.

'Yes' said Mr Eames 'I don't remember its bearing so well in years, it's a picture. When the blossom was out the missus and I came along and sat under it of a Sunday with the baby.'

'There'll be a pound or two off it when they're ripe.' Changing tone he said he had seen Bert Jones back at work in factory that morning.

Mr Eames said he had not noticed him yet.

'Ah he's back and 'e ought never to've gone away.'

''E didn't 'ave any choice.'

'I didn't mean it lay with him, what I meant was they 'ad no right to send one away and do nothing to t'other when it was the same offence.'

'Well I suppose they can do as they like doing.'

'That's where you're wrong Fred, there's the law of England. And the pity of it is they ain't forbidden to go on as they do, one man a favourite and nothing too bad for the next.'

'Well they 'aven't trespassed against the law.'

'I'm not so sure they ain't. But leaving that as may be 'ad they any right to treat young Alfred Parker the way they did eight months back?'

'I ain't got nothing to say for that.'

'Now I'm asking you a straight question, 'ad they any right?'

'No, they 'ad no business to do it.'

'It's wicked, that's what it is. And look at that feller Whitacre. 'E was 30/- short in his money when they sent it to 'im so 'e writes to 'em about it and by the next post they tell 'im they're done with 'im and 'e can go tramp over England looking for another job. 'E wrote for 'is money again what 'e'd earned by labour but didn't get an answer. Is that straight?'

'Why don't he take it to the Courts?'

'What would they do? 'E'd get 'is marching orders quick enough. They'd 'ave a lawyer, so's the firm shouldn't get a bad name and 'e'd be tied into knots in no time. I shouldn't wonder if it ended in 'is being tried for perjury.'

'Well I don't know anything about that but what you just said there – it ain't anything but 'is story is it?'

'I can't say I've seen 'im personally to talk to, but 'e's a truthful feller mind you. But you ain't going to believe their tale are you?'

'I don't see myself believing either of 'em.'

'Twisters that's all they are, dirty twisters. And I'm waiting for 'em, I know the laws of England and once they step over on the wrong side I'll bring 'em into court, I'll sue them with me own money. They'll see soon enough. Why with the lavatories as they're now it ain't decent for a woman to come through the works.'

'I ain't seen one of the girls from the office come through in seven months. I shouldn't like a woman to do it with the language some use.'

'No nor should I. But the lavatories ain't made it any better for 'em.'

'Why?'

'Well it's not decent a man timing you in and out, it's contrary to nature. Any road I ain't told the wife about it. Besides she 'as 'ardships enough keeping her and me alive on our money without me telling 'er the pinpricks you get all the time at our place.'

Bentley filled pipe.

'It's downright wicked' he said going on.

He lit pipe. Smoke from it went slowly up through bars of sunlight here and there which came between leaves of apple tree.

'Ah it's a fine crop' Mr Bentley said, changing tone, 'and it's a good thing for a man to get away in the evenings out into the air.'

As they went downstairs in to dinner he had been shouting to one in front – this was only but nervousness because her he was taking in was so pretty – so when they sat down and he turned to her it was first time he had spoken to her.

'Didn't we meet at dinner with the Masons about a fortnight ago before going on to somebody's dance' he said.

'Probably, I expect so.'

37

'Whose dance was it, I can't remember, I'm so bad at names. Anyway I know I've got to go on tonight to Lady Randolph's afterwards to pick someone up.'

'Isn't it Lady Randolph's we're going to?'

'Isn't that lucky? Think of it, going to the dance one's going on to.'

'But it may be boring, and boring waiting on so long.'

He thought why couldn't she say 'you' may be bored: flattery, he thought, flattery, you could count on fingers of two hands only the girls who flattered you at dinner and that surely he thought was next most important after champagne at dinner parties. Was danger these people they were dining with would not give champagne, he saw glasses did not look like champagne.

'Brilliant' he said letting no break in conversation, 'brilliant' thinking more of himself 'of course it will be ghastly waiting, and it was for two o'clock when we were going on to a little place I know of' he said. 'But of course I can go away and come back again: you don't think that's rude do you?'

She thought what a priggish boy and hadn't heard more of what he said than his little place he knew of. Why speak like a serial she asked in her mind.

'It's done a great deal' he said after waiting for her 'I've done it but perhaps it's rude.'

She thinks it rude he thought, she's half witted and why not take up his quotation 'a little place I wot of' he cried in his mind.

'D'you go much to the dog races?' he said changing conversation.

'Yes I do.'

'Isn't it astounding the crowds that go there.'

'Crowds' she said.

'And all you hear about the lower classes not being able to live decently when you see ten's of thousands there every night.'

'Perhaps that's why.'

'No I can't allow that' he said. 'If they really couldn't afford it they wouldn't go' he said.

'I don't know.'

'Well we've got a factory in Birmingham and I know if you really can't afford it there you don't go.'

He didn't know but why had she taken him up and he was desperate.

'Are you in business then?' she said.

'Yes I am worse luck.'

'Everyone's in business or in the Guards now' she said and, satisfied, he leaned back in chair and said to himself what incredible, incredible things you heard, he would tell it to Mary when they went on to Princes, she would laugh.

'Another thing I can't understand about the lower classes' he said 'is this business by which they pay 1d per week for all their lives and get a whopping £60 funeral at their end.'

'Well they tell me it's because they don't like their families to pay for it, you see, as it's hard on them after they're dead.'

Why be well informed at dinner he said to himself. And would be no champagne; it was claret. Would he tell her what wrong it was not giving champagne at dinner, but was she the hostess' daughter, anyway what was her name. Not even cards on the table he said to himself looking round, and saw she was talking now to next door neighbour and he turned to his left but that one talked also to neighbour next door, and he refused claret then, asked for lemonade, took water, was no lemonade in house.

Monday night Mr Craigan and Mr Gates in bowler hats went along Coventry Road to public house. Mr Tupe saw them. He said to young man he was with was no man so deceitful as man he could see walking on other side of road if he looked. No man like it for deceit. And didn't he think a deal of himself for never saying much when that was easy as picking a tart up in this street. 'I could hold my gob for a day and a year if I so wanted' he said. 'Pity was they hadn't killed him when they nearly did.' Wire rope breaking had nearly caught him day or two ago. You never heard such a hulla-balloo as there was over him. It might have been the gaffer himself that had been burnt alive in the boilers. He'd gone about with a look on his dial days after like 'hold it up where it hurts and let mammy kiss it.' 'Deceitful old bleeder' he said. 'Enough to make you go bald'eaded just seeing 'im go up the street.'

Tarver went down to tennis club. 'Hello Captain.' 'How are you Colonel, how's it going?'

Mr Tarver had in him feeling of expectation this evening, sinking feeling in his stomach. Standing behind row of deck chairs from which people watched the tennis he made violent swings with his racket. 'I say look out,' one man said 'Tarver's in form, men.' 'Boy' said Mr Tarver, imitating American slang he saw at the movies, 'if that old ball was our old manager, well, he wouldn't have much shape after I'd finished with him.' Then he went on, but spoke to himself, that already the old devil looked a bit lopsided already. No you couldn't go on like the old man went on, was some justice had got to overtake you. You couldn't victimize the people under you for ever and always, not you. That was a bright lad, Archer. That letter he'd got from Archer was a peach of a letter, a peach.

When these four finished who had been playing he went on the court next with three others. Man served to Tarver. Tarver full of anger and victory against Mr Bridges leapt at the ball as it came and sent it back faster yet. He stood still and watched where it went and this man who had served ran after it, but he won't get to it said Mr Tarver. But this man did get to it, though he could only return it high and soft, like a harmonic.

'What' said Mr Tarver and rushed at this return and smashed it. Indeed his shot went so fast over the net that those two opponents against him in this game could only stand and watch, it came by so fast. They clapped hands who sat on chairs. Mr Tarver looked round triumphant in young manhood. Bridges, he sang in his mind, what could Bridges do against him in the long run, he sang. You can't keep a good man down. You can fill him with pins like a pincushion but he will come up again. And at this moment ball came past him and he was not ready for it – he did not even know they had begun to play again. He could only stand and watch. 'Oh Mr Tarver!' said his partner and Mr Tarver said damn. One of the ladies heard that. 'Careful, ladies present y'know,' she said to him, archly smiling, and he blushed for shame, who was so careful always in his expressions.

Lily Gates was saying half smiling to Jim Dale it gave her creeps Mr Craigan always sitting at home of an evening. He listened to the wireless every night of the week except Mondays. And look what Sunday was, was as much as they could do to get him out to the Lickeys she said. No when you asked he said he would not come, and what for? all the morning listening to preachers in foreign countries, why when you didn't know the language she couldn't see what was in it, and the afternoon and the evening the same, right till he went to his room, she said.

And when it wasn't the wireless he was reading the works of Dickens, over and over again. 'Don't you ever read any but the works of Dickens?' she'd asked him once. 'No why should I?' he'd said. Always the same books, she was fond of a book now and again, but she couldn't do that. He was a wonderful old man.

''E's like the deep sea' she was saying, half smiling.

6

MR DUPRET 'PATER' indeed had fallen on his shoulder after slipping on dog's mess and was in bed now: pretty young nurse read out of *The Field* to him lying in bed, and doctors had said he would be six weeks in bed seeing what he had done at his age. So he had said to his wife, 'Get me a pretty young nurse.'

At the club they said 'Dupret has fallen on his shoulder, that sort of thing is a perpetual menace at our age': at the works they said, 'the gaffer's fallen on 'is shoulder so they say, at 'is time of life you don't get over it so easy as that,' and two men had quarrelled at dinner hour over his age.

So young Mr Dupret was left in charge of business. He came to the London offices early every morning and made great trouble with those who were late. Was all the others let him do. And he signed the cheques also.

Yet Mr Archer had in his pocket letter from Mr Tarver about Whitacre his fitter and this told also of one man suspended for two weeks while the other had nothing done to him though he was as guilty. This was the opportunity. The old man had fallen on his shoulder, young Mr Dupret would be wanting to do something, to assert himself. Now he would work in with young Mr Dupret, now young Mr Dupret could splash about, would want to. Would be rows when the old man came back over what had been done but it could be managed so to fall back on Tarver. Tarver was a fool and did not see whatever row he made was sure to come back on him. Also on young Mr Dupret. So Mr Archer thought and planned.

But he was sincere in his thinking the old place wanted a

rouser and in his thinking he was always building, always building in his thinking.

''Ow you goin' Albert' Tupe asked storekeeper.

'Rotten, I'm all any'ow today.'

'I 'eard a good one yesterday Albert, there was a chap died, see, and when 'e was dead 'e went to 'eaven. Well after a day or two 'e went to the side like and looked to see if 'e could see any of 'is acquaintance down in 'ell. 'E sees one that 'e used to be friendly with and 'e calls down to 'im "'Ow do Ben, 'ow be you goin'?" "Fine thanks Jim." "There wouldn't be no way of my getting down to where you works Ben would there" 'e says. "'Ow's that Jim?" "'Ow many hours d'you reckon to work down where you are Ben?" "Four-and-a-half with the weekends off." "Yus," 'e says, "and it's ten with us up in 'eaven, Sundays and all, there being so few on us to run the place on" that's why 'e wanted to change eh?'

'Yes' she said to Bert Jones 'yes when 'e said 'e was going to the concert in the City Hall' she breathed on H in Hall 'I said let you go and so 'ere we are again, the city orchestra 'ave begun for another season and now I'll be on my own again, Friday nights. I said to 'im, "Yes. But don't consider" I said, "that I'll be a stay at 'ome even if I 'ave to go out alone, no I can go and take myself out for a walk and get a mouthful of fresh air for myself thank you." Still who would've thought it, meeting you in the road like that, I don't know I'm sure.'

'The world's a small place.'

'Yes' she said 'me walking down the road and there you are. Well!'

'I did use to be going out with a young lady but 'er parents 'ave just moved to London where her dad's found a job so she's up there now.'

'So we're both in the same boat, as they say.'

'Ah and it's a lonely kind of a boat ain't it? But you wouldn't be affected really seeing the orchestra only plays Friday nights.'

'Yes, but I got no use for someone that goes off at a moment's notice when I was just looking forward to the pictures for this evening. There's not many in front of us, we'll be inside within a half hour.'

'It kind of puts you out.'

'Yes it does, yes I like to know what I'm going to do of an evening. So when 'e went I said it's no use your sitting moping indoors alone, you go out to the pictures anyway, even if it is alone.'

'But wasn't there anyone in where you live?'

'No you see Mr Craigan was gone with Jim to the concert, 'e says girls can't understand music though I'm very fond of it myself, yes I am, and my dad was out of the 'ouse before you could say knife, soon as Mr Craigan was off to the concert.'

'It makes the evenings long when there's no one in the 'ouse.'

'Yes it does doesn't it. Yes the minutes seem like hours.'

'I like a bit of music myself. And it's pretty fair the music in this movie ouse.'

Why she said when they did get in, wasn't that strange what would've happened to the lights and girl in front turned round to her saying they had been up ever since she'd been in. Lily said with the film going on and all, wasn't it hard on the eyes she said and Mr Jones said he didn't understand it, he'd never known it before like this. Yes man in front said turning back to him, yes all the evening but people in front cried ssh: band was playing softly, softly.

A great number were in cinema, many standing, battalions were in cinemas over all the country, young Mr Dupret was in a cinema, over above up into the sky their feeling panted up supported by each other's feeling, away away, Europe and America, mass on mass their feeling united supporting, renewed their sky.

'They're always playing this tune 'ere' she said looking for opening in conversation.

'They are' he said carefully.

'D'you come to this one often then?'

'Before my young lady went up to London.'

'I think the music's lovely 'ere.'

Later they found seats. Sweetness of agitation in her, both

44

her and he sitting bolt upright. So they continued sitting. And film came round again, that one, to where it was when they first came in.

'Shall we stay on a bit now the band's back again?' he said.

'I don't mind I'm sure.'

So still upright. But she tired.

'We might as well go' she said trembling. He did not see this.

He walked her home, neither said much to other. She no longer trembled and indeed was bored now. In the street they met Gates that was a little drunk. He wheezed, out of breath.

'They're only takin' those that are short of breath up in 'eaven now' he said 'they run short of trumpets there, 'arps is all the go now' he said.

'I'll wager that was Tupe you got that from' she said.

''Ow'd you know' said he.

'Everyone is in the Guards now or in business' repeated he to himself coming in to one of the private rooms in London office. He thought if she had said that as last night she had well then he need not be so humiliated. But he was, oh yes. Last night had been one of those nights, clearly had he seen then extent of tomorrow's humiliation. Aye and clearly had seen himself throwing up bastions around citadel of his personality now all of it retreated back, in state of siege, behind 'everyone now is a Guardee or in business'.

He threw away cigarette.

It was because, all of it, because she was so beautiful, he repeated to himself, so beautiful.

After all I work, repeated he to himself, I work, here I am in London offices of Dupret & Son, general engineers.

Why had they not brought the correspondence? He rang. 'Why hasn't Mr Sewell brought in this morning's letters?' 'He hasn't come yet Mr Dupret.'

'He hasn't come' he said echo echo to Miss Wilbraham. That dreadful night he thought. Mary had been late – that other with fellows twirling small moustaches round about her, she laughing – and Mary, when she had come, furious, he could not find why. May have been she'd bought new hat.

Bother bother. And here was whole day stretching out in front. What had been her name? A – a – Anne – Anya – Nunk – HANNAH GLOSSOP.

'It is not' Archer was saying 'it is not a thing I want to bring officially before you Mr Dupret, for instance I would never contemplate putting the facts before your father, sir, but I would like to bring it to your notice in a semi-official manner. Of course in your position you want to know everything that is going on and I know that you are already "au fay" with everything that goes on. I know that you have already noticed in the short time, comparatively short time you have been in the business that all is not well at Birmingham. I mean this that it is not running smoothly. I always look on a business as a kind of machine Mr Dupret, one unit, I shall never forget my old employer old Mr March drawing my attention to that aspect of trade, and of course when one part is not running smoothly, wants oiling shall we say, then that machine or unit is not functioning to its full productive capacity. Well a few days ago I received this letter Mr Dupret which I should like to place before you. Of course before you read it I must say that the writer never intended it to be read by anyone but myself, Tarver is not the man to do anything behind another man's back, but in my opinion, for what it is worth, I am sure he is one of the most promising younger men in the Birmingham side. Of course this letter is in the strictest confidence sir, I'm sure Tarver would be most upset if he knew I was giving it to you to read and yet I am certain I would be failing in my duty if I didn't bring it to your notice.'

More frightful trouble Mr Dupret said to himself and took the letter.

Intrigue he cried in his mind, still sitting in private room in London office, intrigue and how horrible people are. Of course Archer was working against old Bridges for Bridges ignored Mr Archer and only dealt with him through old Walters. Both these were old, old. How horrible they all were and everyone too for that matter, loathsome the people in buses, worse in trams of course – he faintly smiled.

46

And when you went out anywhere, he went on in his mind about people, how rude everyone, and they did not laugh at your jokes. And when you sat sweating here in daytime when you might be dodging enemies in the Park or receiving rudeness impassively there, here you were dying of it, the badly managed intrigues, another's mistake so ignorantly exploited, mismanaged. They were like children in their intrigues, like little children, cried he in his mind and then casting back to Hannah Glossop, what figure must he have cut when she did not see point in 'a little place I know of.' He might have said 'I wot of' and so it would have been worse, one should never be, he thought, facetious in conversation with a stranger. Still it would have been 'I know of,' yes must have been.

So stupid are they he said still going on, that there is no doing with them, and there his mind stopped and only kept on repeating then, 'no doing with them.'

Later temper began to come up gorgon-headed within him, he flagellated it, words hung across his mind – stupidity, and then – angry, and then – old men. We shall be ruined cried he in his mind, business will go bankrupt, 'to Siam, Siam,' 'not functioning to its full capacity for production': the old men are smashing it, he cried, something has got to be done, must.

'Who would it be?' Mrs Eames said, holding baby.

'Bentley 'is name is' said Mr Eames.

'So that's what you do when you go up to the garden, you stand talking to that class. You ought to 'ave more respect for your child.'

'Well I didn't tell 'im he was right did I?'

'And what's coming to the garden when you're standing there gossiping all the time?'

'It's staying there.'

'Oh gor blimey, you men it's enough to drive us women mad.'

'Well it is staying there isn't it?'

'You hadn't ought to stand listening to a man of 'is kind.'

'I'll do as I please' he said taking off spectacles to wipe them 'and I'm not saying a good deal of what 'e said weren't true.'

'Lord I can't keep mad at you when you take your specs off. You 'ave a look about you of the lamp post outside.'

'I'm not saying a lot of what 'e touched on 'e wasn't justified in saying. To my way of thinking they didn't ought to keep the tackle in the way they do. The crane in our shop ain't safe now and Aaron Connolly driving it don't make it any safer.'

The lathes he said were all anyhow and any time now he said glass roof might fall in if gale of wind came.

'You'll give me fits' she said.

'And the government inspector's meant to look to all that but there's a woman comes to our place mostly and what can she know about it. And there ain't a girl in the whole factory. Old Bentley didn't mention that no nor did I for I thought 'e might never stop if I went suggesting things to 'im.'

'That's right' she said 'don't get into argument with that sort.'

''E's a decent enough feller all right.'

'Don't you go talking with them.'

'Why shouldn't I?'

'It ain't going to do no good to your wife or child.'

'What ain't. You talk too much that's what it is. If Eve hadn't've started off clacking the serpent wouldn't 'ave caught 'er in his trap.'

'Oo began it, the serpent or her, tell me that.'

'Well I don't know if I remember for sure which of 'em it was.'

'You don't know the Bible, that's what's the matter with you my man.'

'Well what if I don't know, where's the Bible come into it anyway?'

'Never you mind.'

'What's Adam and Eve got to do with Bentley?'

'You begun that, I don't know.'

'I did not.'

'Why you know you did.'

'I did not.'

'I don't know I'm sure,' she said, 'but you did, I know that. Well anyway what's the use in arguing. I'm going to bed.'

'I'm about ready too.'

Halfway upstairs she turned round and said to remember to lock front door for turning then to baby in her arms 'love' she said 'they might come in the night and steal you away. And what would we do then, and what would we do then?'

'Well when are you going to let us have some of that Bryson order?' asked Mr Walters.

'In a twelve month' darkly said Mr Bridges.

'Someone at it again?'

'The day I got the specifications from London I sent them to the drawing office and now I can't get anything. Everything's done that I can do. Seven days they've had 'em and not a thing on paper yet.'

'What's Tarver up to then?'

'I don't know' cried Mr Bridges 'don't ask me. But 'is nails take a long time paring.'

'We've got to have them' (Walters' voice today was dull as felt).

'You can't get drawings out of him, everyone in this place knows how I've tried to get on with 'im. I could go up there and cry my eyes out but dirty Shylock he's like stone, and he'd leave the place straightaway, quick as knife, if anyone went into his place. If I went in he'd knock me on the head. I never go near him, just to keep him in a good temper I daren't do it, he goes up in smoke if you so much as look at 'im.'

'What are we to do then?'

'Don't ask me I'm telling you.'

'I'd better see him.'

'Only a week or two ago I had to have a word with him over that Smithson plant he was seven weeks with, only a week ago. He said Bumpus had been ill and he wanted another man as well. Where's the money going to come from to pay that extra man, eh, tell me that? If we can't keep overheads down where are we? And still there's not everyone could do so nice a job when 'e's in the mood. But we'll be out of business before he's done. It's all fine enough to be pleased with yourself as punch but there's others can do the job just as good and in half the time. That's what it is in business now, they take any job so long as you do it quick.'

'I'll see him, Arthur.'

'You look out what you're doing. Something's up, you haven't got to be blind to see that. I gave 'im something to chew that other day and had 'im on his knees before my chair there where you're sitting. He was sick as if I'd been Mussolini and given him cod liver oil. And then he looked so perked up a day or two after I didn't know what to make of it. Now the young fellow's coming down. What's there in all this?'

'Archer and young Mr Dupret have been a lot together lately' said Mr Walters with muted drama and called through to office for Miss Maisie Alexander to get Mr Tarver.

'Have they eh? And d'you know what Tarver said I was to Maisie, said I was off it, crazy. Can you work with a man like that, and when he's old enough to be your son. What are you going to say to 'im?'

'You leave it to me Arthur.'

Then Tarver came in.

'How are you Mr Tarver? Keeping fit?'

'I'm fine thanks Colonel. Feeling on top of the world.'

'That's good. Is the wife well?'

'Fit as she can be.'

'That's good. Look here about that Bryson order, they telephoned me yesterday –'

'Yesterday? How's that?'

'They're expecting that jacket right away.'

'Why I only got the rough drawings three days ago.'

'Three days ago' cried Mr Bridges.

'Three days ago' said Mr Tarver.

'What's that?' said Mr Walters.

'I don't know when anyone else got 'em' said Mr Tarver 'but we got the specifications Tuesday in our office.'

Then they lied for some time all of them.

Was no record of when specifications went from office of works manager to drawing office and Walters said perhaps they had been lying about in cost office before they had gone through to Tarver, but Bridges and this one did not listen.

One waved newspaper, other clenched fist over rolled up handkerchief in his hand and bit at ends of it

Gradually they got quieter.

'What we want' said Mr Bridges 'is the work to go through.'

'That's what we are all trying to do in our different ways' said Mr Walters and Mr Tarver said 'We're working just for that and nothing else.'

'Of course it's got to be a good job, an engineer's job' Bridges said. 'We've got the best name in the trade for the quality of the work we turn out' Walters said.

'But how'd you expect anyone to turn it out in three days, that's what I can't get hold of' Tarver said.

'But as you were saying just now Arthur' Mr Walters murmured as if he had not heard Mr Tarver 'the whole trend of modern business is that they don't care how it is so long as they get the job quick.'

'What d'you mean three days' said Bridges to Tarver, 'more like three weeks, and that's not guess work it's observation, I haven't sat watching you these days and days with what I've seen going in at one eye and out of the next.'

'Where'd you get three weeks. It was the day before yesterday when I got those measurements.'

'Day before yesterday, Thursday, Wednesday, d'you hear that Tom' to Mr Walters ''e's on a new talk now, it was six days I remember him telling us not three minutes back.'

'It was not.'

'I'm not saying any more' Mr Bridges said 'you go on and talk it out between you if talking helped anyone ever.' He went out.

'There goes a fine man' said Mr Walters. 'Look here' he said speaking like as of earthquake or the deluge 'look here we're all Brummagen men all three of us let's face up to this, John, like fellow citizens. I know and you know Arthur's hard to work with when he's got one of his tantrums on him, I've had some times with him, my word, but you know he's got a lot better in the last few years. But in the old days my word, it's nothing to what it used to be. And of course you're a young man and this place will seem to you a dead alive sort

51

of hole but you've got to take into account mind you that there's not more than ten per cent of the engineering firms in this country making above three per cent profits.'

'That's all they declare' said Mr Tarver.

'I don't know, that's a big thing to say. In London you get a pretty good view of the whole thing and from what I've been told I say it's that myself. Now look here John you won't find another firm that'll give you so much scope, you haven't got much to do, you get time here to work out your ideas and put 'em on paper. Let's get down to it and live in peace. Why when I was with Watsons you were lucky if you got away with it of a morning without someone about the place resigning or getting the sack. There was no time to work or know whether you were on your head or not. But here you've got your own office pretty well, and there isn't all that amount to do.'

'That's just what there is. I can't get through it with Bumpus bad on and off like 'e is. We've got to do something, though it'll take two years to do it in this place. And I must have another draughtsman because as it is now he' nodding to door 'he's on at me the whole time like a can with a stone in it at the end of a dog's tail so that I can't do anything for worry three parts of the time. You can't work with him.'

'I've had terrible times with him myself, terrible times, don't I know it. But I've stuck it out and I've done better for myself in this firm than I could in most others. Though you might not see eye to eye with him, he's a fine man, you can't help respecting him. There's not everyone could have done what he's done for himself.'

'But what's 'e do for the firm?'

'He's done more than anyone for it except myself John.'

'Oh well I'll say this, squire, I've got nothing against him personally.'

'No that's right –' and so Mr Walters quieted Mr Tarver and the door opened minutes later.

'That bed-plate' said Mr Bridges coming in, 'it's a worry, every time I go into the works and go by it I could go crazy. Crazy' he said remembering Miss Alexander, 'crazy, of course you can't expect much of a man that's crazy especially when he's manager. Little things like date remember that.'

'What's wrong with the bed-plate said.

'It's cracked, you can put the blade o quarter of an inch. I'm having them fake there, they've only got to spot it and the m

'You cement it and no one will notice.'

'The vibration of the engine when it's set right across' said Mr Tarver.

'Oho' said Mr Bridges 'but when you've seen a any bed-plates as I have my lad you'll tell a different tale to your grandmother. Why I remember one bed-plate I saw at the H.B.S. and the moulder put his trowel right down into it and it's working now on a liner.'

Mr Tarver was smiling.

'Well that's all Tarver for the moment' said Mr Walters but as soon as he was gone Mr Bridges cried out "ave you seen anything like it, smilin' like a mandarin, what's 'e got up his sleeve? And he talks about engineering, why if it came down to drawing a door knob 'e couldn't do it. That's what we're coming to, eh, cubs like 'im and 'is little master trying to teach us. And I've given all I know to this firm, you know it, we all know it, I've worked my heart out. It makes you want to hang yourself by the window cord from the window. Years of work and now this.'

'The chief isn't dead yet' said Mr Walters 'and now he's fallen down in the street maybe he won't be so fond of walking across them as he was before, so he'll add another ten years to his life. You can't do it now unless you're a young man' said Mr Walters to Mr Bridges and soon he was talking of the difference in Birmingham and London streets and by much talking of such things friendly to both of them he dressed Mr Bridges' wounds.

'That bed-plate' said Mr Bridges – 'come along John as you're there. They were at me this morning on the 'phone calling me names. I might have been anything, a urinal, anything.'

'Their man said he'd put his walking stick into the one we

knows how he did it I don't, it was a wee crack, only put my knife in a bare eighth. What's he want a walking stick in a factory eh, d'you call that business. It beats me how he's the cheek to say that over a public service like the telephone.'

Bridges and Tarver hurried down through works to iron foundry.

'It's going to cost a fortune, eh, we've got to cut the old one up and this one to replace it will take two men and a boy five days to ram up and six-and-a-half to finish, then it's got to be dried. We can't stand it. It's a worry.'

They came to iron foundry.

'They've put Craigan on it then' said Mr Tarver when he had seen what, as he told Bumpus later, he had not believed when he was told.

'I told him (meaning foreman) to do that. Craigan may be a bit slow now but he's sure. It'll be a fine job when he's done with it' Bridges was singing with sureness almost. 'We can't afford to have another like the last one.' His mood changing 'By God' he cried 'but look at the land it's taking.'

We can't afford to have them at all thought Mr Tarver. But I'm not saying anything yet awhile he said to himself.

'Get on with that bed-plate man' Bridges said rushing threateningly on foundry foreman Philpots.

'Yessir' foreman said 'they're tearing into it.'

Tearing into it thought Mr Tarver, two old age pension men and one young feller which looks like girl!

'We're doing over on it' said Philpots, foundry foreman.

There you are said Tarver to himself overtime and so much more on the job and one that I wouldn't answer their enquiry if I was manager. You can bet, he thought, they had to circularize all the old county to find a fool big enough to try and cast a thing that shape and manage to make a good one. Robbery, just robbery.

'It's robbery, dirty robbery in daylight, making us do another' said Mr Bridges to Philpots, 'I put my knife in that crack and it was a bare quarter yet they sent it back. But we can't afford to quarrel with them. Don't you leave it day or night Andrew' foreman's name was Andrew Philpots, 'it's worth your job to you, and mine to myself. The chief'd soon have me chasing if this happened twice in a year.'

'There they are' Joe Gates said of Mr Bridges and Tarver to Dale and Mr Craigan, ramming. Gates shovelled sand.

'More sand' Dale said.

They worked fast for another hour.

'Hold on' said Mr Craigan and then straightened backs. His eyes were like black stones with anger.

Later that evening, when they were home he said again he was getting to be old man. Lily and Jim Dale separately worried about his saying this, Joe Gates was too tired. He had never said that before, either said in his own mind.

7

THEY HAD TAKEN bus. They had gone Saturday afternoon to Mr Jones' uncle and aunt that were lodge-keepers at gate of big house one mile out from bus terminus.

They had taken bus and had walked out. They had come in time for tea. They had stayed for supper. Lily Gates took pleasure in feeding chickens, it was infinitely amusing for her, and she had on new dress.

After supper they had started back for bus terminus towards ten o'clock. They had talked. Lily thought Bert Jones was great on talking. She had said what kind of a life did they live up in the big house which his uncle was gatekeeper of and he said there was three young ladies, daughters of the house, but were no sons, father employed a lot of men in Birmingham he said. She said when they married, those three, would the eldest come with her 'usband to live in the house so it would stay in the family, and he said he couldn't tell and she said she wondered what kind of lives they did live there.

She said it seemed a pity there wasn't a man the house wouldn't come to though girls were as good as men but still. She said they'd go out to dances every night probably and have a high old time. He said perhaps he kept his daughters in and didn't let them out much but she said that class never did that, the girls were free as the fishes in the sea and as slippery, using words her father would have used. And more than that she said, she had asked his aunt and she'd seen them come out of an evening scores of times, so she said.

From joking with him and from the long day talking with him her laughing went out all at once into confidences. Coming closer to him she began to tell what she had not meant to tell anyone, as if he had taken her will from her. She said how low Mr Craigan was often now in his self, and that once when he came back from work some time since she had thought he was finished.

''E's the man in our house really too you see' she said 'and he ain't never said it out like that before. When he an' dad gets too old for work I don't know what'll 'appen. I know I don't.'

'Well, of course,' Mr Jones said, 'he wouldn't be so young now' he said and was moved at her confiding in him.

She pressed closer to him.

'No, that's right, he ain't. But he loves his work. What'll come to us when he an' dad gets too old for it I don't know. Grandad won't know where he is. Yes I often lie awake o' nights thinking 'ow 'e'll manage. And how us'll get on, dad and the rest,' she said and was silent. As they walked, then Mr Jones had rush of feeling. He saw everything one way. 'Us working people we got to work for our living,' he said passionately, 'till we're too old. It's no manner of use thinking about it, it's like that, right on till we're too old for them to use us. Then our children'll make provision for us,' he said and stopped and suddenly he kissed her for the first time. She pressed up to his face, her eyes shining. Then for a long time they kissed each other, murmuring and not hearing what they murmured, behind cattle shed in field they had been crossing.

He sat at home alone in a chair picking his nose.

'The other day I met a girl called Glossop' he said in his mind. He remembered he had asked Mary about her and she had known her by sight, had seen her at dances. Then how had he not seen her? But sometimes in reading, he thought, you will find word you do not know and when you learn the meaning then for a few days you come again and again upon that word. So perhaps he only noticed same people at dances. He thought you made a little circle and yours reflects other circles. Death, death, sackcloth and ashes.

When Lily wakes, her eyelids fold up and her two eyes soft, brutal with sleep blink out on what is too bright for them at first. She stirs a little in the warmness of bed. Then, eyes waking, she sees clearly about her and stretches. She brings arms up above her head and takes hold on one of those parallel bars up behind pillow, and pulls her heavy thighs and legs out straight. Till she brings head up against that bar and till it forces head down on her breast, so she pulls. This done, she sits up, awake.

She saw in images in her mind how Mr Dale was to her like being on the verge of sleep, in safe bed. She laughed and stretched again. She turned to thinking of this new day and what she would have to get for the house today. Then she laughed again for she saw that was how she was with Bert Jones; with Jim she forgot, but with Bert she remembered. When she was with Bert it was like she had just stretched, then waked, then was full of purposes. But with Jim, it was like end of the day with him. Yes, she said, Bert's someone to work for, yes there's something in him she said in feeling and jumped out of bed.

Now Miss Gates and Mr Jones went out often together.

When they were out together once, after that, she saw clearly how unjust her life at home was to her, staying in all day, 'I never see another girl but over the garden fence and all the housework to do, yes, sometimes I could sit down and cry. And look at old Craigan now,' she said, 'I get black looks from him every time I come in after being out with you, he wants me to go out with Jim you see. But women aren't what they were, I'm not going to stay in an 'arem of his making, we're educated now. Yes he's made it pretty plain he wants Jim and me to be married but 'e can keep me in all day if he likes but he won't pick my husband. You've no idea, the 'ouse has got to be shining, there can't be a speck of dust or he'll say "what's this my wench?" Yes, that's what he says.'

'He won't let you go out to work?'

'No, he won't 'ear of it, I've got to stay in and wear away the linoleum by scrubbing,' and she said she did not know how she'd stood it up to then. She went on talking when he, more to draw her sympathy on him, said wasn't all that much enjoyment in factories.

'Oh yes, and how would you like to stay in all day by yourself and keep a place tidy, you're like all men, and then when they give you the 'ouse-keeping money Friday night to have nothing but black looks,' and seeing all this clearly in her mind she was scornful with him. He too, then, began to be angry.

'But when we're married, won't...' he began but she sprang at his face and then it was like so many other of their walks over again.

Later, still exalted, she drew back from him and said, whispering, surely he would not expect her to be like those other women, 'you won't be like dad,' she said, 'that had never any idea of bettering himself. You wouldn't want me to slave all my life till I was a bag of bones.' She said she was not afraid of the work, yes she was used to that looking after three men, but she couldn't do it if she didn't believe there was nothing better coming, 'we shan't be like the others Bert?' and he said of course they wouldn't be, at the works he was a picked man already.

'Come on then,' she cried jumping up, holding out arms to him, 'I can't sit still.' He jumped up and she ran backwards at that, her head held back and her arms now behind her back. But running forward to catch her he fell full length, cutting his forehead slightly.

She sat cross-legged and making resting place for his head in her lap she spat on handkerchief and wiped cut on his forehead, disconsolate, wiping blood off his forehead. Then he was happier than he had ever been before.

They came into front room after supper.

'Have you caught a chill or something?' Mrs Tarver said to her husband.

'I don't know. I don't think I feel well.'

'You ought to be in bed.'

'The young chap came down today.'

'What young chap's that?'

'Where's your mind? Why, young Dupret. Doris' he said to only child, 'what have we got there?'

'Young Mr Dupret,' breathed Mrs Tarver and moved her

chair nearer his. 'Darling' she said to the child, 'don't worry daddy now.'

'Don't talk to her like that mother, you'll upset the child. What's that you've got in your hands, answer your daddy.'

'It's only a toy ukulele she got at Mrs Smith's party, dear. What did he say to you? You ain't going to say he didn't see at once who was right, and the wrong.'

'I don't know. Here, Doris, come and sit on daddie's knee and show him the ukulele. Well, ain't you a ukulele lady now!'

'I am!'

'Johnikins you don't say you couldn't see him so's to get your word in first.'

'Yes I saw him.'

'What did he say?'

'He didn't say anything.'

'Didn't say anything? D'you mean to say. . . . Then what did he do?'

'Nothing. Well he did this. He took the man off they'd put by the lavatory door checking the men in and out.'

'Daddy, don't you like my uku – uku – ukulele?'

'Was that all he did?'

'Don't you like my ukulele, daddy?'

'Don't worry daddy now dear. Go and play over there and put the doll to bed. What did he do that for?'

'To please himself I suppose.'

'And didn't he give you another draughtsman?'

'No.'

'What did he say to you, then?'

'He had a lot of this educated jargon, I didn't understand much of it, though I got a bit nearer to it than old Bridges. He went on about what a fine looking chap – beautiful, that's the word he used – a man in the iron foundry was. I don't know how an iron moulder can be beautiful but there you are.'

'He must be a dandy though if that's all he thinks of in the works. I suppose he 'as ladies trailing round him once he gets home, and a lot of good they'll do him.'

'He's soft.'

'But did you go through the works with him?'

'No, I was coming through the iron foundry from the fettling shop when I ran into him and the old man.'

'And didn't you speak to him?'

'Of course I spoke to him, what d'you think I am?'

'Johnikins, why don't you tell me something?'

'What can I tell you? I was there for about five minutes and he went back to the offices and turned round to me – "I'll come along and see you before I go" lardida he said and went into the old man's room. So I waited for him in my department and the next thing I knew was the noise of him going off in 'is Bentley.'

'Then how d'you think it was him who took the man away from there?'

'Ah that's where I come in. I sent down Bumpus to get some stamps in the outside office and to look about him and make eyes at the girls when all of a sudden out bursts the old squire right up in the air and behind him was the young fellow saying – "but come Mr Bridges it's nothing very terrible" (fancy saying that to the old squire!) "it's nothing very terrible, surely, such a small thing, lavatories . . ." and then he banged the door right in the young chap's face and went off. Bumpus comes back to tell me and the first thing I did was to get up to go and catch him in there with the old devil out of the way, when I hear the noise of his car. I run to the window and there's the young chap driving himself away.'

'Did he? What d'you say to that?'

'I don't know.'

'So he didn't come up and see you after all?'

'Doris, come and play to Daddy on your ukulele, daddie's tired.'

'Leave the child alone, do, you'll be the death of her. What d'you think? Didn't he say nothing about another draughtsman?'

'Not a word.'

'Well he's crossed old Bridges in one thing, and that's to the good, the old scarecrow.'

'Yes, but what do we know went on else. He was there some time, must have been. And if he'd crossed the old man before then the old scarecrow would have been out of the

61

room before that and Bumpus would have seen him. You can depend on his always rushing out when he's crossed.'

'I see they've took the man off from there,' nodding to lavatory door said Mr Tupe to Mr Bentley.

'They had to.'

'Why's that?'

'They were made to' Bentley heavily said. 'As soon as ever I saw a man put on there I said that's a thing a woman won't stand. I 'ad that factory inspector in me mind's eye. I thought to myself she'd never stand for it. And she didn't, that's why he's suspended.'

'But she 'asn't been through, not since that man was put on. 'Er angel feet've not crossed our thres-bloody-'old.'

'She must've 'eard then.'

'Well if you want to know, the young feller took 'm off. And the more's the pity I say.'

'Young Dupret?'

'That's 'im. Now it'll be the old story again, 'alf an hour's work and then twenty-one minutes in there for a smoke and a chat. They've got no conscience to the firm or to theirselves.'

'As the fly said to the spider. Of all the dirty swine – excuse my saying so – you're one of them. And if it was young Dupret 'e was made to.'

''E wasn't, 'e did it on 'is own from what I can 'ear of it. Probably 'e was 'alf witted enough to suppose 'e was pleasing mangy young Russian tykes like you.'

'I wonder at a man of your age swallowing what you swallow.'

'Speaking of beer' Mr Tupe said genially 'I could get down twice what you'd had after you couldn't drink no more, when your head was communing with the stars: if you'd care to try any night, you paying the drinks?'

'My poor old man, how are you?' Mrs Dupret said coming into sick room, 'how do you feel in yourself?'

Mr Dupret lay propped up on pillows. He related how his nurse had told him that he was 'naughty to ring so often and should be spanked.' Courageously he made a comedy out of it.

Mrs Dupret asked what tip should be given to this nurse when she had packed her things, for her one line of original research was into the question of tips. Mr Dupret decided at once and when his wife said surely not so little, since Archie, when he was ill, and had had a nurse for about the same period, had given her quite six shillings more he said no, he would give her that amount and no less. She said how very interesting that was to her. He said she would call him mean perhaps but she said not the least bit in the world, only it was so fascinating what tips people gave. The most absurd person of course was Proust, she said – her voice hazed with wonder. He had given enormous tips, big, huge, it was fantastic, she said sitting down by the bed, he had thought nothing of giving 200 francs to a waiter who brought his, his – well any little thing, but then he was not a gentleman she murmured, enviously almost. For what she wanted most in the world sometimes was to give huge tips but had never dared, she thought the waiter might take her for an actress. (She was of that generation of women which still feared actresses.)

Mr Dupret said Jews had brought the Continent to a ridiculous state with extravagant tipping, that was why he would never go abroad. 'I know dear,' she said. But he went on that it was really to spare her the anxiety of having to give them, he said she knew she never slept the night before moving out of a hotel abroad, and to spare her the disappointment when ten per cent was added to the bill so that there were no tips.

'I've got such a clever book here for you dear' she said, 'it's called *Lenin and Gandhi*. You ought to read it.' He put it down by the side of the bed.

'There's a thing in it which I thought so amusing darling,' she said 'which is where he says the Brahmins or Hindus, one of those people I don't know which, sit for whole half hours saying the same word over and over again. Of course it's very unkind, but it's so like Dickie when he's in love.' She said didn't he know that Dickie was starting another affair and Mr Dupret said another one? and she said yes, a girl called Glossop, a very nice girl from all she could make out, 'but very dull, I'm afraid, like all Dick's young ladies.' There was a certain stage in all his affairs when he sat and repeated to himself over and over again darling, darling, darling, like that, so like those old men squatting on the mountains. Mr Dupret laughed 'ho, ho!' Then he asked how she knew. 'Why the darling' she said 'he always tells me in spite of himself all those things like that about his girls. Then he has to go and make out a reason for his having told me so he shan't seem to have given himself away without meaning to. He is rather a darling, isn't he, Jack?'

'He's a nice boy but he's very silly still' said Mr Dupret. 'He's got no head.'

Mrs Dupret said she thought he wouldn't marry for another nine years at least but now her husband was bored and began to give instructions, summoning people and sending them off, all on business, and he dismissed Mrs Dupret. Going away she thought how nice it had been and still was while he lay ill though he wasn't really ill now any more of course, he was just pretending and it was high time he got about again. But how nice it had been, she had seen so much more of him since he had hurt his shoulder, usually he was working when he wasn't asleep. He worked all day.

She marvelled at the correctness of the tip he had decided on for that nurse, and to decide at once like that, he had a genius for tips, she thought. She went to get ready before going out.

But still, poor old man she thought, there was something about it which she didn't altogether like. His staying in bed like that made her uneasy. And when the doctors said there was nothing the matter with him now, why didn't he get up?

Again, some other morning, she was in his bedroom and they were talking about young Mr Dupret, Dick, and she said how she had seen this girl Hannah Glossop several times again and that she was giving a dinner party for her soon, though of course the party was not to look as though it were hers; Hannah – from talking about her to Dickie she called her Hannah now – would just, to all appearances, be one of the other girls.

Mr Dupret was listless and asked how Dick was getting on

with the Dupret and son business and his wife said she thought he was so interested. Why was it, she asked him, that all this time he had not once asked after that 'side' when he had been managing all his other interests from his bed. He answered that he had decided to give him a free run of the place till he got back to work again, 'there is nothing like the actual experience for teaching you' he said and that when he got back he intended altering every single alteration the boy had made 'just to show him.'

Wasn't that rather cruel Mrs Dupret said, and he said no, of course not. For one thing, if he had done anything it was almost bound to be wrong, and then if you let them have all their own way, young men lost their keenness. After that he sank into a greater apathy and although he did not send her away, which was in itself, she thought, a sign that he was not right, she could hardly get anything out of him.

After Sunday dinner, when Lily Gates had cleared table and had put back on it bowl in which Mr Craigan kept tobacco, she said to those three what were they going to do that Sunday afternoon.

'Where are you goin'?' said Mr Dale.

'I'm not going anywhere.'

'Aren't you goin' out?'

'I'm not goin' anywhere without you go.'

'Don't trouble about me' Mr Dale said. 'I'm used to that.'

'I didn't mean you particular, I meant all on you.'

'I'm stayin' in with me pipe,' Gates said half asleep. 'You go and get the beer.' Mr Craigan reached out and took wireless headphones which he fitted about his head.

'I thought you couldn't mean me,' said Mr Dale.

'No, I should think I couldn't.'

'But don't you put yourself out for us. You go on out.'

'I got nowhere to go.'

'What, ain't 'e waitin' for you at the corner?'

'Who's that?'

'Who's that!!' he said.

'Well what business is it of yours if 'e is?'

'I wouldn't keep 'im waitin'.'

'I tell you I'm not going out this afternoon.'

'Then what's it all about. 'Ad a lover's quarrel or what?'

She smiled at him and said what business was it of his and her smiling made him shout that most likely he had to take most of his time keeping his other loves quiet. Dropping voice he said people of that sort which took other people's girls from them, were not content with one only, they had several, wife in every port and married women some of them most likely, he said, voice rising. Still she smiled when, jumping up, he said he would give her smack across that smile. Craigan took off headphones then and said 'you go and get the beer Lil.' When she had shut door behind her he said to Dale to leave her alone. Mr Gates slept noisily in chair.

Mr Dale sat down. He leant towards fire which made room thick hot. They said nothing for a time. He looked up then towards Mr Craigan and said:

'I've been thinkin' I'd better change my lodgings.'

'You'll do nothing of the kind' Craigan said.

Again was silence.

'It makes it awkward for me' he said 'staying 'ere.'

Mr Craigan said nothing. Dale kicked Joe Gates: 'Joe' he said 'I've been thinkin' I ought to look out for other lodgings. Our wench and me don't seem to 'it it off any more, Joe.'

Mr Gates looked at Mr Craigan. Craigan said:

'You'll stay 'ere Jim.'

Dale kicked fender and upset poker which clattered and crashed on floor.

'I won't stand by and see 'er marry Bert Jones.'

'I can't stand by and see that feller go off with Lil' he said later. 'If her likes 'im better'n me well then let 'er 'ave 'im but I'm not goin' to be there to watch it.'

'I'm telling you she'll not marry Bert Jones' said Mr Craigan and again was silence and furtively Mr Gates watched Mr Craigan. Then Craigan said to Mr Dale: 'You go on off out, Jim, don't sit moping inside.'

'That's right' said Joe Gates. 'Lord love me, you ain't jealous of 'im are you? 'Im?!! Why 'e's nothing more than something to look at, though 'e's as ugly as your backside. But 'e's got no use to 'imself. You didn't ought to worry

66

yourself about him. An' talkin' about women, the times I 'ad with 'er mother before we was married. Why if any dago stopped in the street her was after 'im.'

Taking hat Mr Dale went out of the house. He took a different way from where she had gone to fetch beer. Those two sat and said nothing. Then Gates said:

'I've a mind to 'ave it out with 'er.'

'You sit still.'

'She wants a good clout. You do it then.'

'If you touch 'er I'll break the poker 'cross yer legs.'

Mr Gates stayed silent then and Mr Craigan said no more. But he did not put headphones back on his head so later Gates said:

'Without meanin' any offence, what d'you think on it?' but Craigan did not answer and little later Mr Gates slept again. Mr Craigan sat on. With thinking he forgot what was to have been greatest treat, concert from Berlin.

Then, one morning in iron foundry, Arthur Jones began singing. He did not often sing. When he began the men looked up from work and at each other and stayed quiet. In machine shop, which was next iron foundry, they said it was Arthur singing and stayed quiet also. He sang all morning.

He was Welsh and sang in Welsh. His voice had a great soft yell in it. It rose and rose and fell then rose again and, when the crane was quiet for a moment, then his voice came out from behind noise of the crane in passionate singing. Soon each one in this factory heard that Arthur had begun and, if he had two moments, came by iron foundry shop to listen. So all through that morning, as he went on, was a little group of men standing by door in the machine shop, always different men. His singing made all of them sad. Everything in iron foundries is black with the burnt sand and here was his silver voice yelling like bells. The black grimed men bent over their black boxes.

When he came to end of a song or something in his work kept him from singing, men would call out to him with names of English songs but he would not sing these. So his morning was going on. And Mr Craigan was glad, work seemed light to him this morning who had only three months before he got old age pension, he ought to work at his voice he said of him in his mind and kept Joe Gates from humming tune of Arthur's songs.

Every one looked forward to Arthur's singing, each one was glad when he sang, only, this morning, Jim Dale had bitterness inside him like girders and when Arthur began singing his music was like acid to that man and it was like that girder was being melted and bitterness and anger decrystallized, up rising up in him till he was full and would have broken out – when he put on coat and walked off and went into town and drank. Mr Craigan did not know he was gone till he saw he did not come back.

Still Arthur sang and it might be months before he sang again. And no one else sang that day, but all listened to his singing. That night son had been born to him.

And now time is passing.

Mr Dupret had fallen into a greater apathy, nor was there anything which pleased him now. Nor was he ever angry.

Nothing interested him. Mr Dupret had sent for his friends. Those who came he recognized and they talked to him but he could find no answer to their questions or anything in their conversation which would rouse him.

The days come and then the evening, morning papers are hawked about, last editions of the evening papers are sold in the night while men sit writing morning papers. It rained. The summer was passing. Young Dupret would go into the sick room but while old Mr Dupret recognized him and once or twice thought of what he could say, he never arrived at wishing him more than good morning. If he came in the evening as soon as he was in the room old Mr Dupret said 'goodnight' and if he ignored this then the old man would lie with eyelids shut over his eyes. And his wife was treated in the same way.

Then Mrs Dupret had him moved to the house in the country. Young Mr Dupret used to come down for the weekends. Doctors came and went. Electrical treatment was given him, many other remedies were tried, even the most strikingly beautiful nurses were found to tend him, once a well-known courtesan was hired for the night, but the old man still showed no interest and little irritation; he said good-morning to his wife, son, doctors and nurses, good-night to the harlot.

Lines came out on his wife's face. He never mentioned the City or his interests, whenever he spoke it was about the needs of his body. He spoke of no more than these to the nurses, it is not known for certain if he spoke to the harlot. No one could find the face to be present when she was introduced into his room. He had constantly, before his illness, betrayed his wife and she had known it. Nothing really was simpler for her or more natural in such an emergency than to arrange for the lady to come down, what was odd was the doctor of that particular moment allowing it. Mrs Dupret could have no official knowledge of her coming, she could not see her and had to invent many ruses that the servants might not know.

Richard had to receive this lady and show her to the bedroom, and he stood outside with the doctor and one of the nurses. The doctor insisted on standing close to the door as he said he feared 'the possible effects' upon a man of Mr Dupret's age, but his son stood further away, lost in embarrassment, particularly as the nurse seemed nervous and insisted on standing by him. After thirty minutes the lady reappeared. She lit a cigarette. The doctor said 'well' in a threatening voice and she answered that nothing had passed between them, she had done everything in her power, had done her utmost, she was ready to try again although she had packed up her things in her suitcase and if they liked they could go in with her and see for themselves, (she was plainly intimidated by the doctor and cast imploring glances at young Dupret), but she insisted that all he had said was goodnight and then he had shut eyelids over his eyes, 'the good baby' she said.

Some time passed before young Mr Dupret could recover from his surprise at this visit. To his friends in London he talked with horror about the cynical attitude of older women towards sex. There was so much horror in the tone of his voice that his friends asked themselves what could have happened to him and talked of it to each other. But while he soon recovered his old assurance it was some time before he could go into his father's room. Secretly he was annoyed that his mother had not asked him for his opinion, and for the rest of his life he spoke with venom of doctors.

So nobody knew what the old man thought, though everyone was certain that his brain was still working. A submarine is rammed and sinks. It lies for days upon the bed of the ocean and divers tap out messages to it and the survivors tap out answers to the divers, asking for oxygen and food. Above, on the surface of the ocean men work frantically but the day grows on into the evening, night falls, there is another day, another night, and as everyone realizes gradually that they cannot hope to raise the submarine in time, their efforts are not so frantic, they take a little longer over what they do. In the same way fresh doctors were still fetched to Mr Dupret, but no daring experiments were expected of them. They all said very much the same, that his frame was worn out and that only complete rest might bring him out of his illness. More they did not say and Mrs Dupret though she had never been very fond of him, was now thinking how very fond of him she was.

It was hot and it had been hot all day. Mr Gates had gone out, quite often now alone he went out, and Jim Dale had gone out.

When Lily had tea things put away she came with some darning to back door which opened onto the garden. This evening Mr Craigan sat there.

He smoked pipe. She brought chair and sat on it. She began darning.

Almost whispering he said:

'I'm getting to be an old man.'

'Why grandad, you're not.'

'I am.'

'It's the heat of the day's tired you.'

'It's been very hot.'

She darned his socks.

'I bought those socks three years ago,' he said and she said was another twelve months' wear in them yet. She asked in her mind what he was talking for, and was he going to talk to her about it? She waited.

'My mother' he said then, 'knitted socks that wore longer'n that, and they came farther up the leg. They was very good socks.'

She waited.

'This day' he said 'brought me to mind of the days I was in the fields there and the cider we 'ad. The farmer was bound to give us cider. It was good cider, but it's not such a drink as beer.'

So much talk from him frightened her.

'I mind' he said 'yer Aunt Ellie well.' He spoke cheerfully. 'She was older by nine years than your mother. She married a drover by name of Curley. I remember their getting married. I was in the choir.'

'Was you in the choir grandad?' Lily said from nervousness.

'Ah, I sang in the choir. I ain't been in a church since. Nor I shall go even if I 'ave to bury one of my own.'

'Wouldn't you go the funeral.'

'I would not. Yes I sang when them were married. They made a fine show. I ate myself sick at the dinner there was after. She went to live with 'em up t'other end of the village. We lived next door to yer mother's parents so I didn't see much of 'er after that. But you'd say she was contented if you'd seen 'er. Curley was a nice young chap by what I can remember of 'im and yer aunt was a great upstanding woman. But she 'adn't the looks your ma had when she grew to be a woman. Any road she ran away from 'im three years after. No one knew where she'd went, she just gone out through the garden and down the road.'

'Didn't they put the police onto 'er?'

'No, Curley was frightened to do that. She went off. I ain't never 'eard of 'er since, nor nobody ain't.'

'And didn't you go away grandad?' She was trembling.

'Yes. Her going off like she did, that worked on me, and I

71

thought I'd try my luck. And it was years after when I was settled in this town and earning good money that I wrote to yer father – I'd been pals with him though younger'n me – to find out 'ow my old folks was getting on. And when 'e read in my letter 'ow I was doing 'e brought your ma and you over to Brummagem. You was a baby then. But I'd've been better where I was. I wouldn't 'ave got the money but I broke the old people's hearts and where am I now, with no one of my own about me? I got no home and the streets is a poor place after the fields.'

'But you got me, and there's Dad, and Jim.'

'You'll be marrying.'

'Well, if I do we'll live in this 'ouse if you'd let us.'

'Would 'e like it? Maybe while you couldn't get a 'ouse of yer own. But not after.'

Neither spoke.

'Ah,' he said, 'she left 'er man and went off with a flashy sort of card, 'e was a groom to some hunting people that lived a mile off. And I left my people soon after without a word to tell them I was going, thinking it was a fine thing to do. I wanted to make my way up in the world. But I'm no more'n a moulder, a sand rat, and will be till they think I'm too old for work. Three pounds a week and lucky to get it. I'd rather be in the country on twenty-five shillings. And what's 'appened to yer Aunt Ellie? D'you suppose 'e's kept her? That sort never do.'

Lily was crying. She feared and loved Mr Craigan.

'No that sort never do' he said, and smoked pipe and did not watch her crying. He got up and went inside and listened in to the wireless.

In morning Mr Dupret came to office. Soon Mr Archer came into his office.

He said good-morning sir and said how was the Chief and Mr Dupret said they hoped to move him into country tomorrow afternoon. Archer said change was bound to do him good and when he got to country home he would be different man altogether and would come back nine years younger.

72

'In the meantime' he said 'I think we are carrying on very nicely with you at the helm Mr Dupret. It's being a most interesting time for all of us, sir, working together as the team we shall be when you take over the old ship.'

Mr Dupret said crew would be very different when he was captain, would be more able seamen in it, and he could not help laughing at this and Mr Archer tittered.

Then he looked serious and said: 'Look here, Archer,' and Archer said yes sir, 'you know I didn't touch on the subject of Tarver's having another draughtsman when I was last in Birmingham three months ago but I think we ought to see how the land lies about it now.'

Archer said he thought time was ripe. Mr Dupret said he did not want to go too far with old Bridges, after all, he said, Tarver is still subordinate to the old man and must be while Bridges is still works manager, but that was no reason why Tarver should not have one, he said.

'We've lost several orders through it, Mr Dupret.'

Of course, Mr Dupret said, Tarver can't get his drawings out when he's understaffed. But Bridges must not be offended, or rather must be offended as little as possible. What did Archer think Walters thought about it?

'Of course' said Mr Archer, 'Mr Walters is a first class engineer, or was, and you know as well as I Mr Dupret that he's probably done more for the old firm than anyone – always excepting your father, sir. But I cannot get on with him, heaven knows I've tried, but his methods are not mine, his slowness grates on a nature like mine Mr Dupret. I should certainly not like to try sounding him on the matter.'

'No, I haven't asked you to.'

'Precisely, precisely, but I was afraid perhaps you were expecting me –'

Mr Walters came in. He was loud-voiced this morning.

'Good-morning Dick, how's your father?'

Why should he call me Dick, young Mr Dupret said in his mind, his familiarity was jovial but then he went on thinking any joviality was offensively familiar and was smiling at that while he answered Mr Walters his father was being taken down to country day after tomorrow.

Walters said they were all looking forward to seeing Mr Dupret back amongst them, which angered young Mr Dupret. Then they talked about business. Soon Walters began looking at Archer, expecting him to go and later Walters was glaring at him, but still Archer stayed on, very self conscious, till Mr Walters went off and was first to leave.

Young Mr Dupret saw this and dismissed Archer and was miserable and annoyed at both of them.

Another day and he was talking to Mr Archer about how Bridges would take idea of another draughtsman for Mr Tarver. He said he was not afraid of old Bridges and had taken man off lavatory door just to show Mr Bridges only that. And was also another reason. He thought it had interfered with reasonable liberty of men in the works. He said he thought they would work better for being left alone with as far as possible. After all, he said, it was comfortable factory and the shops were as safe as they could be.

Mr Archer replied yes, they had been very lucky in matter of accidents, but for the one they had had in iron foundry some months back.

'What accident?' said Mr Dupret sharply.

'Why, sir, a wire rope parted and one end in coming down narrowly missed a man.'

'When was this? Why wasn't I told?' Mr Dupret rose from out of chair.

'Three months ago I think sir. I only heard the other day and I didn't mention it to you as of course I thought Mr Bridges would have reported it to you.'

'This is disgraceful, I didn't even know of it!' Mr Dupret was furious. 'What happened?'

'The wire rope parted, sir, and nearly caught an iron moulder called Craigan. Of course it would have killed the man if he had met it.'

'Of course, yes. Why didn't Bridges tell me?'

'Mr Bridges certainly should have reported the matter. I did not mention it as I felt he was sure to have done so.'

'I suppose he thinks I'm a back number and mustn't be told what's going on. What if he'd killed what's-his-name?'

'He is getting an old man now I'm afraid, Mr Dupret, and he doesn't go round to see for himself that things are in a proper condition.'

He thought to himself yes, yes that was it, hush it up and think he wouldn't get to hear of it, incompetent old loafer. he'd see who was the boss, he'd teach him. Where was Walters? He'd let him see what he thought. He'd show them in their dotage they weren't still kings of old castle and they couldn't impose on him as they'd done on his father. Where was Walters? But perhaps he had better wait till he had calmed down. Yes, he would wait till tomorrow.

'All right, Archer,' he said, and Archer went out delighted.

Had anyone ever heard anything like it, young Mr Dupret shouted to himself, serious accident and no word about it said to head of the business. That swine Bridges. Damn them.

Soon as hooters in these factories sounded for dinner hour young man took his dinner over to where Mr Craigan sat every dinner hour eating bread and meat. This young man was in great state of agitation. He spoke quickly and was saying Andrew (foreman in iron foundry shop) had been at him again, it was persecution, Andrew had said he was used to getting eight of those brackets he was doing now to the five he was getting from him. But he knew, he said, Andrew was lying there as last time any had been off that pattern Will, who was in thick with Andrew, had done not more than four with no word spoke to him. He was saying to Mr Craigan Andrew was dead against him, lord if was another job going he'd go to it quick enough, and he'd like to see Andrew do eight off that pattern himself, he'd have eight wasters, you'd see, when they came to be cast. Anyroad, he said, if it was possible for a man to do eight it was a day work job anyway, was no bonus or piece work on that job. It wasn't right, he kept on saying, it wasn't right.

Mr Craigan said to go back and do what the foreman told him. When you were young you had to go about and into different shops to learn the trade, but he had not been in this foundry long, which was good shop for experience in general work. Besides that, Mr Craigan said, was no work going just now, and he didn't want to be out of a job, surely.

'You go back and do what the foreman tells you,' he said, and soon this young man said well he would see how it was going to turn out, and if Andrew had in mind to go on dogging him and making it misery for him to work under him or no.

'You go on back,' Mr Craigan said, 'in my time foremen 'ave asked me to do a number more than eight off patterns similar to what you're workin' off.' He said no more and then this young man went away.

Mr Craigan sat there all the hour as he did always and when hooters sounded once more in these factories to tell men was only five minutes before work, he went to gate to put his check in, which he did. He went over then to drinking water tap. It happened Tupe was there. Stream of men was coming through gate. They put in their checks. Tupe was very angry. He had no money left for beer and it angered him to drink water. No one would lend him money. Mr Craigan waited till he was done and then took white enamelled cup which hung down from nail on the wall and which Tupe had been drinking from. He rinsed it out. Mr Tupe saw this and for benefit of men who were coming in he began joking about Mr Craigan rinsing cup out. But he hated Mr Craigan, and, from crowd of men being about, anger rose in him and he made personal injury to himself out of Mr Craigan's rinsing cup out. Then veil passed on his eyes and he shouted insults though he did not mention Mr Craigan's family. Men stood round. Mr Craigan meantime was drinking water. When he was done he rinsed cup out and went away. As he went through the door into factory he said 'ow do to one who was standing with other men there. When he was gone all turned backs on Tupe.

Mr Dupret, after he had waited three days, dictated letter to Mr Bridges in Birmingham. He dictated with many pauses for he was not used to it, but he wanted all London office to know what he had put in this letter.

'Dear Mr Bridges,' it was, 'I have just learned of an accident which happened in the iron foundry some months back which might have caused serious injury or cost the life of a moulder named, I think, Craigan. I am sorry that you should not have notified me re this matter. In future I would be glad if you sent me a full report in the event of similar occurrences. Yrs faithfully,' and he signed name after that and had office girl to type managing director under signature. He was pleased with letter as being very restrained.

So soon as Mr Bridges read it he telephoned to Mr Walters in London. When Mr Walters came to telephone he asked him had he heard anything about letter which he had just got from young Dupret and Walters said no. What tomfoolery was it now, Mr Walters asked? Mr Bridges said it wasn't tomfoolery, news of today was that he was resigning. Mr Walters said come now Arthur. Mr Bridges said he was and Mr Walters said what, Dick? and Bridges said no, Arthur Bridges was sending for his cards after fifty-four years' work. Walters said what was it for God's sake, and Mr Bridges said listen to this and read young Mr Dupret's letter to him. 'Managing director, d'you get that rightly' screamed he down telephone. Mr Walters said bloody cheek. He said he would speak to young fool now about it and rang off then, leaving Bridges wildly talking.

Saturday afternoon. Lily Gates and Bert Jones went out together.

'Old Mr Craigan was on at me' she said, 'the other night about our going out together.'

'On at you was 'e? What did he say about me?'

''E didn't say anything about you. It was all about my Auntie Ellie.'

'What did she do?'

'She ran away with a groom, yes, when she was married.'

'What's that got to do with you and me? Are you going to run off with some other chap when we're married?'

They kissed then.

'Go on' he said, 'don't listen to that old cuckoo.'

''E's been like a father to me Bert.'

'Is that any reason why 'e should 'ave you all to 'imself?'

'D'you really want to 'ave me?'

They kissed.

'Yes,' she said. She drew a little back from him. ''E said some terrible things.'

'What did he say then?'

'I don't know, not what you might like put into words. But to one who knowed him!'

''Ow old are you? Are you still a kid?'

'What d'you mean?'

'D'you mean to tell me 'e can frighten you into trembles just by talking about something else to you?'

''E never says much in the ordinary way of things you see.'

'You're a girl' he said, 'I suppose that's how it is. But we're respectable. I don't see what 'e's got against me. If my father and mother lived in Birmingham I'd've taken you to see 'em long before now. We've been out to take tea with my mother's sister. And I've often said, often 'aven't I now, that I'd like you to come to Liverpool to see the ma and dad. I'd better go and see your old man, shall I?'

'No, Bert, no you mustn't go and see 'im.'

'Well what about your father?'

'Oh dad, 'e does what Mr Craigan tells 'im.'

'And so do you from what I can see of it.'

Moodily together they walked. Revolt gathered in her.

Later she was saying, exalted:

'Yes we're different to what we were, we've a right now to know things and choose for ourselves. Time was when a girl did just what her parents told 'er and thought herself lucky to do it, yes but we're different now. Why shouldn't I go out with you and 'ave a good time on me own? 'E's getting old, that's what it is. Of course I'm fond of 'im, 'e's been like a father and mother to me since my mother died when I was born so to speak, but I've worked for 'im ever since I was old enough, yes I've earned the right to think for myself. I cooks for all of them, 'im and dad and Jim Dale that lives with us as a boarder.'

'Well, I mean, you're a 'uman being aren't you?'

'Yes, girls now can pick for themselves. It's not like it was in the old days. Yes, I've chosen and 'e can say what 'e likes.'

78

Under this hedge again they kissed. Later again she was saying: 'Oh Bert we shan't be like the others shall we dear,' and he said if Duprets didn't appreciate him he would move some place where he was appreciated. And was a place he had written to, had got friend when they were boys together from Liverpool there, who would put in word for him and was more chance there, for Duprets was old fashioned, you couldn't get on in it. And when 'flu had been so bad January they had sent him out to that very firm with a fitter to put job up and manager there had said kind things to him, 'you should 'ave 'eard 'im,' said he. Lily Gates, listening, saw him as being foreman one day soon.

Old Mr Dupret lay in bed and as, day by day, he said a little more, so the hopes of each one in his house were raised little by little. Mrs Dupret even was becoming her old helpless self again. In the past he had always done all her thinking for her, then, while he had been so ill, she had been forced into being practical to a certain degree, and now, as he seemed to become daily more and more competent to deal with what was about him, so her sanity, what there was of it, so it ebbed and she was drifting back again to the gentle undulations of her spirit which heaved regularly with her breathing like the sea, and was as commonplace.

One day even he called for his letters. Of the first six letters they opened for him one was from Walters, one of his weekly reports. After describing the progress of several orders Walters went on to say how well Dick was doing, only that he had slightly overstepped the bounds of his authority when he had told Bridges to take that man off the lavatory door. But perhaps Mr Walters wrote, Mr Dupret himself had authorized it. After reading this Mr Dupret sent for Walters and a stenographer.

He was never so well again.

The next day Walters arrived and Mr Dupret had strength enough to dictate and sign a letter in which he ordered a different man to be put on at the lavatory door to check the men in and out. He whispered to Walters, when he had signed, that Dick's having done that must have made Bridges very angry, 'who is so young for his sixty years,' Mr Dupret whispered with a sly smile and then lay back and shut eyelids over his eyes. Thus Mr Walters was unable to tell him of the letter his son had written to Bridges because the old man was so visibly exhausted. Even if the doctor had not come in at that moment and ordered him out, he would have crept out then.

Walters went back to London, by Birmingham. He called at works on his way. He gave Bridges that letter from the chief and told him old man was very bad, he said it looked to him he might be dead any time now. Bridges said nonsense. His father, he said, had gone that way, but would be about again soon like his father had been, you'd see. And that letter was just what he wanted, said he, this would show young chap he wasn't cock of the roost yet. Had he told him about young chap's last effort, Mr Bridges asked, but Walters, eyes dimmed, said no, what manner of use was in talking of that to a dying man. 'He was a grand fine man,' Mr Walters said, 'a grand man,' in his dull voice. 'Is 'e as sick as that?' said Mr Bridges.

8

SHE LAY, ABOVE town, with Jones. Autumn. Light from sky grew dark over town.

She half opened eyelids from her eyes, showing whites. She saw in feeling. She saw in every house was woman with her child. In all streets, in clumps, were children.

Here factories were and more there, in clumps. She saw in her feeling, she saw men working there, all the men, and girls and the two were divided, men from women. Racketing noise burst on her. They worked there with speed. And then over all town sound of hooters broke out. Men and women thickly came from, now together mixed, and they went like tongues along licking the streets.

Then children went into houses from streets along with these men and girls. Women gave them to eat. Were only sparrows now in streets. But on roads ceaselessly cars came in from country, or they went out into it, in, out.

Smell of food pressed on her. All were eating. All was black with smoke, here even, by her, cows went soot-covered and the sheep grey. She saw milk taken out from them, grey the surface of it. Yes, and blackbird fled across that town flying crying and made noise like noise made by ratchet. Yes and in every house was mother with her child and that was grey and that fluttered hands and then that died, in every house died those children to women. Was low wailing low in her ears.

Then clocks in that town all over town struck three and bells in churches there ringing started rushing sound of bells like wings tearing under roof of sky, so these bells rang. But women stood, reached up children drooping to sky, sharp boned, these women wailed and their noise rose and ate the noise of bells ringing.

But roaring sound came in her ears and a sun, dark half cold, pressed onto her face. Bert kissed her. She woke. She heard tinkling sound of a pebble in a can which boy was dragging along path. Till all women she remembered, to each one a child, and she clung to man and said she had dreamed, had dreamed, dreamed.

And then in bed, after, rigid, she cried in her, I, I am I.

I am I, why do I do work of this house, unloved work, why but they cannot find other woman to do this work.

Why may I not have children, feed them with my milk. Why may I not kiss their eyes, lick their skin, softness to softness, why not I? I have no man, my work is for others, not for mine.

Why may I not work for mine?

Why mayn't they laugh at my coming in to them. Why is there nothing that lives by me. And I would do everything by my child in the morning and at evening, why haven't I one? I would work for him who made child with me, oh day and night I'd be working for them, and get up in the night to feed him and in morning to get father's tea. I would be his mother, he his father, why have I no child?

Lord give me a child that I might wash him, feed him, give him life. Yes let him be a boy. Give him blue eyes, let him cling to me with his hands and never be loosed from me. Give him me to love that I'm always kissing him and working for him. I've had nothing of my own. Give him me and let him be mine, oh, oh give me a life to work for, and give me the love of him, and his father's.

Young Mr Dupret sat in their country house picking nose.

Why, he said in mind, why could not the old man die? Of course was gratitude and all that of sons to fathers but, old mummy, why couldn't he die. He had made mother's life misery to her, he had never done anything for him but to pull him up, all the time, taking him away from school, and again, little things, whole time. Then to pretend collapse, question was if he wasn't just shamming, when dinner party for Hannah was to come off, so it had to be cancelled. And how did fathers expect sons to learn business without making mistakes? Now after what had been done he couldn't go back to Birmingham. He couldn't look Bridges face to face.

How pleased Bridges would be.

He wasn't, he said again in his mind, going back to business till old man thought better of it. Besides mother wanted him. And what picture she had made of him and herself and of father with that ridiculous harlot. To put her into bedroom where he lay and all of them waiting outside – disgusting, filthy, revolting. He'd made that plain to her and it seemed to be telling on her. She mustn't do that again, or something like it. Pity was the old man did not get rush of blood to head and die of it, malicious old figure head.

Doctors said was no hope for him now. He felt he could go up now to room and say 'die, old fool, die.' Trouble was of course he was not an old fool, but clever like the devil.

Mr Bridges went down through works in Birmingham till Tupe he found.

'What about that Craigan?' Mr Bridges said.

'What about 'im ?' Tupe said.

'What I want to get at is' said Mr Bridges, 'is what happened when that wire rope gave some time back.'

'Nothin' didn't 'appen.'

'Didn't it come down somewhere by Craigan?'

'I know it daint,' Mr Tupe said. 'It broke sure enough but there weren't much strain on it that moment and it wouldn't've bruised 'is arse if it 'ad fetched 'im one. But God strike me 'andsome if 'e didn't raise 'is ugly old dial an' start blubberin' an' made such a 'ullaballoo as if 'e might be dead, or the only one in the shop. That's 'im all over.'

'So it wasn't nearly all over with 'im.'

'All over with 'im? No! But it would've been a good thing for this factory if it'd caught 'im and so killed 'im. There's only one man in that shop by 'is way of looking at it and that's 'im. There's always trouble between 'im and Andrew (that was foreman in iron foundry shop in this factory). You listen to me, sir, the men'll go to 'im before they go to the foreman, it's God's truth I'm telling you. There'd be 'alf as much more work done again in there if 'e weren't in there. 'E's a trouble maker, like you find in all factories, but there ain't been a place I've worked in where there's been the like of 'im.'

''E's the best moulder I've got. I'd give £100 for another like him.'

''E may be a good enough moulder, Mr Bridges, but look 'ow slow 'e is. 'E works to suit 'is own convenience, not the firm's.'

Mr Bridges was moving off.

''Ow's the gaffer, sir, if you don't mind me asking you,' Mr Tupe said to change subject of conversation and because he could not abide seeing Bridges going away.

'He's pretty bad. The young chap is down there with 'im, and aint been to work this week. It looks bad.'

'Well, I don't know,' said Tupe, cunning, 'that dandy 'e daint ever go to work, do 'e!' Mr Tupe said and Bridges, laughing, went away.

'I knows what the old man likes, it's butter, not margarine, an' I gives it to 'im,' Tupe said, in his mind, rejoicing.

Later Mr Bridges sat in chair in his office.

Mr Bridges in his thinking and in most of his living was all theatre. Words were exciting to him, they made more words in him and wilder thinking.

Sometimes liquid metal foundrymen are pouring into moulding box will find hole in this, at the joint perhaps, and pour out. Sometimes stream of metal pouring out will fall on patch of wet sand or on cold iron, then it will shower out off in flying drops of liquid metal. To see this once or twice perhaps is exciting. But after twice, or once even, you just go to stop hole up where metal from box is pouring.

So with Mr Bridges.

You were to him speaking, and he began quietly answering, then, suddenly, he was acting, sincere in feeling, but acting, and words were out pouring, fine sentiments fine. At first you said, 'fine old man' in your mind, at last you were thinking only how to plug him. And with him this was not only with his talking, it was also in his silent thinking.

So in his thinking he thought now Mr Dupret is dying. He thought how he'd worked fifteen years for Mr Dupret. 'And never a cross word between us.' He began now in his thinking. He made Mr Dupret into angel beaming from sky, he saw Mrs Dupret and all their servants weeping in front parlour. He saw slavey bring Mrs Dupret cup of tea from the kitchen, 'from humblest to the highest' he was saying in his thinking, without her ever having asked for a cup. He was seeing doctors, great surgeons going in and out of room where the Chief was lying. Inside he for life was fighting. Mr Bridges thought then how all had to come to it, 'great and small, King and navvy.' He thought one day he would die, the wife would die.

And he thought then, sobering, he was too old to get another job and what would happen when young Dupret was head of business? And he couldn't afford to retire, wife had made him spend all the salary, were hardly no savings. What would happen to them? But then he thought the Chief was sure to put someone older as partner to young chap, or adviser, or trustee. You couldn't put kid like that at head of business, government wouldn't allow it. No, he thought, forgetting grieving.

Young Mr Dupret sat at bottom of garden down by where flowed river Thames. Autumn was about. Down this river leaves came floating on the water, yellow leaves, and with each coming of the wind yellow leaves left trees and came floating down on to the water, quietly settling on the Thames. So now thoughts settled three by three in his mind and soon he thought no more but as river Thames slipped away to the sea so drifted into sleeping.

Sunshine was pale. So drifted into sleep. Yet came party from Maidenhead in launch up the river, men and women, a silver launch. Laughter came like birds from women in it. It came on slowly and he opened eyes and it went by, this laughter reaching him. He stretched and watched it go. Laughter from it fluttered back to him and then in wide circle launch turned leisurely and came back past him and he thought why did they turn it there. Why did they turn it there he thought and then man on launch played dance tune from the wireless they had on it and it went on down with stream till he could see them no more but still hear them, then he could not hear them any more.

Women were on that launch, he envied the men. They would be back at Maidenhead for tea, he thought.

He thought and saw in his mind was no good his staying here with father getting no better nor any worse, and he saw what he most needed now was the company of women, like on that silver launch. Hannah. He thought he would go back to London. Also mother needed rest, he would try and bring her with him.

Again he thought was no use in struggling against that one defeat with Bridges. He would go back to work, and if Bridges and Walters mentioned man being put on at lavatory door he would tell them just what he thought. It was hollow triumph of theirs he thought and he would show them just how hollow. It would not be long now before he showed them.

He shook afternoon from off him and went back into house.

Still flowed river Thames and still the leaves were disturbed, then were loosed, and came down on to water and went by London where he was going, by there and out into the sea.

Mr Craigan with Joe Gates and Dale that was his mate in iron foundry, these sat at supper and Lily brought food in to them. Happiness moved with her where she went. Yet Bert was not going out with her that night, he had business. Yet in all she did showed happiness.

Dale wanted a knife, but, getting up from table, for himself fetched it.

And Gates asked to pass bread. Lily stretched for this, but Mr Dale leaned, he pushed bread forward over to him.

When plate of meat was eaten he handed plate to her and Craigan's that was next him.

When supper was over he fetched beer. The two old men had settled in chairs and were smoking. He said then to Miss Gates if she was going out tonight. She said not tonight. He said would she care to go to the movies? She said she didn't mind. They went off.

When they had got seats even at cinema he said nothing, like he always did say nothing. She for this was grateful and sat apart from him in her seat in glory of secret happiness. He felt this and he was miserable. She was so grateful to him and he said nothing and she hardly watched film, she thought so of Bert.

So.

9

HANNAH GLOSSOP.

Her father also had been sick and she had gone home, in country, over the weekend. Doctor had motored down from London to see her father. That night his chauffeur had been watching machinery which made electric light for this house in country. He watched too close, caught in fly-wheel he was killed.

She had never seen him but when she heard she cried. She cried all the weekend. Nothing had ever been near her before. No one had ever been badly hurt near her.

They said: 'darling, but you never saw the poor man.'

She said: 'I know,' and cried.

They said: 'darling, the doctor's providing for his family.'

She said: 'I know,' and cried.

'You never saw him, he can mean nothing to you,' they said to her, and she said again and again, 'to think of his dying!'

She cried all weekend, and she got quite weak. Doctor became quite worried over her. At last he told her mother was nothing physical the matter with her he was sure. What really was wanted he said was for something to do to be found for her, some work for her to do he said.

Her mother said work? What work could she do? It was true, she said, she had enjoyed enormously General Strike when she had carried plates from one hut to another all day, that was true enough, but what work could she do? Doctor said of course to be married would be the best thing for her but 'in the interim' he thought some kind of work was what she wanted, and he went away with hired chauffeur.

*

88

Another night. She had cleared table after supper. She went off out. Jim Dale stayed a little, then he got up.

'Where you goin' Jim?' Mr Gates said. 'To the boozer,' and he went off out.

'Goin' to the boozer, did you 'ear that?' said Gates to Mr Craigan, 'that's what she's doing, she's drivin' a good lad to go and wet 'is troubles. 'E daint ever use to go before. And 'e's a good lad. Why can't I give 'er a clout?'

Mr Craigan was silent.

'It's wicked I reckon,' Mr Gates said. 'Ah and she gave him a short week the other week, that day when Arthur was singing and he put on his coat and went out. An' she don't wash up of an evening even, but leaves it till morning. She's got too much money, that's what it is, and you can wager she pays for Bert Jones into the movies.'

Mr Craigan put wireless earphones over his head.

'You and yer wireless,' Gates softly said, 'it's enough to make anyone that lives with you light 'eaded, listening like you might be a adder to the music. I'll go and 'ave one,' he said. He got up, 'I'll go to the boozer and 'ave one.'

Mr Gates went to public, to public where Tupe was.

Tupe drank with Gates and Gates with Tupe. 'Yes,' said Mr Tupe finishing story, ''e said to her, them are one and nine.'

'Them are one and nine, 'e said to 'er,' Gates chimed, and this story was done. He drank of his beer in pot.

'Ah,' he said easing trousers, 'that's the 'ang of 'em. Females is like that right enough. Take our wench. What do she do with the money?'

''Ow much d'you give 'er Friday nights?'

Mr Gates drank again.

'Mind, I'm not askin' as some would,' confidentially Mr Tupe said, 'I'm not Paul bloody Pry.'

Because Mr Gates was a little drunk, he leaned, he whispered.

'Strike!' Tupe said, 'You give 'er all that much?'

'Ah!' said Mr Gates flattered, 'we daint ever stint in our 'ouse.'

'Stint!' said Mr Tupe, 'I wonder 'er wouldn't choke you with grub on that money.'

'I never did hold with stintin' the grub, nor Craigan daint.'

'Nor I do. But on that money my old woman'd keep three kids as well and them'd ave more'n enough to eat. It's wicked, Joe, 'er's twistin' yer.'

'Twistin 'is 'er?'

'All that money and 'er says it goes in grub. You can bet it daint. I give our old woman three bob less'n that and there's enough an' more to eat in our 'ouse, an' 'er gets 'er own clothes and anything for the 'ouse.'

Mr Gates banged fist then on table.

'I'll wager she pays for Bert Jones into the movie.'

'Why in course she do. Look 'ere Joe, what's Craigan at in your 'ouse.'

'It ain't my 'ouse, it's 'is'n.'

'What's 'e at, anyroad.'

In another public Mr Dale alone sat about, not drinking.

'What d'you mean, what's 'e at?'

'Do 'im pay 'er Friday nights,' Mr Tupe said.

'I think e' do,' said Mr Gates. They talked and Gates confided more in Tupe who got mysterious more and more. Each spoke in broader country accent they had come from to Birmingham, speaking louder.

Getting more drunk Gates forgot seriousness and said what good thing that Dale went to pub, which he did not do before, it would anger Mr Craigan. He was good lad, Gates said, he did not expect you to do your own and three others' work, like some expected. A drop of beer would do him good, say who would water was lion's drink. But Craigan now, if you looked up two moments at work he was down your throat, and then in evenings, in their house it was like being in a hearse with wireless to it: 'Dirty ice-faced 'ermit,' Gates said, holding sides, he was laughing at own image in a glass, ''e'd listen to the weather reports so long that 'e wouldn't tell what it was doin' outside, rainin', snowing or sleet.'

Few young men go to public houses in Birmingham, then, only when they are married. So when Mr Dale went he was alone, nor did he want to talk.

Mr Gibbon said after he had done the Holy Roman Empire

he felt great relief and then sadness at old companion done with. Mr Dale wanted to feel relief but felt only as if part of him was not with him, and sadness of a vacuum.

Griping sorrow was in void in him, but felt he could draw into him all winds of air for sympathy with him, that he must take hold on someone and clutch him so he would not go away and say all the sadness that was in his heart to him, and suck the sympathy back from that one.

But then he could not do all that (what would people think of him?) so he went to where was warmth and noise, were many people and talking, nor did he drink but sat over pot of beer hoping to be distracted.

– This is substance of what he wanted, though he did not know what he wanted.

Also young Mr Dupret was restless so he came to London, and Miss Glossop also came to be distracted.

They met at dinner party. They sat next each other. She did not remember him but soon they were talking. And from their mouths this time went words that seemed like to sink into each other's eyes.

Soon he was saying what trouble parents were to their children and she got very interested.

(She thought mother was real cause of her not getting married. She would not let her do anything, when she enjoyed washing up – which she had never done but three times at picnics and the General Strike. She blamed mother for uselessness feeling she had just now, and but for that useless feeling she would not have cried when chauffeur was killed. So she got very interested.)

Then he said how his father was dying now, and how sad it was. How he had had to drag mother up here away for a rest. He said the doctors told them would be months before he died yet. Now bending her face to his she shone out feeling over him.

'It's so awful,' she said, 'I can't get used to the feeling of death. A doctor came to stay with us last week. His chauffeur got caught up in the thing that makes our electric light. He was killed. Poor man, he was dead at once and it's so awful

91

to think that it can happen to anyone. Of course it's different for old people because they're old, but young people like us, we might go and die any time.'

They talked so, all through dinner, and hostess noticed. She thought in her mind young people didn't play the game nowadays but talked only on one side of them from soup till dessert if they were interested. 'Mr Dupret has talked to Hannah all through dinner,' she said in her mind, 'and there's poor Di next him absolutely starved. All she can do poor child is to listen to what's going on across the grapes over on the other side of the table. Henry's just as bad as the other boy, he won't speak to her either.'

So he talked to her throughout dinner and when ladies went and port was sent round he did not join in conversation then, he did not talk because he was still finding more in feeling to say to her. When they got into cars to go on to this dance, they went in different cars. He sat silent thinking of presently when they sat out.

As she sat in car misery came back over her, he was so clever she thought, and she must have seemed so silly talking to him all dinner when it hadn't been much, not worth all the notice it attracted, their talk. Also she felt fat.

When he came out of cloakroom he waited for her at foot of stairs in crowd of people. When she came out of cloakroom she looked happy as happy. Why, thought he, can this be for me? He pressed forward to her. She let him take her upstairs.

She hardly knew he was there, truth to tell!! As they had got out of motor-car, there, in doorway, just going in, Tom Tyler, back from Siam. Tom Tyler!! 'Tom!' she had screamed, 'Annie!' He was here!

As they went upstairs, so the music came nearer to them from room was dancing in.

Chandelier hung from ceiling on a level with half way upstairs. It was like bell-shaped, and crystal, cut in all manners, formed it. As they went up he looked at chandelier. Chatter of people going up and down past him and he thought this great brilliant thing, you are like her only she is not so cold, but how like you are, he thought, all these people ascending, descending, and then, as first tones of dance music came down through chatter about, chandelier thrilled all through and light tumbled down along it, like it was a bell and notes trembling from the clapper.

So, as they went upstairs, and she had put her arm on his (she did not know it), so happiness tumbled down his spine. They went slowly, were many people. All these were talking as these two went further so dance music got much louder and louder, and so she glided up into bliss:

Your eyes are my eyes
My heart looks through

sang the band: bliss again to be in London, and Tom Tyler being here, just think of it, bliss, and she said to notes of xylophone, darlings, she said, darlings.

And again, this was to be lucky night, was no one to receive them and they danced straight out into the room, marvellous band, Roberts, and she was thinking Dick was Tom Tyler.

Your eyes, sang they again,

Your eyes are my eyes
My heart looks through

'Oh' she whispered, 'Oh' and he felt quite transported.

Just then Mr Dupret in sleep, died, in sleep.

''Ow are ye Albert?'

'Middlin' Aaron. The sweat was dropping from off me again last night from the pain.'

'Them,' said Mr Connolly nodding to group of men, (it was lunch hour in Dupret factory and men sat about) 'them tell me the old gaffer am dead.'

'Ah, he died in 'is sleep. I can't say it makes a deal of difference to me, I ain't ever seen 'im only the once. How old would 'e be in your estimation?'

Mr Connolly said he had had fine innings and then they talked of young Dupret's age. They said he was twenty-six and didn't the old chap have him late on in life, seeing he was seventy-eight when he died.

'It's the food and the comfortable life,' said Mr Milligan.

'It am' said Mr Connolly.

'Ah' Mr Milligan said, 'the young chap's no older than Bert Jones there that is just turned twenty-six.'

When Mr Dupret came back to office in London Mr Archer went in to him.

'Mr Dupret, sir' he said, 'the office have asked me to come on behalf of them all to convey their condolences in your bereavement, which is also ours, sir, but to a smaller degree of course. It is an honour I very much appreciate, if I may say so, in that I did not have the – the honour to work under him as long as some who have been in this office all their lives. But every day we were here we were learning from him sir, every day, I am sure no one knows that better than I do. It was a pleasure to work for him Mr Richard, always a kind word for everyone. I remember once as I happened to be sharpening a pencil he came up behind me without I heard him. He put his hand on my shoulder and said, "Archer, go on as you are going on now and you will be all right!" I don't think I shall ever forget that, Mr Dupret, as long as it pleases our common father to spare me. The Lord giveth and the Lord taketh away, sir.'

Mr Dupret, embarrassed, said wreath they had sent looked very beautiful on the coffin. Archer went away delighted.

Mr Dupret thought how like father to say that to Archer and make joke for himself out of it in a wry way, knowing Archer would never see barbed end of it. How like too, to be always mistaken in his best men, good men like Tarver he thought nothing of while men like Bridges he exalted in his own manner, though without ever praising them.

'Well, Arthur, he's dead.'

'Yes' said Mr Bridges to Mr Walters.

'They weren't there when it happened,' said Mr Walters, 'he died all of a sudden with none of his own to hold 'is 'and.'

'Where was the young chap then? Wastin' up in town?'

'He took his mother up there, Arthur, to give her a change.'

'Yes, he's dead,' said Bridges.

'There was a fine man,' Mr Walters said, 'loyal to those under him, you knew where you were with him.'

'Yes,' cried Mr Bridges, 'yes and now we might be like in the desert with a pack of wolves as escort and at night when we lie down scorpions,' he cried, 'poisoned snakes for pillows.'

'Not so loud Arthur.'

'I don't care who 'ears me,' shouted Bridges clinging on to mantelpiece. 'I'd like to call 'em all in and say to 'em, we are like a flock that 'as lost its shepherd with the night coming on. I loved that man. Why, I'd 'ave laid down my life for 'im. And now where are we, tell me that? 'Ere, I'll tell you what he'll say. He'll say we're too old for our jobs. That gang in your office up there will be at 'im all the time, and what am I to do, I got nothing put by, if I can't 'old this job I'll have to go on the streets with the wife and die like any dog in a 'ole.'

'Arthur!' said Mr Walters.

'Aye,' Bridges was out of himself, 'aye and since I came 'ere I've built this side up stone by stone and made a job of it. Waller, of the O.K., said to me only a week ago standing where you are now, he said you turn out better work here than I've seen in the trade. Now there's a man of experience, mayn't I take part of that on myself? No, it's now as I might be a 'orse or a dog turned off because their old man 'as died, or like an Indian widder woman that is burned beside 'er dead 'usband.'

'Well, there's other firms.'

'They wouldn't take us on at our age.'

Walters quietly said he would work for young Mr Dupret as he had worked for father.

'And so will I,' Mr Bridges said, abating, 'but you see what's coming to us, 'e's gone out of 'is way to make me a fool before my own men, you'll see,' (rising again) 'he'll bide 'is time till 'e can get us off without a pension, forcing us out of a living. And that's what comes to a man that 'as worked all 'is life for another. My bones in my body they ache all day now but when I've worn 'em out in 'is service 'e'll sell 'em as scrap to the rag and bone. That's 'ow it will be.'

'You ought to take a day or two off Arthur.' Then Mr Bridges began again at that, saying did he want him to starve right away. Suddenly he covered face in hands, he burst out into sobbing, and Walters sent for brandy.

Miss Gates went out in afternoon to buy food in shops and now was last sunshine of winter on the streets. She came into high road and trams went by her rocking, roaring sound came from them and sound of their bell like metals. Along line of shops which were on each side of this road women in dark clothes went in and out of them.

She passed by and black man passed by her. She had in mind to turn back and look at him. But she saw chest of tea in shop window. She stopped by it. She thought of film she had seen which was advertisement of a tea firm, she had seen in it black women that gathered the tea, and how delicate she had thought them and she remembered now, how delicate their arms and hands which did not seem touched by the hard labouring.

Were tins of pineapple in that shop window and she wondered and languor fell on her like in a mist as when the warm air comes down on cold earth; in images she saw in her heart sun countries, sun, and the infinite ease of warmth.

'Well, Albert,' said Mr Gates, who came to fetch chaplets, to Mr Milligan storekeeper, ''ow are you feeling?'

'Middlin', Joe.'

'Ah, and the old man's looking ill and all.'

'What – 'Tis 'im? Ah, 'e came by the other day and I said to myself, I said, that man 'as the shade of death on his face.'

'I said as much to Jim, when 'e went past. It's a shame there couldn't be a double funeral, the old gaffer and 'im.'

Mr Milligan laughed.

'Well, there's double weddings, ain't there,' cried Mr Gates 'and double beds bless my 'eart,' he said, 'all for the enjoyment of mankind, so why shouldn't we see two dirty sods put underground at one go off.'

'They buried the old gaffer some time back. I don't say I 'ad anything against the man. But it's marvellous the state these

96

worryers get into, I don't reckon I'll be far out when I said Mr Bridges is done for.'

'Ah, and look at our foreman, Andrew there, 'e takes it 'ome with 'im. I'll wager 'is missus is a good moulder. I'll wager 'er 'as to listen to 'is troubles every night, 'ow this job blowed and that'n run out.'

'That's right. But, come to look at it, wouldn't Bridges and Tupe be all right in a 'earse together.'

Mr Gates did not relish this.

'I'd like 'im dead,' Mr Gates said carelessly. He meant Mr Bridges. He meant to keep off topic of Mr Tupe.

Milligan said indeed Tupe should be in a grave and Mr Gates asked for chaplets. When Mr Milligan came back he said to mark his words and that would be big changes in this factory soon. Yes, he said, they would see a lot different, whether for better or worse he couldn't say.

Well, Mr Walters said in his mind, I must try and like the young chap, and he came into Mr Richard's private office.

'Good morning, Dick.'

'Good morning' Mr Dupret said cordially. 'I hope you're well.'

'Pretty well thanks. But it's marvellous what the weather's been doing to people.'

'Yes, two or three of my friends are down with the 'flu. It's a wonder we're alive, Mr Walters.'

'Yes, it is that, and I'm worried about Mr Bridges, Dick. He's not as well as he ought to be, not by a long way. Everything seems to have got right on his mind lately. I shouldn't wonder if he didn't have a breakdown one of these days.'

'A breakdown?'

'Yes, he's right down on his luck. A good deal of it was your father dying as he did – (as he did? wondered young Mr Dupret) – and then he takes everything to heart very much. I think we ought to send him on a holiday.'

Mr Dupret said he was sorry to hear that and who would take over if he did go away.

'Cummings will take over.'

'What about Tarver, Mr Walters?'

'Cummings is senior to Tarver, Dick, it wouldn't do to put the younger man over the older one.'

'Wouldn't it give him a useful experience of running the works. After all, Tarver is our coming man isn't he, Walters?'

'Well Mr Dupret,' said Mr Walters, rage rising in him, 'I don't know that Tarver's got the all round knowledge necessary for a works manager.'

'What sort of a man is Cummings?'

'He's a real good man. He came to us as a lad and has been with us ever since. Mr Bridges has been bringing him on ever since he came here.'

'Then what sort of age is he?'

'He'd be round about fifty.'

'Rather a long time to be bringing along, isn't it Mr Walters?'

'Engineering isn't learnt in a day.'

'Well,' Mr Richard said importantly, 'I think I'll go down to the works for a day or two to see how things stand. I'm all for Mr Bridges going for a holiday but I don't quite see my way clear yet about his temporary successor.'

Hoity toity Mr Walters thought and why wouldn't he give him handle to his name, call a man 'Walters' who was old enough to be his father!

Mr Dupret picked up a letter.

'Why haven't these people had delivery yet?'

'There's been a heap of trouble in the iron foundry over that job, Dick. It's an awkward job, but they've pretty well got it weighed up now since I went down there and saw it.'

'Damn that iron foundry,' Mr Dupret said.

'Yes, I've said that many a time,' said Mr Walters. One sentence, like a bell, knolled in Mr Richard's mind, 'Cummings will take over,' sentence said confidently.

Lily came to go and meet Bert. She took short cut that was over piece of waste ground.

Night. Street lamps were lit over where she was going to. She walked across. She had done shopping and men had been fed at evening, now work was done and like as when gulls come and settle on the water so her spirit folded wings, so walked in quietness.

Night was mauve about her, mauve and cold. She only felt warmer.

So, wings folded, as the gull takes on motion of the sea, night flowed over her then in her.

Gathering coat she hugged arms round body and folded in night and buried face in it, in fur of her collar. And so containing it warmness rose in her, drowsed her mind, and came in little ball of warmth top of throat, behind her nose, breathed through her there, till she was drunk, and all of her was dyed in night.

She came nearer street lamps and then stumbled a little. Looking up she saw them, light sticking out from them, and as she came nearer so night left, excitement effervescing in her she put coat straight, and felt cold. When she stepped into cone of light of this lamp, night was outside and it might not have been night-time.

She met Bert at corner.

They kissed. Her warmth and his, their bodies straining against each other, became one warmth. Walking, his arm round her enclosed her warmth and his. So it came from his veins flowing into hers, so they were joined.

They walked from cone of light into darkness and then again into lamplight, nor, so their feeling lulled them, was light or dark, only their feeling of both of them which was one warmth, infinitely greater.

Tom Tyler was the life of the house-party. Before dinner he stood on his head, put a pin in the back of a chair and sitting on the chair leaned round it, bending his body into an arc and took the pin out in his mouth. Then when some other man did this, only not so quickly of course, Tom sent for a tumbler and filling this with water he put it on his forehead. He knelt down, he bent his body back in an arc from the knees, and soon was lying flat on his back with not a drop of water spilled, nor had he steadied the tumbler with his hands at any stage in the course of this delicate operation. No one could do it after him, many got soused

ter in trying to do it, which only added to the
hilarity.

nnah got quite hysterical with excitement.

en he put an armchair in the middle of the floor and
shions at a little distance at the back of it, and he took a
running leap and dived into the chair, turned a somersault on
his head in it and landed with the chair onto the cushions. The
chair was broken. That was a very good joke. Then they all
played hunt the slipper.

All this was good clean fun. If anyone touched anyone it
brought a bruise.

So it was all good clean fun. And when they were bored
with hunt the slipper they sat in a circle, (Tom Tyler directed
all this), and someone, man or woman was put in the middle
and kept themselves very stiff and everyone, each one
theoretically being for himself, everyone I say tried to push
the person in the middle onto one of the others who were
sitting. When that happened, amid screams, the person fallen
on had to go in the middle. So boys fell across girls and then
perhaps took a little time to get up, but it is quite true to say
that there was nothing dirty in all this.

Hannah, for instance, did not even long for Tom to be
pushed over her, nor did she even think of it, it was all – how
shall I say, – all was like the clearness of an empty glass, with
the transparency of light. Yet not transparent. You look into
crystal globe and its round emptiness makes a core in it you
can't see through, there is nothing there only the transparency
is confused. That was like Hannah Glossop when someone
wasn't talking to her, inoculating ideas.

When she went to dress for dinner she told maid she had
never laughed so much in all her life.

Mr Bridges, on his leave, sat in sitting room of a lodging
house at Weston. He was writing letter to Mr Walters. He
looked up and onto the sea grey under dark sky, incessantly
moving, spotted with gulls. He had just written: What I won't
wear about this place is seeing a big ship go down and then
when you're sitting in the same place with nothing to do and
not even a dog to speak to you see the same boat come back

100

up again an hour later. There's times I could go loony wondering what it was up to.

What were they doing at Works, he thought? Young chap would be down there now, and most likely he had only given him the week off so he might play hell with the place while he was away. Some fathers had awkward children by God and to hand the whole show over to them when you were dead, it was like cutting the throat of a whole crowd of people.

What would Tarver be at?

Mrs Bridges came in then.

'She says it's sixpence for a bath!' she said.

'Sixpence, eh?' said Mr Bridges. 'You go tell her she's in competition. Tell her I can get a wash for nothing in the sea there and if she don't cut her prices she'll lose the order.'

'Oh, yes, you bathing in this cold.'

'You tell her I've bathed every Christmas Day since ever I could swim.'

'Why it aint November yet and you can't swim, you know you can't.'

'How'll she know that, eh? If it's going to cost us a tanner for a bath I'll wait till I get back to Brum before I wash the dust off me of this bloody 'ouse.'

Women, he thought, would you believe it, they'd ruin you. Yes, thought Mrs Bridges, and little he'd think of it if it was for a pint.

Cummings, he went on in mind, was a good man, he'd taught him all he knew, but he didn't like leaving works with him, not with Tarver and those sharks about. And he couldn't ring up again, he'd rung up twice this morning already. The waiting till you got back, that was the rub of it, was like having your arteries cut and watching the life blood spouting out.

Richard Dupret came late to that house-party. He arrived in middle of fish course at dinner. He had warned hostess was only train he could come by, having to work late that day in London; but yet, as he passed by open door of dining room to go and dress and saw brilliance of lights there and clash and glitter of women's dresses, and heard their laughing, he had a sickening in stomach.

Older woman asked hostess who was that young man that was arriving? and she said Richard Dupret.

'Sylvia Dupret's son?'

'Yes my dear. It was her husband who died not so very long ago.'

'Wasn't he very rich?'

'Yes very. Poor Sylvia it was quite dreadful for her, she was at the Embassy with a party when they telephoned through and Ian Lampson had to break it to her. Of course it wasn't altogether unexpected but the doctors had said he might linger on for months.'

'Didn't she stay by him at all then?'

'Oh yes, but she came up for a change.'

'She oughtn't to have left him, a woman shouldn't do a thing like that Grizel. It looks so bad.'

'Oh no, it's very unkind when you say a thing like that Katie dear. It was unfortunate I admit but I don't see how she could have helped it. He had been no more alive than a log for months.'

'Did he regain consciousness before the end?'

'Dear Katie, I don't know whether he did or not.' And they talked of something else, man sitting between them changed topic of conversation. But that woman thought obviously he had regained consciousness and that Grizel hadn't liked to admit it.

When our Richard came down, others had finished. The men even had done with the port. He ate alone, nervousness growing in him and served by footman that was anxious to get to his meal, so hurried Mr Dupret through his courses. Why did she have no flowers on table? thought he in interval of nervousness. When he had had glass of port footman announced him into the room where now all houseparty was concentrated. Shutting door behind him footman yawned in the passage and went quickly to supper. Now dinner table lay in empty room like a grave that has dead flowers on it.

Small hush was as Mr Dupret went to greet hostess. He shook hands with older people. Mary came up and then he was in midst of his contemporaries, was introduced to two or three, and then saw Hannah Glossop.

Mr Tyler went on with his plan of a game. It was like 'prisoner's base' only played in darkness and Mary, whose house this was, said they would take over the North Wing and turn out all lights, and play there.

All younger people went off. Walking with Miss Glossop Mr Dupret had now lost feeling of nervousness.

After breakfast assembled women in one room, men in another.

Older man was saying he had only seen woodcock on the ground once, which was by great bit of good fortune as he did not know what made him look in that direction but there it was, on the ground, twenty yards from him. He was saying this to Tom Tyler, who upheld that conversation.

Mr Dupret thought that was how it was, once he had been going upstairs with Hannah at a dance and chandelier which hung there had trembled as it might be at sound of the band which was beginning to play, so light on that chandelier was beginning to move. What difference is there, thought he, between my chandelier and his woodcock, one or the other moved one of us? And yet how much better if he could be excited at sight of woodcock on the ground for excitement over chandelier was at light moving over it, caused probably by someone stamping on the floor above. The woodcock was on ground by no agency of man, its being there was a natural phenomenon, and he thought his chandelier and how it moved him was a spurious emotion.

He thought this was a parable. Darkness he thought was merely opportunity for Tyler and Miss Glossop to play a game in, where to him it would be another thing. That seemed centre of it all to him. For in their games they sublimated all passions, all beliefs. That was why Tom Tyler cut him out with Miss Glossop, who did not care to talk. And so he saw these games they were always playing to be charades of the passions. So was there no other way to her heart?

10

LEAVING HOUSE-PARTY Mr Dupret went to Birmingham. When he heard Mr Bridges was already gone on leave he was glad. He did not want to see Mr Bridges. Indeed, now he knew it was not for him but Tom Tyler that Miss Glossop smiled and lilted, heart was out of him.

So when he came he sent for Mr Cummings and just said he hoped everything was all right. Mr Cummings made no impression on his mind. When he had gone Mr Dupret sat on in office. He thought, and slowly tried to gather up energy inside him. At last he went up into Mr Tarver's office.

'Very glad to see you sir!'

'I'm sorry Mr Bridges is ill!'

'Yes, it's a shame he's bad.' (Mr Tarver was in great spirits this morning.) 'But you mark my words squire,' he said, 'they'll all go together.'

'What on earth do you mean, they'll all go together?'

'Well you see Mr Dupret' said Tarver and he went red, 'I meant they were getting on, you can't be sixty-one and expect to feel on top of the world.'

'I don't want any intrigue Tarver,' Mr Dupret said in tired voice, 'we've all got to pull together or we'll be nowhere in no time.'

'You mustn't take what I say wrong, sir, we all work for the good of the firm, we all pull together, though we're all sorts and different sizes.'

'That's it,' said Mr Dupret, and felt like he was nurse at school for infants and surely this man Tarver was mad. Why did he call you squire?

'Mr Tarver, I thought when Mr Bridges came back I would

suggest to him your having another draughtsman. And really if Bumpus is always getting ill like this we had better part with him.'

'Don't take Bumpus from me,' Mr Tarver said dangerously. He rose from his chair. 'I couldn't do without him, Mr Dupret, for God's sake.'

This one was pleased. The man had spirit. 'Right you are,' said he, 'I didn't know if you thought a lot of him, that's all. And I promise to get you another. Or rather you and Bumpus, and of course Mr Bridges will have to choose a further draughtsman between you.'

'It's been needed, I only said to the wife the other night I didn't see how I could go on short-handed like this with the new machine I'm bringing out. But with another man we'll eat it up colonel.'

Beaming he came up and shook Dupret by the hand.

Mr Dupret thought perhaps he was mad after all but enthusiastic anyway, not all words like old Bridges, and he was a young man, Arthur thought well of him. Yes, damn it, he would show them and give Tarver pat on the back. So he asked Tarver if he was coming round works with him, and together they went round, Tarver visibly glad.

As they went round works, Mr Dupret and Mr Tarver, behind them was Cummings. He dodged behind machinery and everything they did he noticed, every time they stopped to look at something he took it to be complaints.

Mr Milligan, standing in gateway of stores department, saw him following and said in his mind who would believe it who did not know? Who would be in position of authority now, even to be storekeeper? You had to be strong man, nerves of steel, or it was more than your health would stand.

Didn't they make themselves ridiculous the way they behaved, look at Cummings, everyone in the place laughing at him so soon as he was gone by. That must have been a knock for him the young chap going round with Tarver. Yes, and their health couldn't stand it, some of them. Andrew, foreman in iron foundry, many a time worry was too much for him and he'd go off and sit in a corner where none could see him with his hands over his face. Was many would not believe that but with delivery, delivery always being shouted at you, in tricky work like iron founding were many foremen took their lives and those that didn't take them had their lives shortened by the worry. Andrew had been looking done up just lately, Mr Milligan said in his mind, and thought of when he himself was last in hospital.

Mr Dupret and Tarver came to iron foundry shop. 'Have they had many wasters here recently, Mr Tarver?'

'No, we've been very free of them for the last week or two. But they're slow in this shop colonel, terribly slow.'

'Well I suppose that's all right as long as they don't make bad ones.'

'You're right there Mr Dupret, but they ought to make sound castings quicker, like they do in other foundries.'

'Sometimes these people don't seem to be able to make good ones quick or slow. Do you remember a few weeks back –' and they talked of job which had given trouble. Dupret used what he thought was Mr Tarver's language.

'What d'you put it down to Tarver, ought we to have another foreman?' nodding to Philpots who was busy and yet watching them, in corner of foundry shop.

'Andrew's all right,' said Mr Tarver, 'no it's the men he has to work with. You can't get old men to work fast squire, that's natural, and old men like Craigan keep the weight down.'

'Then why do we keep him on?'

'Mr Bridges says he couldn't do without him.'

'Well,' said Mr Dupret, 'I suppose Mr Bridges has his reasons,' and they moved off and into machine shop.

Mr Cummings darted into iron foundry. He went to Andrew Philpots.

'Did 'e say nothing to you Andy?'

'I didn't like to go and speak to 'im, I waited 'ere till 'e should come to me if 'e 'ad anything to say.'

Mr Cummings went off. What are they up to he asked in his mind. What is it?

'Well dear' Mrs Dupret said, 'did you go down to Birmingham today?'

106

'Yes,' said Mr Dupret.

'What's the matter, Dick, aren't you feeling well?'

'No, I'm feeling quite all right' said Mr Dupret lying, 'but the works are so depressing, it's all so incompetent. They are all such awful people.'

'Well from now on it's your own fault, darling, if you don't like them, isn't it? I mean you're head of the business now. When your father was alive you had to do things more or less under his supervision but you are your own master now, aren't you dear? Still I expect the more you look into it you'll find your father right.'

'Yes. But it's not altogether the works. The fact is, I've gone crazy over a girl again.'

After Mrs Dupret had said what was fit and appreciative and had let him tell her that it was Hannah Glossop – he had told her some months ago only he'd forgotten that – he described Tom Tyler and the way she did not seem to notice anyone else.

Mrs Dupret comforted.

Mrs Dupret said that sort of man exercised a fascination over girls which soon wore off. 'He is young and fresh looking and full of spirits,' she said 'but they soon see there is nothing much in him after all.' She told him to keep away from Hannah a bit, above all not to run after her just now, and she proposed that they should have that little dinner party for her which they were to have had before his father fell ill. Hearing little of what she said, he went on about how the thought of her was perpetually running through his mind, and sometimes the thought of her came in spasms upon him, it made him feel quite ill, physically ill. Mrs Dupret said 'poor darling,' and 'we'll see if we can't get her to dinner, shall we?'

Miss Gates. Now, as has been said, evenings were drawing in, now they could no longer go out in the evening, winter, or at most they allowed themselves one cinema in the week.

So it was often that she stayed indoors and Mr Jones began going to technical school where she sent him. Sitting at home with the family she darned their socks and mended clothes in the evenings, and Mr Craigan with her father and Jim Dale were there. Now again it seemed for Craigan like times when Lily had kept company with Jim. Their evenings were as they had been and that was comfortable for him.

She had begun saving and she made Mr Jones save. This was why she was so much quieter, but Dale thought perhaps those two were tiring of each other and soon they might quarrel, then she would come back to him again. So he took heart and went no more out in the evenings nor gave her much attention now he began to feel sure of her again, only Gates went more and more out and was often seen with Mr Tupe.

Mr Bridges put back receiver on its hook. He went back into sitting room of the lodging house at Weston. His wife asked him about the news. He said the young chap had just left works, he had had Cummings on the 'phone. Mrs Bridges asked if he had done anything?

'No, not a thing.'

'Well that's a bit off my mind.'

'How's that?'

'You know how I mean.'

'It's not what he does, he don't do anything, it's what 'e means to do Janie. And now the father's dead what's to stop him doing it.'

'How do you know what he means to do?'

'You can see it in 'is eye. He looks at me now and again with a look as if I'd murdered 'is best girl or got her be'ind a hedge.'

'You!'

'It's a vindictive somehow. That's why I shouldn't ever've come here. You'll see he'll use it some way against me.'

'But didn't Mr Cummings tell you nothing else just now?'

'Cummings? Ah, I was keeping the best for the end. The young chap wouldn't go round with Cummings, wasn't good enough for 'im, no he 'ad to go round the place with Tarver for everyone to see. What d'you make of that eh?'

Mrs Bridges shook head over that.

'Cummings said 'e went round after them but couldn't make out they'd said anything particular. That's a good man,

Cummings. I wouldn't take £1,000 for 'im, not if I 'ad the choice. That's where it is. I ain't got the choice of me own men, I have to be told now if a man's a engineer or not.'

'Don't get talking so, Phil, young Mr Dupret ain't done nothing to you yet.'

'Ah, but what's 'e going to do? There's nothing that comes I can't see coming, all my life or I shouldn't be where I am. And Tarver? Aren't I as nice and easy with him as a man could be, cooing like a dove to 'im, yes, and I'd turn somersaults like other pigeons if that's what he preferred. Ah Janie I'm glad we're leaving for old Brum tomorrow. It's got on my nerves sitting here. But there's this to it, I feel grand, grand after this ten days.'

He went over and gave wife sounding kiss. She laughed: 'you get 'is girl behind a hedge!' she said.

HANNAH GLOSSOP STAYED over into next day when rest of house-party had gone. All the men had gone back to offices but Tom Tyler, who was on leave from Siam. So she had him all to herself.

All afternoon went they for a walk across fields and she asked him what his life was. He was unpaid adjunct to British resident at Siam. He told about shooting they had and how you could get a game of squash racquets there. He said how once the resident's wife came down to official dinner with her dress back to front, and the difficulty he had had to let her know. The way he had done it was to turn his plate upside down and being a clever woman she had understood. Dropping suddenly to the intimate he said evenings there were marvellous, and between them they had got together quite a good little dance band at the country club.

He was bored with this walk because she made him do all the talking and was serious, but she – as sometimes on a ship when is sun and spray so do you see rainbows everywhere, on the deck, on wave-crests, so as he spoke wonder was round about all he said for her.

As soon as Mr Bridges had gotten back he went round works. ''Tis 'im' the men said when they saw him. He went round. He thought in his mind it was fine, fine to be back. 'The men have but to come to me when they're in trouble, I'm a father and mother to them,' he cried in his heart, 'aye, I am that.'

He talked long with Tupe, very hearty with him. Cummings came up then to greet him for Mr Bridges had gone straight into works when he was back. Loudly Mr

Bridges met him. He said he felt fine, fine. He asked how things were and Mr Cummings said everything was going on all right. Then moving a few yards away so Tupe could not hear above the noise of lathes working in this shop Mr Bridges asked what about young chap? As heads of these two moved towards each other at that, men on lathes winked one to another, while Mr Cummings grew mysterious look on his face. He said he had only just heard, Tarver had come boasting to him he said, boasting the young chap was giving him another draughtsman. 'Our overheads won't stand it sir,' he said, though he did not know much about such charges.

Mr Bridges said: 'There's a grand thing to welcome you back.'

He stood silent.

'Another draughtsman, eh?' he said. He swore.

At last he said why couldn't Tarver have come and said a word to him when he got back (forgetting he was but just arrived), no bit of friendliness in that man anywhere, it made life misery for you, why if you'd been so nearly dead you'd had a chat with Peter at the gate Tarver wouldn't say a word when you got back.

'Isn't 'e a beauty?' Mr Bridges said.

That evening Mr Bridges went through works on the look out for trouble. Mr Tarver had not come to see him or ask him how he was. Bridges went through works on chance of finding someone to vent anger on.

That day Mr Bert Jones had one of his spells on him. Were days when he could not work, his mind was not in it. It was not that he couldn't concentrate because he was thinking of something else, but rather as if his mind was satiated by the trade he worked at, as if he had reached saturation point as day by day, year by year he did very much the same things with almost identical movements of arms and legs. So sometimes when you are working daze comes over you and your brain lies back, it rocks like the sea, and as commonplace.

So he stopped working.

'What's the matter with you Bert?'

'There aint nothing the matter?'

'Well come on then.'

But Mr Bridges came up behind. He made a row. Only that, he did not suspend him. But he relieved choking feeling he had in his chest. He went away satisfied.

Mr Jones worked for rest of evening without stopping. He felt like quite desperate.

That evening, half past five, and thousands came out of factories, the sirens sounding, and went home.

Mr Craigan, with Gates and Jim Dale, went out of Dupret factory together, when Mr Tupe came up with them. He walked with them. He said:

"Ow do you think the old man's lookin'?"

Mr Gates said holiday didn't seem to have done him much good. Anger rose in Mr Craigan at Tupe's coming up to them.

'Aint it a bloody shame' said Tupe, 'the way they try and drive a man of 'is age to the mad'ouse. Did you 'appen to see Tarver and young 'opeful goin' round together not above a week back? Well and now Tarver won't come and bid the old man good day when 'e gets back after goin' away for 'is 'ealth.'

"Ow d'you know, know all,' Mr Dale said.

'I knows young feller because 'e told me 'imself.'

'O he did, did 'e?'

'Ah, 'e did, and I don't reckon they've any right to treat an old man the way they're doin'. 'E's told me things. When a man gets on in years they should respect 'is age I reckon, what d'you say?' said he, turning to Mr Craigan. This one made no answer to him.

'Yes by rights that's what they should do' Mr Gates said, nervous. 'Ah, and 'e 'ad a row with young Jones, which wasn't nothing but those others trying to down 'im, that bein' a good lad' said maliciously Mr Tupe. Dale asked eagerly if he had suspended him. 'Suspend 'im' said Tupe, 'suspend a fine chap like that, not on yer life, 'e does the work of three in that shop.'

'Well 'e was suspended in the summer wasn't 'e?'

'Yes, 'e were suspended' said Mr Gates hoping to close conversation.

112

'Ah,' Mr Tupe said, 'and what was that but Aaron Connolly, I know the man, nothing's too low for 'im, I saw 'im go and tell Bridges 'imself Bert was in there, and being as it might be in front of witnesses, the old man 'ad no choice.' Here Mr Tupe had inspiration. 'That was why 'e daint suspend Aaron' he said triumphantly.

Mr Craigan went then to other side of the street and Dale followed him. Then at last Mr Gates followed them, because he feared Mr Craigan. Yet was he ashamed at leaving Tupe.

So came they home at evening. They went in to the house, they washed, and Lily had evening meal ready for them. Mr Dale was excited in his mind. He thought if Bert Jones was sacked chances were he would find no other job in Birmingham. Then he would leave the town, would have to, and go back to that home he said he had in Liverpool. Thought of this put Mr Dale in a good temper.

Lily began saying how Eames' child next door had grown. Mr Gates said Eames was poor sort of a man. But subject of the works was in Mr Dale's mind and he asked how much truth was there in this talk about old Bridges being crowded out.

'I don't know what 'e's told Tupey' said Mr Gates, 'but there's only men of 'is age and young men in that place, so trouble's bound to be between 'em, the younger lot trying to push the older out of the light. There's none that comes between 'em, speakin' of age. And the young chap's crazy like any lamb in the field.'

'He's not so crazy as some,' Mr Dale said, 'now take "our" Bert, that's the second time 'e's been suspended in four months.'

'Suspended! Where did you 'ear he'd been suspended? The old man daint suspend 'im' said Mr Gates.

Lily smiled. But Mr Craigan broke into conversation. He said:

'If I 'ad a son I wouldn't educate 'im above the station 'e was born in. It's hard enough to be a moulder and 'ave the worry of the job forty-seven hours in the week but to be on the staff, or foreman even, with the man above you doggin' at you and them under you never satisfied, like the young chaps never am nowadays, it aint like living at all. In course they're getting rid of Bridges like they'll get rid of me, seein' I'm an old man now. Another month and we'll be getting the old age pension Joe, and we'll get the sack then. Like Bridges will get the sack, seein' 'e's getting an old man, same as we.'

That same evening Lily Gates went out to meet Bert Jones.

When they met she saw for the first time white, cutting anger in him. He said they must get away, he said that! who had always been the one to draw back. They must go right off at once he said and anxiously she asked what the trouble was, for she knew him that he was not dependable worker. He said trouble? He said what was the matter with her who was so keen on their going and now, when he said they must go directly, wanted to know why?

'Aren't you on a line!' she said pleasantly.

He told her about Bridges, but she thought when they were married he would be quieter, it would be the responsibility would make him so. She told him he must not worry about that. Indirectly then they talked of their going like it might be tomorrow, yet both questioned in their hearts if they would ever go. Then she quieted him. They kissed. She made him talk of other things. Soon she felt him contented again. So again they let their time slip by.

Mr Craigan felt he must act. Tupe now was so thick with Joe – it looked bad his having the face to come up and talk to them – and Lily with her Bert Jones. All this in images appeared in his mind before him.

Home was sacred thing to him. Everything, his self-respect was built on home. If he had no home to go back into an evening then he would have to move to another town where none knew him. As it was shame for the Hebrew women to be barren so in his mind was it desolation not to have people about him in his house, though he had never married.

He also had noticed Lily seemed quieter and while he saw in his mind it was winter kept them indoors, yet, because he wanted to, he saw Lily did not look so enchanted, she had talked more, she had not lately always been waiting, waiting till moment came to put on her clothes and meet Bert Jones.

114

So when Mr Gates had gone out, as he did every evening now leaving Jim Dale and he alone, he called Jim and said to him why must he be chipping Lily about Jones, why not leave her alone more? If you spoke to a female nowadays he said they made grievance out of it and took care to go another way to yours, whether it was their way or not, only to spite you. 'And females,' he said, 'like to think you're thinking of them, and afraid for 'em, and once they know you're that way they try and keep you at it.' He said Jim's talking of Jones would give that man importance in Lily's mind which he did not deserve 'being like 9,000 other wasters in this town. Let her forget 'im.' Mr Dale did not answer.

Mr Gates went to public house, where already Tupe was.

'It made I laugh,' Tupe said, 'to see the look just now your old man give me when I come up. 'E daint like it, did 'e? No, we're not good enough for 'im, Joe.'

Gates was relieved that Mr Tupe had not taken it wrong, his crossing the street and leaving him for Craigan.

'That's the truth,' he said 'us ain't.'

'But I got in a good one, eh, when I said that about Aaron Connolly? There's a dirty sneakin' 'ound for you. Anyroads 'e ain't no better'n a peasant, you can tell it by 'is speech.'

'I don't know I got anything against Aaron.'

'Well Joe, you're a marvel. It's no wonder to me you're put upon. Got nothin' against Aaron Connolly? I know what you mean but that's the lie of it, 'e daint ever let no one see t'other side of 'is face. I know 'im. No there ain't nothin' above board about 'im, that's just it.'

Later Mr Gates repeated what Craigan had said about how, soon as they had old age pension coming to them, they would be stopped off. Mr Tupe ridiculed idea of that. He said it was done at Thatcher's but in old fashioned place like Duprets you could bet your life they'd never do anything of that kind. Then he gave all the old arguments for old men being better than young. Soon came in more friends of his, all labourers like Tupe himself. (This was loss of caste for Gates to be perpetually with them, as he was step above a labourer.) They sat drinking.

This was time of year when people that did not shoot came back from Scotland to watch shooters shooting pheasant instead of watching grouse-shooting. Also hunt balls were beginning. Now for Hannah Glossop, and Mr Tyler too, it was party after party in country houses, and they met at many of them.

Almost at once Mr Tyler began kissing Hannah when they were alone together, goodness she did like it. She made little rules about this for herself, one was she must not kiss him too often but let him kiss her. So when he kissed her, in little ecstasies she closed eyelids over eyes. He could not see of course that she rolled eyeballs under the lids when he kissed her. Yet she feared he would feel that in her lips so she did not often let him kiss her mouth, coy, coy, and did not often kiss him – well bred kissing.

Soon, after one or two more houseparties, he kissed her no more, though almost she stood about in dark places. He thought it was disgusting to kiss her who was so dumb then, and yearning.

Then he was rude to her.

Miss Glossop asked Tom to stay and he would not come.

Leaving house, going into the garden 'he does not care' she said aloud.

She walked in misery. She tried not to think of him. But as sometimes, coming across the sea from a cold country to the tropics and the sky is dull so the sea is like any other sea, so as you are coming tropical birds of exquisite colours settle to rest on the deck, unexpected, infinitely beautiful, so things she remembered of him came one by one back to her mind. And as the ship beat by beat draws nearer to that warmth the birds come from, so her feeling was being encompassed then by the memory of him and it was so warm she sat down on the wet ground and cried.

12

MR JONES CAME back to his lodgings after work.

Man and woman who owned the house sat down to evening meal with him.

Their name was Johns. Mrs Johns said to him: 'What's the matter Bert? You've been that restless these last two days.'

'What's up with 'im?' husband said. 'It's nothing but one of you women've got hold on 'im.'

'Then what's your young lady been sayin' to you?' asked Mrs Johns smiling.

'It's what 'e said to her' cried Mr Johns, 'that's what 'as caused the rumpus. You women can't never take a thing right.'

'Yes I dare say but then men never could tell which was right or wrong. But I'm not talking to you, I've spoke enough to you these thirty years, I'm talking to Bert and I don't like to see 'im low like 'e is.'

'Take a tip from me young feller, don't do it, don't go and marry. I know.'

'Marry, why shouldn't 'e marry?'

'That's it, go on, ten bob down and fifty bob a week for the rest of your life, nothing wrong with that is there? That's why women are so keen on marrying, and I don't blame 'em seein' men is such fools. But I don't know where all the money goes.'

'I'd like to see you managing this 'ouse.'

'Oh well' he said winking, 'I aint never regretted it when I married you.'

''Ave some sugar candy,' Mrs Johns said to Mr Jones, 'oh my listen to my 'usband.' Husband and wife laughed but they both looked at Mr Jones who did not laugh, and they grew serious.

'I don't reckon to meddle in any man's business' said Mr Johns 'but seein' you've been 'ere some years you won't take it wrong if I ask 'as anything bad 'appened.'

'No it aint nothing that you can call bad, but I'm fed up, that's all.'

'Fed up, are yer? Yes, we've all been fed up in our time, and it's not a thing that gets any better as you grow older either. 'Ad a set-to with the foreman?'

'No, it was this way. I 'adn't put down the six inch file I was using about twenty seconds, just time to blow my nose and the old man – we call 'im 'Tis 'im in our place – was all over me and threatens to suspend me. Well that's not treatin' you right. I tell you I'd like to get out of that place. It's old fashioned and there's no getting on in places like that. Tell you the truth I'd been thinking of clearin' out into a new country.'

'They aint no places for a woman' said Mrs Johns.

'She's more keen on going even than what I am.'

'Ah, that's all very well,' said Mr Johns, 'but what if she wants to come back after a month or two out there. Females is funny things.'

'You don't know 'er,' Mr Jones said. He spoke like he was sorry Lil was as she was.

'Women'll tell you there's nothin' they want more but then when it comes to doin' it they won't 'ave it.'

'Oh yes' said Mrs Johns, 'but who eats the 'ouse up, tell me that.'

'I'd go alone if I was you,' said Mr Johns, 'and then 'ave 'er come out after if you've fell on yer pins.'

'That's what I'll do' said Mr Jones triumphantly.

''E don't seem any too sorry to get away from 'er,' said Mr Johns to wife who said: 'but when's this comin' off, not any too soon is it? I mean we shall 'ave you stayin' on here a month or two yet, will we? We don't want to lose you, you know.'

'No, missus, it won't be for a month or two.'

'Where would you be thinkin' of going if I might ask,' said Mr Johns.

'Well she, I don't rightly know yet,' he said and Mr Johns looked at wife and winked. Jones went on to say Mr Herbert Tomson had gone out to Australia and just because he had not found job there except on the land, which he was not taking, it was no argument why you mightn't go to Canada. Then for a time they fell to talking how wrong it was to expect men who had worked in factories to go back to work on the land.

'It aint fair on the females,' Mr Johns was saying.

'No, my young lady wouldn't stand that,' Jones said.

Later, when they were alone, Mr Johns said Bert would never go out and to look at way he told Lily Gates he went to technical school in evenings when he never went after first three times. Mrs Johns said no, he would never go. He hadn't the stuff in him, she said.

When they had had supper and again Mr Craigan was reading Dickens and Joe Gates was gone out, Dale stared at Lily washing up. (She washed up now because this was not evening for going out with Bert Jones.)

Mr Craigan smoked pipe, already room was blurred by smoke from it and by steam from hot water in the sink. She swilled water over the plates and electric light caught in shining waves of water which rushed off plates as she held them, and then light caught on wet plates in moons. She dried these. One by one then she put them up into the rack on wall above her, and as she stretched up so her movements pulled all ways at his heart, so beautiful she seemed to him. Mr Craigan would never have windows opened at evening so was a haze in that room, like to Dale's feeling. When she had done and was drying red hands, he said would she care to go to the movies with him again. He was so humble, and then Bert and she were saving, Jim would pay for her into movie, why yes why not, she had had hard day's work, (it had been washing day), yes she would go. 'I don't mind,' she said, and went to change her clothes.

He thought of her face shining from the steam, and if it were his to touch it. Feeling of confidence rising in him he thought he would bite it. Yet when they came to cinema again

119

helplessness came over him. Sitting next her in intimacy of the dark and music yet she was far from him.

This film was of the tropics and again as when she had seen that black man in the streets all her muscles softened under the influence of dreams and imagination of that warmth. She felt in her heart it must be a soft thing, not the cruel beating heat it is.

And he did not understand her, and how sitting beside felt her hard and cruel, and hating him. He did not see she was all dreams, all her own dreams.

But Mr Craigan saw this. *Little Dorrit* laid on his knee, he thought it was selfishness that was all of Miss Gates, like it had been with her Aunt Ellie. He began talking aloud to himself. 'Yet she's a good wench,' he said, 'there's not many of her age would keep the house so clean.' Was a silence. 'An' she aint been out so often with Bert Jones,' he said. He fell to picking at his coat. Then he held up finger and squinted at it. He chuckled. 'Her blubbered when I told 'er of her Aunt Ellie' he said in whisper. 'Ah' he said 'but as the tree leans so the branches is inclined.'

Suddenly he broke out into loud voice: 'I wouldn't educate my son above the station 'e was born in,' he said and then whispering 'what is there in it, old Dupret 'ad to work twelve hours a day to keep 'is money I'll be bound 'e did.' Was a silence. 'An' a motor-car, aint we better on the feet our mothers bore us.' No, he thought, she was good girl, and this trouble would go by. She'd see Jones hadn't the making in him to work. She would go back to Dale that was an honest lad.

And indeed, now tropic film was over, she said two words to Dale. She was grateful to him again, this time again for keeping quiet. Kindness in her voice bewildered Mr Dale.

'Well if we do go' he said in a bad temper, 'where'll we go to.'

'If that's the tone of voice you're using, Bert, to think of our goin' away in, well then,' she said, 'we'd better talk of it some other day.'

Sunday. They were walking out along road into the country. Air was warm and moist. Silence was between them then.

'Go on, dear,' she said. 'I didn't mean any 'urt.'

'It's this weather gets on my nerves.'

'Yes, I'm sure when I came out I didn't know what to wear yes I didn't at all. But I brought the old gamp,' she said and made a little wave with umbrella at clouds above.

'Don't you like our goin' to Canada?'

She said yes in undetermined sort of way.

'Yes or no,' he said.

'Aint I said yes. I don't know what's been the matter with you lately I'm sure, no I don't.'

They squabbled then a little and she dragged gamp behind her more and more, most mournful thing to see. Her face paled to sicklish colour. Her mouth grew stiff and grim like that umbrella looked. He said didn't she want to come, was she going to draw back, was she afraid of work he said. She smiled. 'Work,' she said, 'why you're a wonderful worker to be suspended twice in six months.'

He got very angry. He said he hadn't been suspended but the once and didn't he go to technical school so many nights a week, was it his fault he'd been suspended it being all along of Tupe, that her father went about with now. If she didn't want to come he didn't want her.

'You don't want me,' she said and she went paler. 'Don't want me,' she said and she began crying. Large tears came down from eyes down her still face. He turned. He saw these and as the sun comes out from behind clouds then birds whistle again for the sun, so love came out in his eyes (at the victory, at making her cry) and he whispered things senseless as whistling birds. Lastly he said, 'and what would I do if you weren't coming!' She clung to him – aching tenderness – and she thought how could he be so cruel.

Mrs Eames said to husband had he noticed Lily wore woollen stockings quite often now and he said no did she? Lily was in love, Mrs Eames said: she knew, she knew. Then it would be Jim Dale Mr Eames said, and Mrs laughed at him. 'Observant, lord save us!' she said and went on about Bert Jones saying he was the one Lily was after and he worked in Dupret factory. 'Works at our place?' said Mr Eames, 'ah, I know the one you mean. Given up silk stockings for 'im? Well that's not many of 'em would do that nowadays, goin' to work of a morning you don't see nothing but these art silk stockings.'

'No, I don't reckon you would! Yet what these girls put all their money on their legs for I don't know,' she said, 'seeing how some are made.'

'It's a bloody marvel to me they're alive all of 'em, getting their legs wet coming to work and going back of an evening.'

'Don't you go thinking about things like that my man. You've never told me about getting my feet wet. But what I like about Lily is she's got the spirit to do what's in 'er mind.' Mrs Eames said were not many girls would have courage to go out in woollen stockings and not paint her face, to go against the tide like she did to save money. Real pity was she did not dance, Lily, she said, had met too few men. What's this Bert Jones like? she said.

'I can't say I've spoken to 'im more than two or three times in the last year. 'E seems like a lot of the other young chaps, you know, he don't seem to 'ave much interest in nothing. But 'e's good at his job I've been told. 'E's one of them that are always smoking cigarettes.'

Mrs Eames said she would laugh if Lily married him instead of Jim Dale as old Craigan intended.

''Ow's that? Jim's all right, there's nothing wrong with Jim, he's as steady a man as any woman could wish.'

Mrs Eames said she would like to see the laugh on old Craigan. Mr said so that was it was it, but what had she got against Mr Craigan who was most respected man in the works. He never interfered in anyone's affairs and there was nobody didn't like him. Well, said Mrs Eames, it was Joe Gates really. She didn't like that man. Once a bird had got caught between windows over at their house and they had sent for her to come over. It was one of first times Lily had been out with Bert Jones. Well after she got tired out, that Gates had started telling her dirty stories like she wasn't respectable.

'I'll go over an' 'ave a bit of a talk with Joe Gates now,' he said.

'Now don't you go and get quarrelling. There ain't nothing in it to be worrying over, or to act foolish, it was all months ago.'

Mr Eames was angry. But at last, when she told him it was really nothing, he said he never could cotton to Joe Gates. 'I don't like the way he goes about with Tupe,' he said, 'who's no better than a low down spy of Bridges'. And seeing he lives in Craigan's 'ouse 'e's no business to go about with Tupe. There's no love beggin' between old Mr Craigan and 'im. The dirty 'ound, the names he's called 'im before now, and to his face.'

'Oh well I expect you know the old man best. But what's 'e keep that girl shut up for like he does?'

'It's none of my business what 'e does,' said Mr Eames, 'but if I 'ad a daughter of her age I don't say I wouldn't do the same.'

'Then you'd be a fool, my lad.'

'Maybe I would but I wouldn't 'ave things going on in my family like there is in houses no farther'n this street.'

'Listen to you !' cried Mrs Eames. 'Well, and d'you know what's goin' to 'appen to them all. You listen to me and I'll tell you. She's going to marry Bert Jones and Craigan'll go and live with 'em, while Gates goes off and lives with Tupe most likely.'

'Most likely the best place 'e could be,' said Mr Eames, 'but what exactly did you say 'e'd said to you.'

13

'WHAT'S IN YOUR mind then about where we're going to?' he said to Lily, on their Sunday walk, later. She rubbed his arm between palms of her hands. She said was nothing particular only instead of this Canada 'e was always talking about why couldn't they go East. He said what did she mean by that? She told him then of film she had seen.

'A tea plantation?'

'Yes,' she said, 'a tea place, a place where tea grows.' He said would not likely be any factories there to work in. She answered him he would have to give up his trade. What chances were in engineering now she said. If they went to Canada it might only be out of the frying pan into fire. 'There's no money in that trade and won't be for years. You chuck it up, Bert.'

'Well if we did go out where'd we get the passage money from. It's not like Canada, you'd have to pay the train fare to those places.'

'Mr Dupret would lend it you.'

'Oh would he, 'ow'd you know? I 'aven't been at his place more than three years. Anyway what's the hours and wages in a tea plantation.'

'I don't know for sure, but it'll be more than in factories.'

'Yes, but I don't know the trade.'

'They'd learn you. You see Bert there's not so many white men out there, here there's too many, that's what keeps wages low. I say go out to where a working chap's wanted, not where there's too many already.'

'Well and if we did go out, what about the 'eat. Could you stand the 'eat. It's the tropics where tea grows you know.'

'Oh yes I could stand it, yes I like it where it's warm.'

'Ah, but it's hot out there. How'd you know you could?'

'H.O.T. – warm,' she said and rubbed arm between palms of her hand. 'I know I could dear,' she said and he kissed her while she laughed at him. 'Crazyhead' he kept on saying to her then.

Miss Glossop was downcast. We have seen her feeling, when she thought of Tom Tyler, had been like a tropical ocean with an infinite variety of colour. As her boat came near dry land you could see coral reefs and the seaweed where in and out went bright fishes, as her thoughts turned to him so you could see all these in her eyes. Further out, in the deep sea, in her deeper feeling about him when he was away, now and again dolphins came up to feed on the surface of that ocean. And in her passage she disturbed shoals of flying fish. These were the orchestration of her feelings, so transparently her feeling lapped him and her thoughts, in shoals, fed on the top, or hung poised for two moments in the shallows.

All this was so when he had come back only more so – the dolphins played more often and her boat, thrusting along, disturbed more flying fish. In the shallows was a greater activity, halcyon weather. Every day shone the sun, every day the sea took on new values. And every day at that time there was a look about her eyes of an excited stupefaction at these things.

Then, as we know, it was taken away. When he repulsed her it seemed she was on a boat surveying that discoloured feeling, that desolation in the sea when sky is grey and dark. And always the boat was circling round that land. Then, as we have seen, tropical birds came out and rested on this ship. One by one they reminded her she was on a particular sea, and near land very particular to her. Weeping, weeping, when she was reminded in this way of how bright her conceits had been, weeping she added to an ocean made up, as she was then thinking, of tears shed at the perfidy of man.

Her mother, seeing this, insisted that she must go out often, to be distracted. So when she came to dinner with the Duprets, that dinner which had so often been put off, she was still circling round her memory of Tom Tyler, only each day she circled a little wider, a little farther off.

But stretch this simile, and, having given Tom Tyler one island, make archipelago about him – though each day she circled farther from Mr Tyler yet she did not draw any nearer to where Dick lay. Nor any nearer to her mother's island.

Mrs Dupret had told son she too had heard Miss Glossop was in love with Mr Tyler but that he was not in love with her. She told him he would catch the girl on the rebound. So when at last Miss Glossop came to dinner this moment seemed of great importance to him.

When she came into room he dared not look at her. At the same time he could not answer girl he was talking to so she thought sudden blankness in him must be because of pains in his stomach. Mrs Dupret called out: 'Dick, where are your manners, darling? Here is Hannah,' and he went over. Then girl he had been talking to saw just how it all was, that he was in love. He went over. He shook Miss Glossop by the hand. He could not find anything to say to her. At last he said in despair: 'What have you been doing? I haven't seen you for ages.' She said something about country house-parties and hunt balls and he thought 'Oh if she could have said – I have been in love and have been thrown over then oh then he would have said – I am in love, but my love is not returned!' Then would they have talked of this, each sympathizing with the other and then gradually he would have taught her it was she he was in love with. Then she would have seen what miserable sort of man was Mr Tyler.

As it was she said nothing and was another silence between them. Then he said he wished they would hurry up with dinner and she answered she was sorry she was so dull that he must long for escape to a meal. 'Not at all, no, no, it's only that I'm hungry. Heavens, I didn't mean . . .'

'Oh all right, all right. Don't let's go on with that,' she said and said no more. He moved off feeling if he could shoot himself he would do then.

Very disturbed he went to his mother and drew her aside. He said she must change places at dinner, he could not sit next to Hannah. Mrs Dupret became helpless. She said what was the matter? and he answered Hannah was angry with him, would not speak to him.

'But how can I change all the places now dear. Look here comes Pringle now.'

'Dinner is served madam.'

'No dear, you must sit next her, it's too late now. And I don't suppose she is angry with you, darling. How can I change all the places now. I can't, can I?'

Terribly disturbed he took her down to dinner. People on either side of them began talking away from them, they were left high and dry.

When party went he stayed on over – was nothing for him to do in London, the business ran itself, nothing to do but sign cheques on Thursday and this was Tuesday. He took boat and rowed on the river. What a new year, he thought in mind, what a new year, father dead and now Miss Glossop was over, that was done with!

River was brown and flowed rapidly down to the sea. On either side the violet land under this grey sky. Trees on either side graciously inclined this way and that, leaning on his oars he watched these and rooks that out of the sky came peaceably down on fields.

He thought in his mind here was end of another chapter, another episode done with (Miss Glossop had been rude to him whenever she could be rude). He thought his mistake had been at all to mix with these people, he had no place here, he was like father in that who had never really mixed but had led his own life. Why, he asked in mind, should you leave your life lying about to be cut in pieces by Miss Glossop. And, when it was cut to ribbons, for other Miss Glossops to watch it lying there and be diverted by it. One should go away he thought.

One might go to foreign countries but what was in these but nausea of travelling, hotels, trains, languages you did not know, Americans? Besides it was work he wanted.

So gradually he decided he would go to Birmingham. Hadn't mother told him it was his own fault now if works

127

were not satisfactory. He would take Walters and Archer and they would spend a week or two there. They would have a grand clear out, Tarver was not having a square deal – an early spring cleaning. Work, that was it, he would work.

14

Tuesday afternoon Mr Dupret went to London. He went to offices. He found Mr Walters and said he wanted him to come down also to factory tomorrow. Mr Walters said he was too busy, and what did he want him for? Mr Dupret said he was going to make thorough study of the place, such as he could not do when father was alive. He said he was taking Archer with him. Walters asked why he wanted to take Archer?

'Because I want to!'

'Right you are Dick. How long will you be down there?'

Mr Dupret said he did not know yet. When Walters was gone he was very angry with him. He thought Mr Walters couldn't be bothered to come down could he, and oh yes Walters ran the business didn't he! Well, Mr Dupret was going to run business now.

Meanwhile Mr Archer was telephoning Tarver that they were coming down, he did not know what for.

Meanwhile Mr Craigan was in bed. He was coming to work in morning and a shower had caught him, had wetted his clothes through, and all day he had worked in wet clothes so that next morning he stayed in bed with a fever. His hands trembled, trembled at the bed-clothes. Lily was very frightened.

What was most on the old man's mind was thought of Bert Jones. He felt pretty certain Dupret factory would not turn him off when he got old age pension, when he had said they would it was only because he was depressed, yet you could not go on always working and he looked forward to living in

129

Dale's house, with Lily his wife, till the end. They were both grateful to him, he had saved, and was more money in their house than in any on the street. But if she married Jones then those two would go off, Gates would leave him, he would be alone as he was when he first came to Birmingham.

Year after year Lily had grown to be his daughter, not Gates' daughter. Craigan was fonder of her now than if she had been his own. And Bert he knew, he knew was no good, he would never bring regular money to the house.

Lily came in then. Mr Craigan suddenly began talking and before he knew when or how, he was having it out with her.

He spoke calmly. He said Jones was a decent living man but that was it, he was too quiet a man he said, he knew the sort. They would never stay long in the same job that kind, he said, and what a woman wanted was man who brought in the money regular. Then look at his trade, were too many in it. He said he had worked for years and years now, best part of half a century, and he had learned it was not governments nor good times or bad that raised wages, but the demand for men. She had also thought of that.

'Take foundry work,' he said, 'the young chaps won't 'ave it now, it's too dirty for 'em and too hard, you can't get lads to start in foundries nowadays. In a few years there won't 'ardly be any moulders left and those that can do a clean job then will get any money, any amount o' money!'

He said she ought to think it over. 'Love's all right for them that 'as Rolls Royces' he said, 'but for the wives of working men it's the money that comes in regular at the end of the week that tells.' He went on, unfortunately, saying didn't she have any gratitude towards him? What sort of life would she have had with her father, didn't she think he, Craigan, deserved a home when he was too old for work.

'Why, grandad,' she said, 'you ain't too old for work, there's years in you yet' she said and loved him. Going away she thought of these things. She thought how faithful Dale was to her. And all this time heart had been sinking a little before adventure of going away. (Mr Craigan of course did not know they planned to go away.) She thought more of Jim Dale. He was more practical. And as Mr Craigan said it was the practical that tells. But really it was most practical to go away.

At cinema.

'It's like this Lil,' Mr Jones said in whispers, 'when I get out to Canada I may not get a job straight off. I may 'ave to look about a bit and with no money coming in I expect we'll 'ave a tightish time of it to start with. It stands to reason we shall. Then what's the good in your coming out with me just at first. You wait till I get settled in and I'll send word to you.'

'Yes then yes, then you don't want to 'ave me,' said Miss Gates in a calm voice.

'Get out, of course I do.' He tried to kiss her but she turned face away.

'Yes, that's it, off you'll go and leave no address and I'll never have another word of you.'

'I tell you I'll send for you, of course I will.'

'Will you?'

'Crazyhead.' He kissed her. She drew back.

'But I'll go out along with you, thank you my man,' she said. 'It may make two mouths to feed, yes, but there'll be four hands instead of two. They say there's any amount of work for girls out there.'

'Well I 'adn't thought of that. There's something in that Lil.'

'In course there is, silly. I know you're trying to get away from me. But just you try it on. Yes you were.'

'Crazyhead,' he said, but nearly all spontaneity had gone of their relations to each other.

'Oh Bert I wish your dad and mother did live in Brummagem and not in Liverpool. It's costly when we want a talk and it's raining and we 'ave to go to the movies to be out of the wet. 'Ow's your technical school going?'

He lied. He said it was interesting, that he had not missed any classes.

Walters had telephoned Mr Bridges to say Mr Dupret was coming down. The line had been bad, Bridges had not heard what time he was coming or how long he was staying. So

131

when he arrived Mr Bridges was still making last minute inspection of the factory.

When Mr Dupret arrived he went with Archer straight to Mr Tarver's office. Cummings found Bridges and told him Mr Dupret had just got in with Archer with him, and had gone to Tarver. Mr Bridges stood still and then, at hearing this, an arrow as it might be pierced him, transfixed his heart. Mr Dupret comes into Tarver's office, Mr Archer with him.

'Good-morning Tarver, how are we this morning,' said Mr Richard, hearty, thinking he was using Mr Tarver's language.

'Why squire' Mr Tarver said. He pretended to be surprised, 'Come in sir, come in. The fact is we've not much work in but we're always busy in this department. How are you Archer? As a matter of fact I believe Mr Bridges is going to start the men on short time tomorrow. But this is a bit of a surprise isn't it. Fancy seeing you down 'ere' he said to Mr Archer.

'Short time, that's a pity' said Mr Dupret. Why wasn't I told he said in mind?

'Yes here we are on a little expedition down into the provinces' said Mr Archer, 'isn't that so sir? We've left the gay metropolis to pay you a little visit John.'

'Didn't you know we were coming?' said Mr Dupret.

'No sir, I didn't hear a word.'

'That's funny' Mr Dupret said, 'I heard Mr Walters telephone the general manager, I thought he would have told you.'

'Mr Bridges didn't say anything about it,' Tarver said and thought he would say it was just like him not to say a word, but he remembered then how he had said similar things to Mr Dupret before and it had not come off. So he thought he would let silences speak for themselves.

'Didn't he?' said Mr Dupret and Archer winked at Tarver, Tarver winked back.

Was a silence and then was loud noise on the stairs. Mr Bridges came in. Effusively he greeted young Mr Richard. Then he saw Archer.

'Why dammit it's Archer' he said shaking hands violently. 'What are you doing down 'ere?'

'Holiday-making,' said Mr Archer, 'holiday-making.'

'Well he won't get much of a holiday down here will 'e John, if that's what he's come for, it's work down here by God, work all the time.'

'When you don't put the place on short time,' Mr Dupret said.

'Ah, I hate to do it, I hate to see the men not drawing their full money at the end of the week. But what can you do? There's no place in all Brummagem that isn't the same. There's no money about, there's nobody buying now, they make do with the old stuff till times get better. But come along to my room will you Mr Dupret.'

As they were going out of the door Mr Bridges said he was sorry he had not been there when they had arrived, but he had been in the shops. 'What train are you catching back to town so I can order the car.'

'Well we shan't be going back tonight,' said Mr Dupret, 'we've come down to have a thorough look round the place. We'll be five or six days here.'

'That's grand,' said Mr Bridges and asked in his mind – what was it now, what was it? Why hadn't Walters told him, he cried in his mind, not that he had anything to hide, but just so as to know to be able to keep him from Tarver and so forth.

Mr Dale was very solitary kind of man. So when Thursday came and was no work at Dupret's (for it was first day of the short time that was starting now), being a fine day he went walking into country.

This day he was bad-tempered. He was young man and he knew he could get work in another foundry he knew of where was better money to be picked up on piece work, for in Dupret foundry was only day work. He was young man, the hard piece-work would not hurt him and again he ought to work in as many shops as he could to learn his trade, as all foundries have different ways of working. And now Dupret's were on short time, he was getting still less money. But he was grateful to Mr Craigan, he could not leave the old man, who was too slow now to work on his own.

Craigan had private money. Mr Dale was more

comfortable in Mr Craigan's house than he would be elsewhere and he had to give Lily less money than he would a landlady because in their house were three wage-earners and but four mouths. If he went to work in another foundry he thought Craigan would not let him stay on.

And was Lily.

He was half hoping he would come across them walking, he knew they were out this way together. Just now he hated her. It was she was keeping him back and on low wages, gratitude or not he would have left Craigan if it hadn't been for her. And he would look at no other girl.

Just then he came across them. It was at crossroads and they came from behind houses there, walking together very close.

Lily was excited at short time being started in Dupret factory. Eagerly she and Mr Jones had talked of this. More and more she wanted now to go away. She called to Jim to come and talk with them, to discuss how long this three day week would last at Dupret's. But Mr Dale made as if he did not hear.

She called again, much louder. Then Mr Dale, anger bursting over in him, picked up small stone and threw it at them, as a boy might, and at once he walked away.

Mr Jones to make show of dignity shouted hey, hey, no more than hey because the stone had not come near them, but Dale went off.

That day Mr Dupret sat alone with Bridges in his office. He was very calm, he hated all of them now in a bored way.

'Mr Bridges,' said he 'we've got to have what the French call a little explanation.'

The Froggies, Mr Bridges said in mind, nerves on edge, the Froggies what have they got to do with it damn 'em.

'The point is this, I'm head of this business now and everything must go through me. You see it's only fair, all the money that's put into it is mine.'

'Of course it's yours,' said Mr Bridges 'and . . .'

'No, let me do the talking. The point is that my father with all the whole lot of interests he had hadn't the time to go into everything. Well I'm not on any boards, this is practically the only concern I'm in, and I want you and Walters to get out of the habit of doing things above my head and without my knowing it.'

'What d'you mean? I . . .'

'I mean this, that you and Walters for better or worse, and quite naturally, pretty well ran this business on your own before my father died. But it's different now, I want to take a hand in it.'

'If that's all you know about your father my lad . . .'

'God damn it Bridges will you listen to what I say? The point is this, from now on I'm going to run the whole show myself, or rather it's going to be run through me. Take the question of the men being put on short time. I didn't hear a word about it. Well in future I am going to hear. I'm not saying that it shouldn't have been done but it's only fair I should be told.'

'I think we'd better talk another time. I can see you're in a temper now . . .'

'No, we're going to talk now. The point is this, when I say we're going to talk we're going to talk, from now on.'

'Well you ain't going to make me talk,' Mr Bridges said and walked out.

Eleven o'clock. Mrs Eames had done house. She stood in their bedroom she had just tidied and their son pulled at her skirts.

'Ain't you gettin' active on your feet!' she said to him. She picked him up. She kissed him.

Thought came in her to call on the Craigans. Mr Craigan was still in bed. She thought he had got old very quickly and danger was with that sort if they stayed in bed for more than three weeks they might never get up again. She tidied hair. Then taking son she went next door and knocked. No answer. She knocked. She went in.

'Lily,' she cried, 'Lily.'

'Who might you be?' said Craigan from bed upstairs.

'It's Mrs Eames Mr Craigan, I thought I'd ask after you 'ow you were.'

'I'll bother you to come up missus, seein' I'm in bed. Lily shall be back directly.'

Always Mr Craigan had prided himself on not lengthily talking. 'Many a man 'as lost everything by it,' he was fond of saying. But more and more now he felt a need to talk and seeing this in himself he said in mind that he was getting old.

'Come in if you'll excuse my lyin' here in bed.'

She said again she'd called to ask how he was feeling, and to excuse her bringing son in with her but was no-one in their house, she could not leave him. He said he was not well and when you had got to his age you did not easily get over fevers like the one he had had.

'Where's Lily then?' said Mrs Eames.

He said she'd gone out for a spell and said Mrs Eames, what, to leave you alone like that! But he said she was a good wench, more than daughter to him. She had some crazy notions perhaps but were not many of her age would keep house in such good shape as it was now, or keep him so comfortable.

'An' you've got another coming if I see right,' he said looking at Mrs Eames' belly.

'Yes in three weeks' time.'

He said if it was like her boy there it would be a fine kid. Mrs Eames loved him, he had that way with women. She began trying to persuade him to get up. But he would not.

He would not get up because now he felt everything slipping away from him. Dale was dissatisfied at this short time they were working in Dupret factory and no one knew better than Mr Craigan he should get experience in other shops. Gates now went with no one else but Tupe in evenings. And Lily. What had she gone out for just now? He did not know what was in her heart. Everything was slipping away from him.

15

FRIDAY AND MR BRIDGES talked to Mr Dupret in the office. 'It's like this Dick,' he said, 'Walters telephoned me to say you were coming down but the wire was so bad I couldn't for the life of me hear all he had to tell me. Well when he had had his say I told 'im I thought of putting the men on short time, but the wire being as it was, 'e didn't hear it. That's how you didn't come to know. The fact is we're right up to the quota that your dad laid down was safe to carry stock to. And as there's very little coming in you can't keep the men and 'ave nothing for 'em to do.'

'No of course not. But in future I'd be grateful if you would write a letter to go through our files. What I mean is it looks better if we seem to have a say in it,' Mr Dupret said smiling.

'There's no dirty work going on here, Dick.'

'No, no I know there's not. I didn't mean that. Only you must spare our feelings up there Mr Bridges, you must make us feel a little more important than we are perhaps.'

He was not being sarcastic. They had made up differences and Mr Bridges had said he liked a man who spoke out. But they were quite ready, both of them, to break out again. Indeed Bridges had said to wife, dramatizing, that he only stayed on still out of loyalty to the memory of the chief.

'Well you see Dick, this is how it was. We start our working week Wednesdays. It was simpler to start short time on Thursday or the books would get cockeyed. And I was watching the quota like a cat watches a mouse, watching it all the time. As soon as ever we were right up to it I came down and put the whole show on short time till we could get more orders.'

'Exactly. Well now it's all straight in my mind. But you'll remember about next time. I'm not sure we couldn't carry more stock but still I don't want to bring that up. How are the men taking it Mr Bridges?'

'That's the rub, that's the rub. If we have to work short more'n a week or two all our best men will be leaving us. I got a good team together, it'd break my heart if it was broken up.'

'I suppose it's only the young men will go?'

'Yes, it's the young chaps that'll send for their cards.'

'That's the disaster, to my mind. You're always telling me how difficult it is to get fully trained younger men. And of course the old men will hang on and be a millstone round our necks.'

'Ah I know you,' cried Mr Bridges and hit Mr Dupret on the back with palm of his hand.

'For God's sake don't hit me' said Mr Dupret.

'Sorry' said Mr Bridges, 'but the old men ain't so 'opeless as you young fellers would like to think. In the iron foundry now there's one or two older men I wouldn't part with for love or money. And the crane driver in the engineers, Aaron Connolly, rising seventy, I wouldn't part with him for love or money.'

'The iron foundry is just one of the things I wanted to talk to you about.'

'Go ahead' Mr Bridges said complacently.

'Well you've always told me there's no money to be made in iron founding but – you know, I'm not trying to be quarrelsome – isn't that rather a defeatist policy?'

'Diabetes?' said Mr Bridges.

'No I meant isn't that lying down before you're hit? If we can't make money in that horrible foundry can't we lose a little less at the very least.'

'That's just what I'm working for the whole time, I'm always after that place. But there's not one in all Brummagem but doesn't lose more money than we do.'

'Well look here, I've been talking it over' – talking it over eh? Mr Bridges cried in mind, 'and I think we ought to change our policy. What we do now as I understand it is to let the men work comparatively slow so as to be sure each job is a good one and not a waster.'

'They don't idle Dick,' said Mr Bridges.

'No, I don't mean they work idly but since we are all agreed we can't put them on piece work owing to the nature of the work what I want is that we should get rid of the old men, give the others a bit of extra money, and drive them a bit, taking our chance on the wasters. The point is that the old men keep production down with the tone they give the shop.'

'Taking our chance on the wasters eh?' said Mr Bridges. He laughed. 'No lad it won't do. I remember they tried that at the O.K. when I was with 'em. D'you know what 'appened, they went down on production by fifteen per cent.'

'What sort of a manager did they have?'

'They 'ad a man. 'E wasn't a fairy.'

'Well opinions differ, that's all I can say.'

'Who doesn't think so?' Mr Bridges said defiantly.

'Your subordinates don't.'

'What, Cummings?' Bridges thought he had made Mr Richard give away Tarver.

'Cummings? I'd rather ask Lot's wife what she thought of salt,' said Mr Dupret and was so pleased with that, it seemed to him so in the Bridges tradition, he thought he would go away on it.

'Well, it's lunch time,' he said pleasantly and went out.

Mr Bridges did not laugh.

Friday morning. While Mrs Eames visited Mr Craigan Miss Gates was walking back from Labour Exchange where she had got pamphlets on Canada.

She felt now they must be practical. No longer now she thought of tea plantations.

She thought how Mr Craigan had said it was the demand for men raised wages, only that. It was most practical to go where men were wanted.

They would be married in Liverpool, where his parents were. Then they would go.

But she loved Mr Craigan. She thought then he had been father to her for years and years. Now he was old and he was ill, she didn't ought to leave him, not now. 'But us workin' people, we got to work for our living, yes we have,' she cried out in mind. quoting Mr Jones, 'and go out to find the work.'

She thought how Mr Craigan was rich enough, was no need for him to work with the money he had put by. He would not be comfortable as she had made him but he could pay for comfort.

Mr Gates. She owed him nothing, nothing at all.

(She had forgotten Mr Dale.)

Mr Dupret walked down the street Lily was walking down.

He thought it was not poverty you saw in this quarter, the artisan class lived here, but a kind of terrible respectability on too little money. And what was in all this, he said as he was feeling now, or in any walk of life – you were born, you went to school, you worked, you married, you worked harder, you had children, you went on working, with a good deal of trouble your children grew up, then they married. What had you before you died? Grandchildren? The satisfaction of breeding the glorious Anglo Saxon breed?

He thought how he would sit in office chairs for another forty years, gradually taking to golf at the week-ends or the cultivation of gardenias. All because of Miss Glossop.

But these people, how much worse it was, he at least, he thought, had money. These people had music of course, but second-hand music. Still they had really only marriage and growing old. Every day in the year, every year, if they were lucky they went to work all through daylight. That is, the men did. Time passed quickly for them, in a rhythm. But it was the monotony, as one had said to him.

Coming to a recreation ground he walked into it and made to go across. At the gate he passed Lily and did not notice her, she was so like the others. Here, because it was mid-morning, some mothers had brought out their children too young still to walk. Cold winter sunshine. They stood about in groups while older children with cries ran about, like trying to catch their cries in the air, the boys at football, the girls at some game of their own. Passing through this he shuddered, a sense of foreboding gathered in him. What will they grow up to he thought in mind – they'll work, they'll marry, they'll work harder, have children and go on working, they'll die. He

140

shuddered. Then he forgot all about them and thought about himself.

But Lily coming through the gate saw children running and those mothers and she stood and watched them, feeling out of it. 'I must have babies,' she said then, looking at baby in mother's arms. She was not excited when she said it. Just now she was being very practical.

Going down road after this, to Mr Craigan, excitement took hold on her. Every woman she passed, were mostly women in the streets now, every woman she looked at like she was a queen, they her subjects, was an eagle in her eyes.

What were they to her, they were like sheep and would always be here, was no kind of independence in them she thought in image in her mind, like lettuces in a row they were, yes, separate from one another but in one teeny plot of land.

Ashamed at so much imagining she thought then oh if I could break out now and run, yes and run in to grandad and scream to him I've got them, I got the things about Canada.

But thought of him being against it quietened her. So like any other girl there, only she had no shopping basket, she walked down the street only if you looked it was all over her face, what she was feeling.

Lily went home to get Mr Craigan his midday meal. She did not speak much to him and again he wondered at her. So it was only when she had washed the plates up afterwards that she sat down and read about Canada.

Then she took some clothes that were to be mended. Putting away the leaflets in her dress she went to window of the kitchen, and sat there where she could look over garden at the back and not be seen. In her senses she felt golden light covering a golden land, that was how she saw it from what she had been reading, and she thought how she always did love darning – and what it would be to her when she was mending for someone more particular, or her own child. Something fluttered at her fingers. (How can you darn when as it might be a bird is in your hand, fluttering between thumb and fingers.) Panting she laid her needle down. That's funny, she thought, my not being able to darn, and why, I'm all out of breath.

Now, for first time that year, day lingered noticeably in sky as the hour grew later, clouds were blown away or melted, I don't know, only all of a sudden spring nodded from a clear sky and most beautifully that clear light hung there far into evening. She folded hands in her lap. Everywhere round became suddenly quiet. Then sirens in the factories began sounding, mournful sound.

When she heard the sirens she rose from chair and put bread and cheese on the table, for other than bread and cheese no supper was put out on Fridays. She went upstairs to Mr Craigan to see if he wanted anything but he did not. She hardly noticed him. Now, the sirens having sounded, she was disappointed.

Now also in Mr Dupret's factory the men were being paid week's wages. Every pay envelope had at least £1 less in it as this had been a short week. Mr Gates and Mr Dale came back home silent. Joe was in bad temper because he had less money and because he had been put to work with another man who had more to do than Mr Craigan. Mr Dale was desperate because he had been put onto small work after Craigan's being ill had broken up the gang they worked in, all three of them.

When Mr Gates had finished washing he looked at bread and cheese on the table and spat. Lily said not to spit on the floor but into the grate if he had to spit. He did not listen to what she told him but said you got tired of the women never keeping any money to end of a week, and wasn't he entitled to a hot supper who had worked to fill her mouth. She said it always had been the custom with them to go out to a fish and chip on Friday nights. He said oil they fried the fish in was machine oil. She said particular wasn't he all at once and what about her who had to clean it up when he spat on floor. He said: 'Well, if it's been the custom to go out for a bit of fish Friday nights then it's all along of the same custom that I spit on the floor and spit I do,' he said and spat again.

Mr Dale sat and ate bread and cheese. They had had a short week yet he did not dare to give her less money than he always gave. One day, he thought so to speak, she must remember my goodness, that I would be a good husband to her, bringing the money back regular at end of the week. And if he gave less money than he always gave he did not dare to face her reproaches. He must risk nothing now that might offend Miss Gates. So when Mr Gates' back was turned to the bread and cheese he said here was his money for her housekeeping. Row with her father had made her forget short time they had been working and without saying a word she took it and put it in her dress. She asked Mr Gates what about him? He said here you are and puts down money on the table. She says what, only that much? He says yes and if that isn't enough well she doesn't have any, and snatches it back again.

She said that was half what Mr Craigan had said they should all give. He says well wasn't it a short week and why should he pay for Bert Jones into the movies with money he gave for housekeeping money. Why should he pay for Bert Jones into cinemas at all he says. She began to cry. He mimicked her, he was old, it was terrible the way he did it.

When, after that, in height of their argument Mr Gates hit his daughter she went upstairs to get hat and coat and then left the house. Mr Dale was very angry. He said to Joe to get out of it before the old man heard, Lily he said was gone up now to tell him. Mr Gates did go but he said ever since Craigan had been sick he had felt a new man. He was the girl's father, when she asked for a clout he'd give her one. What business was it of the old man's he said if he had kicked his daughter where it would hurt her most, and that's what he would do next time. He went and, greatly daring, he tried to drink all the money that night he had taken for a week's work, thing he had not done since he was a lad.

Mr Dale went upstairs to Mr Craigan. He thought he would find Lily there but Craigan told him she had not been in after they had come in from work. He was sorry. He had hoped to benefit when he found her womanlike, as he thought, in tears beside Mr Craigan's bed. Or he hoped to make all that might be said about it felt, as she was not one to take being hit quietly and what had happened made him afraid.

*

143

'Joe hit 'er.'

'Joe did?'

'Ah.'

'What did 'e 'it 'er for?'

'Why 'e wouldn't give 'er the money, seeing we've had a short week.'

'Where would 'er be now?' Mr Craigan said.

'I don't know where she would be,' said Mr Dale, 'now you say she's gone outside.'

16

MISS GATES LEFT house, dressed, so quickly that she was before almost the last of Mr Gates could be seen in their street where he went to Tupe and public houses. She walked firmly, quickly. She went to where Mr Jones lodged.

As she clapped the door knocker she thought for first time how he would be now at his evening class. Not used to think at all except about prices of things she was now quickly thinking. When Mrs Johns opened door to her she said with drama, and at once, she was that young lady Mr Bert Jones kept company with and she would leave a note for him if Mrs Johns did not mind. This one said to come in, Bert would be back in two ticks, and would she sit down in the front parlour. Then, as if she wanted to explain asking her into the front parlour, (formal entertaining of so young a girl compared with Mrs Johns) then she said 'You see dear you 'aven't been down our way before 'ave you,' and she says Bert Jones is as son to her in her heart, never having had children of her own. Miss Gates said she would write a letter to him if Mrs Johns wouldn't mind being bothered for paper and ink. This one said wasn't she in a hurry, why he'd only gone down the road to the post office, 'been writing a letter to 'is mum and dad,' said Mrs Johns 'trying to find 'em.' But Lily noticed nothing in this, that he should not be at evening class or that he should be trying to find parents, not even when Mrs Johns went on to say that was why she felt so particular about him, being childless as she was. Lily Gates was now at bow window: ''Ere 'e is, 'e's coming,' cried she, and Mrs Johns left parlour saying to make herself at home please, though she knew the room wasn't up to much! This last Miss Gates did not notice either, indeed she was not noticing anything. This haste seemed indecent to Mrs Johns, and not to bring her manners with her, first time the girl came to his house, this shocked Mrs Johns. She went to front door to tell him not to trouble to come in by the back for Lily was in the front room, and to see what was on his face or if he knew about it whatever it was.

When Mr Jones came in she went back to kitchen where sat Mr Johns. She told him the story and said she gone herself to the front door to see if Bert's face wore any kind of look on it. But no, she says, he doesn't know anything about nothing whatever it is, and when she'd told him who was waiting for him he'd seemed like frightened.

'Time was when I said 'e 'adn't the stuffing in him to go out and shift for 'imself like, but now I seen 'is young lady, that girl could take a man anywheres, men being what they are.'

'That's bad,' said Mr Johns.

'Yes, and that girl's not 'appy at 'ome,' said Mrs Johns. 'I'll lay there's been some trouble at 'er 'ouse and she's come round to tell 'im about it. If I wasn't what I was, but like some I knows on, I'd be listening at that key 'ole this very minute.'

'You think 'e'll go then?'

'I'm afraid for 'im,' said Mrs Johns, 'such a nice lad that 'e is. That's what comes of taking up with foundry people,' she said.

Meanwhile, in other room, Lily was saying like as if everything had been knocked out of her now she was with Mr Jones.

'He struck me!'

''E 'it you? What did 'e hit you with?'

'With 'is fist, yes, I fell down, couldn't help myself 'e 'it out so hard.'

'Striking a woman,' said Mr Jones, 'that's about as low a thing as 'e could do.'

''E's my father you see Bert. Yes 'e's got a right to, one way you look at it. But I can't stay in that 'ouse,' she said and they talked of what they would do. Mr Jones fell more and more silent as this went on, and her temper rose till she said she would see him tomorrow and with that she went. She was afraid she might say something to him about himself which would bring quarrels between them, for now of all times she wanted him for her life.

And now for Mr Jones his position was this: that as it might be foreman had given him a job out of which, if he did it right and it was not easy to do, would come advancement and satisfaction for him.

Foreman set up the job on lathe and stood by then to see if he could do it. Others in the shop looked on from their places, maliciously, some enviously, and others hoped it would come out right for him. So he, Mr Jones, began on first part of what he had to do, and this part was easy for him. With all senses fixed on it yet in a sense he played with the job.

So he completed first stages of what had to be done. He looked at his work and it was right. But this part was not the test. Final, more difficult work on it was coming, foreman began to smile with anticipation at the difficulties that were before him.

If Mr Jones did not want to go on those others watching him, and the foreman, made it into confession of failure to draw back. Also he realized now, what he had not thought of before, that he had indeed begun – bit of metal he was using was scored now, partly used, and if he gave up they might not be able to bring it in for some other job. Also he might never have the chance again and suddenly it seemed so desirable to him that 'I'll have a try,' he said in mind and threw belt of his lathe over into gear.

Now the job, revolving so many turns each second, now it had a stillness more beautiful than when actually it had been still. On the small surface of it was sheen of light still and quiet, for noise of his lathe could not be heard above noise of other lathes working about him. And pace of events bearing on his life quickened so that for two moments their speed had appearance of stillness. Also the foreman and others that were looking on openly by now, had now his appearance and features. He said in mind he had to go on and do the job right. He poised before it, tool in his hand and it might be the sense of power he had and which he felt for the first time, to make waster of that bit of steel or a good job out of it, it might be that kept him still undecided.

Mr Dupret talked with Walters in Mr Bridges' office. He said they had to do something, they could not go on as they were now. If they got into rut of losing money they would never get out of it. He said while he had been down here this last week or two he had seen many more elderly men working than he had thought possible. 'It's not fair on the younger men Walters,' he said, thinking just now like a journalist, 'you can't get away from the fact that younger men work the harder.'

(Walters had been sent for as last resort to deal with Mr Dupret. Bridges now took everything as a joke. But Mr Dupret said constantly in his mind, 'I must work, work.' After Miss Glossop it was most necessary for him to do something tangible violently, and in this Mr Archer, and Tarver also, egged him on.)

Mr Walters saw that no argument would be heard by Mr Dupret and as he was actuated really by a devotion to Dupret's father he forgot about his pride. He thought no great harm would come of this, he would let the boy do it, and then he thought he could not prevent him if he wanted to, and smiled. If he threatened to resign, for instance, probability was his resignation would be accepted. And as all his life he had worked in this business he saw it as his own creation, and did not care to think of that work undone through Tarver's inexperience.

So it was decided that all men within six months of their old age pension (what would it mean, thought Mr Walters, nothing, twelve men at the most) all these would get their cards on Saturday. Mr Bridges had come in by then and smiling he said to make it Wednesday, Wednesday was end of every working week. Mr Dupret said no, tomorrow Saturday, for God's sake do get something done and walked out.

(Mr Archer was in course of being disappointed. Mr Dupret thinking over what had been said, thought afterwards these two had behaved very well and shown a real will to help.)

148

17

LILY STOOD IN hat and coat by kitchen window quickly cutting stairs of bread. When she had stack of these by her she reached to tin of beef that was by the loaf and in stretching she raised head and saw man in garden next theirs digging in his garden. Behind him was line of chimney pots, for next street to theirs in that direction was beneath, hidden by swell of gardens back of their street. This man, then, leant on his spade and was like another chimney pot, dark against dark low clouds in the sky. Here pigeon quickly turned rising in spirals, grey, when clock in the church tower struck the quarter and away, away the pigeon fell from this noise in a diagonal from where church was built and that man who leant on his spade. Like hatchets they came towards Lily, down at her till when they were close to window they stopped, each clapped his wings then flew away slowly all of them, to the left. She had drawn back to full height. Then again she looked at that man and he also had been watching the pigeon. He again began to dig but the clock striking had told her she had time yet and she wondered at him digging in that unfruitful earth and that he was out of work and most likely would be for most of the rest of his days. There he was digging land which was worn out.

She reached to the beef and cut thin slices off it. One slice she put between two stairs of bread and when the sandwiches were all made she wrapped them up into a parcel. She looked once more at man digging and went out into the streets. At a corner some way from their house she waited for Mr Jones.

While she stood there waiting for Bert Jones clock struck the half hour and noise of it came faintly to her from where she had come. Just afterwards the sirens sounded and in Dupret factory. Mr Gates came out of iron foundry with the others and joined in long crowd of other men going out. All were animated at thought of the weekend though many talked still of how that morning nine men had been turned off for age. Laughing, and one man would shout to another ten yards in front of him in the crowd and some boys, separated from each other, threw balls of rolled up paper at each other above heads of these men. Day was dark and white paper balls were thrown above this dark crowd quickly moving to the gate and darkly Mr Gates went with them by side of Mr Tupe. He said his stomach felt like that lathe was working on end of it and he said this day was bitterest he would ever remember, a black day. Mr Tupe did not listen then, he also had got his cards and indeed, from moment that morning when they had been turned off both of them he had no use for Gates any more. By his being suspended he would be short of money so he would have to crawl to Gates now when he wanted a drink (Mr Craigan was said to have money put by), instead of Gates making up to him for his company. Also this had been great shock to him, he had felt secure as Mr Bridges' spy.

Bentley came up outside gate and tried to shake hands with Gates, saying how bad he felt about their being turned off but Mr Gates would have nothing to do with him, his mind was all on himself. Bentley went off with Tupe. One thing only cheered Mr Gates. He had Craigan's cards in his pocket, now he had only to go on living in that house and Craigan would keep him to end of his days. And he would bring the wench to reason, if she married Dale then they were set right till they should die.

As he walked back along streets to Mr Craigan's house he thought how Tupe had made him the goat for all others in public house last night and he thought he was all square with Tupe now, being in the better position. But also he felt hopeless for he saw how he would be always under the dominion of Mr Craigan, and that made him savage with that hang-over he had, and being suspended being on his mind.

When he came into their house he found Dale was before him there. He went into kitchen.

'Where's Lil?' Dale said.

''Ow do I know where she is?' said Mr Gates.

'She ain't laid the dinner,' he said and Gates looked and swore. It was bare except for loaf of bread and the tinned beef so he picked up tinned beef and would have thrown it up chimney with histrionic gesture but he remembered he was now on Craigan's charity. He put it back on table.

'Maybe she's up with the old man,' he said and went to wash.

Mr Dale went upstairs. By time Mr Gates had done washing he calls down from top of the stairs to say she hasn't been up there since half past ten. Carefully putting Mr Craigan's cards in middle of kitchen table Mr Gates went out, bursting to get drunk.

(He had money he had earned from Wednesday to Saturday and still had some of his last Friday's money which he had not been able to drink away all of it.)

Mr Dale went back to Craigan where he lay in bed. He said Lily was gone and Craigan said gone? Mr Dale said yes and she had not laid any dinner for them, hadn't cooked anything. Craigan said he was sorry for that, and this was first time he had ever apologized to Mr Dale, perhaps he could go cut himself some bread and cheese he said. But Mr Dale sat down on chair at side of the bed and Craigan, after looking at his face which was expressionless, began complaining. He said, and lately he had talked more and more, here he lay looking out of his window on the city with nothing but his thoughts by him. When you were old was little else to do but think, people same age as you died and you could not always expect young people to come and talk to you. And somehow, he said, he had lost the taste for Dickens, times were different now to when that man lived – it was funny he said that he should wait till he was this age to grow restless. Then again wireless was no longer what it had been and it got monotonous looking out down on the town hour after hour with days growing longer as they were.

Mr Dale looked past him out of the window and saw the shapes of factories and looked down streets down there below them. He picked out Parker's and out beyond was the Selwyn

151

Motor Co. and over there was Beales and over there was Pullins. Then again picture of Lily running off with Bert Jones came before his mind and he looked down at floor again.

Town beneath them was a deep blue, like the Gulf Stream, with channels which were the roads cutting it up, appearing, being hidden, and they the colour of steel when it has been machined. Above it factory chimneys were built, the nearest rose up almost to level of where they were in bedroom only way away, and others further away came not so high. Rain had fallen ninety minutes before and this wet was now drying off the roofs. But these still glowed with white cold that steel has when it has been machined, and the streets also.

Mr Dale spoke out then. He said maybe she had run off with Bert Jones. But Craigan said why should it bother him her going for a walk with Jones and most likely she had not had dinner ready for them because she had been wild with her father at his clouting her. He said Dale should not worry about things like that, because he was a young man, and to wait till he got to his, Craigan's, age, then was time to worry when was no longer time for anything, when life began to draw away from you.

So Craigan's voice droned on his complaint and Mr Dale thought how much more reason he had to complain and how the old man was losing grip, not to see Lily meant running off with Jones. But Mr Craigan did not want to see and when Dale went off he lay back and looked at the ceiling.

Mr Dale went up to centre of the town, to the Bull Ring and he wandered through markets there and through the Rag Market, joining in the crowds, drifting where they went. Mr Craigan lay on his back in his bed. He did not want to realize, even that he no longer worked at Dupret's (for Mr Dale had told him when first he came in) till turning his head his face rolled over opposite to the window. Sun had come out and showed between two rolls of cloud. Shining on the streets, points of the factory chimneys also caught some of it, and the wet roofs also that were on a path between him and the sun struck out at his eyes with brilliance. Mr Craigan turned his face from it.

*

152

Mr Craigan had gone to work when he was nine and every day he had worked through most of daylight till now, when he was going to get old age pension. So you will hear men who have worked like this talk of monotony of their lives, but when they grow to be old they are more glad to have work and this monotony has grown so great that they have forgotten it. Like on a train which goes through night smoothly and at an even pace – so monotony of noise made by the wheels bumping over joints between the rails becomes rhythm – so this monotony of hours grows to be the habit and regulation on which we grow old. And as women who have had nits in their hair over a long period collapse when these are killed, feeling so badly removal of that violent irritation which has become stimulus for them, so when men who have worked these regular hours are now deprived of work, so, often, their lives come to be like puddles on the beach where tide no longer reaches. But his time being up at Dupret factory woke Mr Craigan. At first, lying in bed after Mr Dale had gone, he was bitter. But when fully he saw that his working days were done he thought it was right he should be discharged, being an old man like he was. He began thinking again about Lily Gates.

When he had lain in bed, when he should have been at work, then rhythm had stopped for him and he had no motive, as rhythm was stopped, to get out of bed. Like as if train had stopped outside a station but now it draws in where he must get out and see to motorbike he rides on from now on. So this woke Mr Craigan, and he saw Lily was indispensable to his being now he had to sit about. Turning head on his pillow he saw shower was gathering over beyond the town and he was pleased. He thought that would drive them in if indeed they were out together.

Miss Gates walked with Mr Jones through streets and she was leading him to field where first he had kissed her.

She stopped him by yard of a monumental sculptor and they looked at tombstones there, both saying nothing and both dark with the white marble. One small stone had 'Reunited' only carved in middle of it and she wondered there should be no name and then wondered how much families got off price of headstones when they let them be shown lettered in the yard. All were recent – to memory of so-and-so 1927 and another, January, 1928.

When we think – it might be flock of pigeons flying in the sky so many things go to make our thought, the number of pigeons, and they don't fly straight. Now one pigeon will fly away from the greater number, now another: sometimes half the flock will follow one, half the other till they join again. So she thought about tombstones and how sculptor made it pay showing so many spoiled ones in his window as it might be. Till she dismissed this from her mind, thinking he would make it pay handsomely and well in any case.

When they came to that field they sat under hedge and he spread mackintosh he was carrying for them to sit on. At once she came to the point. She said they had waited too long . . .

She went on with arguments for their going which we have heard and he. Soon passionate scene was being enacted, as they say. Shower came on, rain welted down on them but neither noticed till at last, as she pushed her face into his yet again, suddenly her arms round his clothes felt his nerves go slack and he said they would go tomorrow.

So, as pigeon when she had watched out of kitchen window had flown diagonally down in a wedge and then recovered themselves, as each one had clapped his wings and gone slowly away, so she drew back from him, her mind unbound, and said to him: 'Why look it's raining.'

It was raining – it's coming on to rain decided Mr Craigan when he noticed it. He thought this would drive them in and he must see her face when first she came in from being with him, if indeed they had been out together.

With great care he got out of bed and went on his knees. He crawled to cupboard where his clothes were. This he had thought out, considering that his legs after three weeks in bed would be too weak to support his body, and he did not want to risk falls. Shapeless hump in his nightshirt he crawled along the floor. He dressed. His fingers trembled. Now and again he doubted if he had been discharged from Dupret factory. He knew he was best moulder in the shop.

With very great care he went downstairs. When he was down he stood at the foot to take breath. Well, he thought, he was down and this evening he would sit in the front room. He opened door into it and like all these front rooms air in it was stagnant but as he looked round for something out of its place, or as it should not be, he was satisfied by it. Was nothing but what was right. Well, he thought, whatever you might say against her the wench kept house clean as a whistle.

She would not keep it so clean if she had some light-witted notion in her head, so he thought and he was wrong for in this case Miss Gates was half ashamed at what she planned and had tried to justify herself in her own mind by doing more on the house than she had done before. But Mr Craigan was growing old, so more easily to be reassured. Still, picking out *Little Dorrit* from the bookshelf, he sat down in his best suit in the best chair and thought of what he would say to her that evening when she came in. Most likely she would be late if she had been with him and that would be added chance of saying something.

He sat. And he was so satisfied at how he had found the house after his time in bed, and above all so satisfied with his legs that had not given way as he went downstairs, as he had feared they would, that he fell into doze over open book.

He slept.

Round about seven Miss Gates came in. Taking off hat and coat she put them on a chair. She pressed palms of hands to her cheeks. Then she began to put out things for supper and to get food out of the cupboard. Her moving about in the next room woke Mr Craigan. He got out of his chair and carefully went to the door. He came in. As he came in she put his cards down which she had just seen on kitchen table. Her face wore guilty look as if he had surprised her prying into his life. She said:

'So you're down.' He was expecting to be first to speak and this put him off his guard but also he had recognized them as his cards which she had been holding, and now what had been uneasy feeling about losing his job was big as a slag heap before him.

'Ah. I'm down.'

She said no more to this and went on getting things out for supper. He was hurt she should take no more notice of his being downstairs, now of all times. But he was not going to talk about his being finished at Dupret's, he was not going to be first to open that. He thought of what to say:

'Maybe that's so much labour wasted o' your'n my gal,' he said, 'maybe they won't come in for supper after there weren't any dinner for 'em.

'Maybe they will, maybe they won't but it'll be there for them, yes, on the kitchen table.'

This was so unlike her that Mr Craigan thought must have been more in her bawl out with her father than Jim had told him. For more you came to think on it more unlikely it was that she thought to run away from him. Where would they go? She hadn't got the banns out or he'd have heard. And his Lil would never stand for rooms, married or not. And there were his cards on the table.

'What made you not put dinner on for 'em?'

She did not answer him.

'Surely,' he said, 'you can't be mopin' like a pup that your dad 'it you?'

He waited to hear her sniff. Time was when anything from him had made her cry. Irritated, he expounded one of the great principles he lived by:

'In this 'ouse,' he said, 'the wage earners must 'ave hot meals every night bar Fridays, if they don't come back midday for it. And on Saturdays there is to be two 'ot meals, and one on Sunday.'

'Well ain't this going to be a 'ot meal?' she said.

He turned and went back into front room. In two minutes he felt he would be complaining to her of his health, instead of taking her to task. Again he said in mind he felt now to be an old man. Yes, and then, he thought, they took first chance they had to deprive you of work. Thinking he would have it out with her Sunday night, not now, not just now, he turned all his anger on to subject of Dupret factory, against his better judgment.

She was so excited anything she handled seemed to be alive. Bert had surprised her, yes, out of all knowledge. Once he'd

156

said he would go he'd let out he'd looked up trains, he'd been so masterful, yes, it was now or never.

Neither Mr Dale nor Gates came in to supper. She waited for them. When still they did not come she put up the hot dish and took some sewing into front room where Mr Craigan sat. He said hadn't they come in and she said no. He said how was that? 'they 'ave no right not to come in when their supper's ready for 'em,' and she was pleased at that and thought her coming in had taken all suspicion from his mind.

She sat in a tumult, trying to keep fingers steady on her sewing.

Mr Dale came in then. She went into the kitchen and brought him his supper. When all had been put before him she said was anything he wanted? but he said no. She said something about bed and went upstairs. Craigan thought it was that she did not want to come face to face with Gates, when he would make her say to Joe she was wrong before all of them. Mr Dale ate and then came into front room where Craigan was. They sat in silence. Then at last Craigan began complaining. Gates being out gave him pretext for his complaint, how Gates was always out and now that they were finished at Dupret's they would not be able to afford boozers. Mr Dale also thought if it weren't for Lily he could go out and see the world now, travelling up and down England. But he would say goodbye to more than that for Lily. Some years of his life had been staked on her, like impaled, he could not think to let them go for nothing, the years and all he had said to her. (He had spoken little or nothing to her all that time.)

Just then Mr Gates came out of public house. He was drunk and in state of righteous indignation. Mr Tupe came out after him. He was in same state as Mr Gates. He said to find her out, to go and give her a good thraipin', ah, to make her give up all these mad thoughts and to marry decent and regular, to a respectable man, to Mr Dale, he said, that everyone in factory respected along with Mr Craigan. This he meant and he was sincere in this for he saw many free drinks in money Joe would get from that old man. But misfortune was following him like a dog for Mr Gates at that moment

157

suddenly became aware to full extent of his own misfortunes come upon him this day. He broke loudly into long recitation of all the oaths known to him. This was more than what policeman on the corner would stand for and this one ran him in, took him to police station, locked Joe up.

18

WHEN LILY GOT to station, bag in hand, she was so tired
with strain of walking through streets seeing in each man or
woman she passed someone who would ask her where she
was going off to with a bag on Sunday morning, and at the
first, leaving home like she had – all those lies and the way she
crept downstairs had so tired her that she could hardly see
who were standing on the platform. Whether were any there
she knew. She said in mind she was in such a state now she
did not mind if there was someone who'd see her. She put bag
down and there, when she looked up again, was Mr Jones. In
his hand was bouquet of tulips.

'Why, what 'ave you got there?'

'I stopped by the cemetery and bought 'em.'

'Whatever did you bring those for?' she said, 'Yes, what
for?' growing hysterical. 'Why I nearly fainted away. Oh Bert,
'ow could you?'

'Why, what's the matter? I thought . . .'

'And me thinkin' 'ow I could make myself less conspicuous,
yes, and then there you are with a great bunch of flowers on
the station platform, why whatever will they think?'

'Think? Oo'll think? What's it matter what they think?'

'You stand where you are while I 'ave a look round your
shoulder.'

Trembling, breathing deeply, she peered round his shoulder
at those who were to travel with them. She stood by shoulder
of the arm below which hung the tulips, his head bent over
hers as she peered round and this movement repeated in her
knee which was bent over heads of the tulips as they hung.
She had on silk stockings today.

She gave up looking at the travellers. She looked now at the tulips.

'Where'll you put them?'

'Where will I put them?' He raised them up till they were upright as they grew.

'Do not!' she said and snatched at his wrist and turned them upside down.

'Oo's being conspicuous now?'

'You go and leave them in the Gentlemen.'

'Leave 'em in the lavatory?'

'Yes, what are you lookin' at me for, we can't take them with us what's come over you, yes, leave 'em in there. Why, at every station the train stopped we'd 'ave porters lookin' in at the window and wondering.'

'Well what's it matter if they do wonder, what do they know?'

'O Bert I do wish I 'adn't come.'

'All right,' he said, 'if that's the way you feel I'll leave 'em there.' He went off to do this. Looking at her shoes she thought in mind why you see they'd telegraph back, telegraphs being free between themselves so to speak, they'd telegraph back along the line seen a young lady with a boy and tulips, something's up evidently, do the police want 'em, like that, yes, O why had he bought them? Look at those people on the platform now watching him going – but they were not watching him, being too disgusted at having to travel on a Sunday to notice anything but themselves.

When he came back without the tulips she breathed easier for it and began to feel for her hair under brim of hat. He was bewildered.

But they were not long without their tulips. Like old stage joke they were brought to them by lavatory attendant. As he gave them to Mr Jones, who did not resist, he said:

'You'm be by the banks of the river Nile, mister,' he said. 'I sees you forget 'em out of the corner of me eye from where I was in the office, and I daint stay longer'n to put me coat on before I was after you.

Miss Gates turned and walked off to end of platform furthest from where other passengers stood.

'You'll 'ave the missus create at you my lad,' he said, 'if you go hon forgetting.' He turned and started back. 'Maybe, again, you'll forget 'erself,' he said, more to himself than to Mr Jones, turning prophetic. Mr Jones went after Miss Gates. Now again tulips hung down bobbing along, thumping against calves of his legs under plum coloured suit he wore. When he got to her she said:

'I come over bad.'

'Sit on the seat then.'

They sat there.

'Give 'em to me dear,' she said then, suddenly reckless, 'I don't care and it's a shame to hold 'em the way you are,' and she took them and rocked them in her arms. He smiled and for a moment had great relief. (For he wanted badly to go to the lavatory and having to leave the tulips had not given him time to have one. Now he could not go back, because of the lavatory attendant. His mind was fixed on possibility of train being corridor train.) At this moment train came in.

As on platform suddenly then she had stopped being afraid to meet someone she knew, now in the compartment, empty but for themselves – and, being Sunday, it was not corridor train – she put tulips on the rack and they did not worry her any more. Now one or two, their heads drooping through meshes of the rack, wobbled at them when train drew out of station.

They sat side by side. Now it was all over she folded eyelids down over her eyes. He thought Derby would be the next stop where there'd be any wait worth calling by the name. Other stations they'd just stop, look out, and be off again.

Tulips, tulips she remembered time of infinite happiness in a cinema when a film was on about tulips. Not about tulips, but tulips came in.

This train stopped at next station. Man came into their compartment. He was working man. They both looked at him, not speaking, and he looked at them and all three turned eyes away from each other's eyes. Then he looked again at Mr Jones and when train started again he said 'Excuse me won' cher but would your name be Pinks?' Mr Jones said no, his name weren't Pinks. This man said Pinks had a double in him

161

then, they might be twin brothers for all you could tell the difference between them. 'Excuse my asking you like that,' he said and he noticed suddenly tulips on rack above his head – (he was sitting opposite to them). He had to lean his head back to see them properly and when he did Lily winked at Mr Jones. Then, bringing his face down to them, again all three turned eyes away from each other's eyes.

Lily looked to see if that man should smile but he did not and she thought it unobservant in him not to smile at meaning of those tulips. Then she was surprised because Mr Jones had winked at this man and jerked with his head to other side of the compartment. Both of them went over there, leaving her by herself, and Bert began whispering to him. Miss Gates did not know what to make of it.

They came into next station and stopped. This man got out. As he got out she heard him say to Mr Jones no, he wouldn't get real chance before Derby. As he went away she plainly heard him say well he hoped it would come out all right for him. She was amazed.

'What'll come out all right for you?' she said and Bert said it was nothing.

'You didn't take 'im into the corner away from me for nothing.'

'I just wanted to ask 'im something.'

'O it's something now is it, instead of being nothin? Ain't I supposed to know.'

'Well no, you ain't, that is . . .'

'Why ain't I supposed to know?'

'There weren't anything in it Lil, it was only I . . . I won't tell yer.'

'You will!'

'I won't.'

But she looked so miserable then that he explained. He went red in the face when she began to laugh at him. 'Ah, but I'm not laughing,' he said and she laughed and discussed ways and means with him. They could find no way out. 'Kiss me Bert,' she said but that was no good as he said he could not, the way he was feeling now. Somehow this delighted her. Their journey, at last, was beginning. Every minute they were

162

further from Birmingham and everything harassing was away behind them now. And they were getting near to Derby.

When train drew into Derby station he ran out of the train and she leant out of the window. When he came back all smiles she opened door for him from where she was on the inside, and once he was in she put hands on his shoulders and pushed him down onto the seat. She sat down across his legs and kissed him.

Then she got down and sat by his side. Train started again. Now at last, she thought in mind, this journey is begun. He kissed her.

But it's not like that. While she expected to be happy she was not and Mr Jones could only think of what they would do when they got to Liverpool.

For as racing pigeon fly in the sky, always they go round above house which provides for them or, if loosed at a distance from that house then they fly straight there, so her thoughts would not point away long from house which had provided for her.

With us it is not only food, as possibly it is for pigeon, but if we are for any length of time among those who love us and whom we love too, then those people become part of ourselves.

As, in Yorkshire, the housewives on a Sunday will go out, in their aprons, carrying a pigeon and throw this one up and it will climb in spirals up in the air, then, when it has reached a sufficient height it will drop down plumb into the apron she holds out for it, so Miss Gates, in her thoughts and when these ever threatened to climb up in air, was always coming bump back again to Mr Craigan. And again, as when we set off impetuously sometimes then all at once we have to stop as suddenly just how little we are rushing off for becomes apparent to us, so, now first excitement was over, for first time it was plain to her just what she was after. She wanted to better herself and she wanted a kid.

At home was Mr Craigan with no more work in him, and her father, and Mr Dale. For some years Mr Dale's life had been part of hers and she thought in mind how she was mostly Mr Dale's life.

We do not want a thing so very badly all the time: just now she didn't, now she came to think on it, particularly want children.

Mr Craigan, what would he do without her? And in his illness, who'd look after him? And wasn't a bird in hand worth two in the bush? Who'd say if they'd be any better off wherever they were going.

Mr Jones jogged at her arm. What was she thinking of, he thought, she was so silent now? Nodding to window, he said: 'Black Country.'

She looked out of window. It was the Black Country. Now series of little hills followed one on the heels of another. Small houses. Lots of smoke.

Train began to slow down. She did hate the country anyway really. You couldn't say anything for this bit but that were lots of towns in it.

Mr Jones then said, wondering still what she could be thinking about.

'Black Country courtship.'

She looked out at once. When she had heard word 'courtship' just now and for some time past heart had tugged at her breathing.

She saw man and girl walking up winding path which had been made up a slag heap. Man was dressed in dark suit with a white stock for collar and wore bowler hat, high crowned. But it was the girl's clothes interested Miss Gates.

Her clothes were so much exactly what she liked that seeing her walking there, it might have been her twin. Not that she could see her face, but it was just what Miss Gates liked in clothes. And she who had been saving to go to Canada where they wore those things you saw in movie pictures, wide hats and blue shirts! Though the older women did dress more ordinary. But O it was so safe and comfortable what that girl was wearing. Temptation clutched at her. She put forefinger to her mouth. She hoped for train to go on. Train stopped. She could not take eyes away from looking at those two, O it was so safe and comfortable to be walking on this slag heap. For where was she going herself? Where would they walk themselves when they got out there. Miss Gates felt she didn't want to walk any place where she hadn't walked before. Or to wear any clothes but what that girl and she liked, and that only where would be others who liked those clothes looking out of train windows or from the roads, wherever they might be.

Looking at her Mr Jones saw she was dreaming. He thought this was a funny way to start off on life's journey, but then women, he thought in mind, were funny things. He relapsed back into his own worries. Fact was his parents had not written to him for three years. They'd be able to put her up for a night or two till he got the licence and he and Lily got married before they went off. Why hadn't Lily liked to get married in Brum. Anyway was no hanky panky about her, it was marry or nothing with her, and that's the way any responsible chap looks at it he thought in mind.

But that was the trouble, suppose he could not find parents. He knew they had changed shop they had managed, and lived over, for another. They had written to say they would write from their new address, but they never had. Suppose the people at the old address did not know where his home had gone. It made you bad to think of it. And his aunt, her who was wife of the lodge-keeper not far from tram terminus, she hadn't had word of them, not since long before he had. He hadn't told Lily, had kept it from her. He'd have to tell her, it wouldn't be right if he didn't tell her. He'd say, just as they were drawing into Liverpool, how he didn't know their address just yet as they'd changed houses and he'd lost letter when they'd written to tell him, but he and she would go to the old address and ask. Made you look foolish when you told all that was on your mind and then there was nothing in it. Yes, that's what he'd say and besides, they'd find them, the people who'd taken over their shop would be bound to know where they'd gone.

Now everything which before had seemed terrible to her, like how if she stayed in Birmingham she would get like all the other women, and Bert the same as all other men, never any better off – only poorer, now this to her put on appearance of the great comfort. But now at the same time she put this from her mind. Wheeling turning her thoughts took on formation ducks have or aeroplanes when they are flying, both of them.

She had come so far. She could not go back. 'Yes, I can't go back now,' she said in mind. Blindly her hand stumbled to get in crook of his arm (for she did not look at him), and crept through like water seeping and round his arm. He turned and kissed her. Then he turned back and watched those two on the slag heap.

They sat. The train was still. She looked at shoes on her feet, he at those two standing on the slag heap above. Her arm was round his arm. She put head on his shoulder, their hair whispered together, both had yellow hair. Train moved on now, smoothly, like water the land glided past outside. He rested his head on hers where it rested on his shoulder. So their heads inclined one to the other, so their breathing fell in one with the other, so they took breath together in one breath as they had been, once before in night. Her arm through his arm felt his body breathe with hers and then her life was deep and strong to her like she couldn't remember feeling before. He did not notice, for he worried yet.

Mr Craigan took headphones off his head.

Perhaps he could have a sleep. He leant back in chair.

He interlocked fingers of his hand across his belly. He crossed his feet. He closed eyes.

No he could not sleep.

He made movement as if to pick up *Little Dorrit* which lay on the table.

No he knew he could not read.

He drew back his hand and picked bits of fluff and cotton off his trousers.

He unbuttoned one more button of his shirt.

His fingers worried then at button of his waistcoat. Then he buttoned that button up again on his shirt, with difficulty, his fingers were swollen.

He thought what was it doing outside? He got up. He went to window and drew aside lace curtains. It looked like rain. He thought if it rained it might drive them in. If they weren't under cover this time.

Coming back to his chair which was by fireplace he saw again photograph of her aunt Ellie. What happened of her. What did her come to?

He knew if he went upstairs he'd know one way or t'other but that's just what he couldn't bring himself to do just now. When a thing's done it's done. When a job's scabbed it's scabbed. He'd talk to her tonight when she came back, her'd know, when she came back. If she did come back.

He sat down again. He looked into grate which had pink paper fan in it. Was clean as a whistle. Her didn't stint her work. If her took on a job you could wager she'd go right through with it, not just play with it. But there, that was it. He blamed himself. He shouldn't have put off bawling her out last night.

He'd see what they were doing now in Berlin. He put headphones on his head. As he did this he remembered again how, out of corner of his eye, he'd seen she go past this door out to the street with something in her hand, might have been a bag. It was no use. He took headphones off his head. He sat for a moment. Then he got up out of chair and made for the stairs. He climbed them. He went into her room.

They sat in railway carriage side by side. Now she had drawn back from him.

He was so sure they would find his parents when they got to Liverpool that he was making plans now of what they would do in Canada, of how well they would do. Again was first day outside, another fine evening. They stopped at station and he let down the window to let country air in onto air they had brought with them from Birmingham, but Lily asked him to close it. He thought how nervous she seemed but then it was only natural in a woman starting on life's journey.

Miss Gates was very nervous. She kept herself by force now, as it might be, from thinking of Mr Craigan. She was now wondering how she could ever happen to be in this railway carriage. Bert seemed like stranger to her, and in these strange stations. And the night air that was coming up, it couldn't be healthy in these parts. But she was frightened, O yes. Night was coming in, she was frightened of this night. In strange house. Not in her own bed. Her underclothes she was now wearing were strange to her, she had made them for this. No, they couldn't have had that window open, it wasn't safe.

Then – he was so confident he brought it out by the way like – he told her how he did not know his parents' address. He told her what they would do.

'Why did you tell me?'

'I 'ad to tell you, love. I wouldn't 'ave been right.'

'But we'll find them shan't we Bert?'

'Of course we will.'

'Then why put ideas into my 'ead. Now I feel frightened,' she said.

He put his arms about her shoulders. He poked his face blindly round in her hair. Strength of his arms about her made her feel safer but all the same her thoughts turned round and round this new thing now, in images. She lay limp against him. She saw them in streets, it getting darker, and they walking and walking till there'd be nowhere they could go. Being with his parents, well it was decent, it wasn't the last word on what they were going to do, she could still then go back to Birmingham, she hadn't burnt her boats as they say. But being alone with him, well there you were. She wondered if she could yet go back, even if his people were in Liverpool. She thought they'd just got to be in Liverpool.

Just then train came into a station and stopped. Mr Jones took arms from off her and looked out of window. Noise of loud voices came from towards them along platform, one man said ''Ere Charley this'd do,' another, 'No Ed let's go farther along.' Terrified Miss Gates watched bit of platform through the window and wooden paling behind it on which was nailed advertisement for Pears Soap. Next that was advertisement for Liverpool paper. Behind road outside was pink house and the sky in bars of red and black. She watched this space most intently. Nine men came into it. They looked into this carriage, she saw one man with white face who had bright green muffler. That was bad luck about, seeing green like that. They went by, she heard 'ere you are – get in 'ere Sid – of course there ain't no bloody corridor one said. Good thing there wasn't a corridor now, even if it had caused a bit of a bother before. Then she remembered these men had been carrying musical instrument cases. She thought what would they have been up to on a Sunday, think, on a Sunday. She did

168

feel so nervous. Porter ran up laughing and said through window to these men how he hoped they were all right. Then he said, walking along by side of train which was now moving, how he did not think the folks down this way would forget them coming for some time yet. The men were all laughing.

This dance band had been hired by vicar to play hymn tunes in church service, for every Sunday now his church was empty and he would do anything to have it full. He had given them tea and while he had gone off to take his evening service and to find the church quite full again, not even standing room, these nine men had come and caught this train back to Liverpool where they lived and worked.

This Sunday had been unusual Sunday for them, by now they were quite worked up. Three sat in racks, six about on the seats. One said to come on and have a tune. As he took saxophone out of case this turned red in sunset light. Pianist said what'll I do? Someone said he could raise his ugly voice. As they got instruments out of the cases they laughed each one to himself, alone, they played a little separately to tune these instruments. Then they all looked at one man. This one did not seem to move yet all at once suddenly they all slipped into playing, all nine of them, pianist played on cushions of the seat, they were one, no more nine of them, one now.

What more could have been wanted to fit in so with Mr Jones' happy feelings? In wonderment he listened. He got up. Forgetting Lily he opened window to listen better to them and hung head out.

'Bert' screamed Miss Gates. She jumped up and pulled at his shoulders.

When he came in again she said: 'whatever were you doing that for? Why a bridge might 'ave come and cut your head off and where would I be then?'

Sharp air of evening rushed in on them. She pulled window up. He sat down and when window was up he drew her down onto his knees. He said had she been scared? He kissed her. But she got down from his knees. She listened to tune they were playing with distrust. She trembled.

As he listened beat of that music, so together, made

169

everything in the world brother to him. As he listened and they played he expanded in his feeling and looking back in his memory for something he might express this by he put arms round Lily. He said:

'In our iron foundry at our place there was a chap used to sing. 'E 'ad a wonderful voice, what you might call a really fine voice, you know love what I mean. Last time I 'eard him sing 'e went on all day. D'you know what it was? 'Is wife 'ad given 'im a son the night before.' He kissed Miss Gates. 'All the chaps used to come round when he sang.'

Again she lay limp in his arms, distraught. Kids, I don't want 'em she cried in mind.

Pianist sang. He was tenor. He sang:

Your eyes are my eyes
My heart looks through

Horror. She looked past Mr Jones' head which was pressing against her head and there was Liverpool beginning. She hated it. Factories. Poor quarters. More and more of them.

She got up and tidied herself by the glass. Her face even frightened her.

So when they got into station and got out she said in mind it was all she could do to walk.

'Aren't you going to take the flowers,' he said laughing.

'What are you talking of?' she said. 'Leave 'em in there for Christ's sake.'

19

WHAT IS A town then, how do I know? What did they do? They went by lamps, lamps, lamps, each one with light and dark strung up on it each with streets these were in. Houses made the streets, people made the houses. People lived in them, thousands millions of lives. Each life dully lived and the life next it, pitched together, walls between built, dully these lives went out onto streets promenaded dullness there. Ugly clothes, people, houses. They went along through these, strangers to it, she did not recognize her own form of ugliness in it.

Thousands of lamps, hundreds of streets, each house had generally a mother and complacent father, procreation, breeding, this was only natural thing there in that miserable thing home, natural to them because it was domesticated. Procreating was like having a dog, in particular spaniels. Fido who I'm so grateful to. Miserable people. Clerks dregs lowest of people these not fat and meat but like bellied fish or schoolmasters, in particular cod.

Sunday is worst day in the world. You can go out Sunday and come back in everything sucked out of you by inquisitiveness in eyes in residential districts, from clerk's fleshlessness. At night they all stay in, most of all Sundays, after a little fiddling walk for the wife to show off clothes after showing them off through a little bit of fiddling church service. Some of them have little jolly card parties with a few jolly fellows. They may be coming walking back from it. But for them, no one about. Getting dark now, each lamp has light and dark to it. By gad didn't know it was so late well better be getting along now or the wife won't have it eh, think

I'm up to some of the old games what well old chap I'll say goodnight now oh I say no I say old man did you see your wife give me a kiss well perhaps it was a good thing you didn't what, Gracie you're the sweetest little woman, with another of course oh, that well dash it all that ever was. Well goodnight and God bless you all – well and my goodness now if he wasn't wiping a little wet wetness out of the corner of his little yellow little eyeballs God bless us.

Or is it the young sweetheart saying goodnight at the gate of the eight by four front garden to the girl chosen for him, her arch as her photographs. And her kiss has lit such a little light in him, like a little flaming candle, he'll warm himself over it all night yes he will. Inside the old people draw up nearer to the fire, out at the garden gate, Mary, when we were young what a glorious thing life was, Mary, glorious youth – but there's life in these old bones yet he said thinking Fido, only Fido wasn't biting.

They had come on tram to outskirts of Liverpool. They were walking in the direction back in now. They looked for address of shop. Mr Jones knew his way. Smell of the sea was at her, forcing itself on her.

They had been on edge of the Residential District. They were coming now to blinded shops. Roads were broader, lighter by a little. Here was dropsical fatness of shopkeepers' paunches, when they got to address they were looking for they knocked one up. Early to bed early to rise this one's motto. In nightshirt he came to window above. He leaned paunch out over window frame, he let his weight sink on it, bulging. If they'd wait two minutes he would get address for them where their parents had moved and in his place at window showed curling papers like bobbins. Whining voice came from inside of that room – 'what is it ma? Ma, ma, who's there ma, what is it?' His wife poked her nose over window frame. Lily saw nose, one eye, curling papers.

'Well now' said fat shopkeeper they met afterwards squirming along in shadows of the street looking for a bit of fun – these courting couples in the doorways y'know, y'know you can see a bit o' fun o' nights – 'well now' he said, 'it's Mulgrave Street you want is it?' He told them, shopkeeper they had knocked up hadn't been able to tell them way to address he had given them and Mr Jones did not know that part of town it was in. Dropsically fat, hatpin little eyes, shopkeeper watched Miss Gates as he told them. Something up here. That gal looked frightened out of her life. But that young chap was up to a bit o' fun. Didn't know how to start with 'er, that's 'ow it looked. Yum yum he felt in huge belly, um yum.

Now first that feeling which had soaked all through about Mr Jones, how everything, everything was wonderful, she was the sweetest girl in the world and wouldn't the old people be glad to see her, now first that feeling ebbed and died in him. He was afraid for her as now they were going into poorer quarter of the town, streets were getting now to be the streets of ports, darkness of waters looked now to be flowing over into these streets. He did not know the way, but he knew they were going towards the docks. He had seen in his mind their coming to that shop and those there telling him to go back the way he had come with Miss Gates, to go back in direction of the Residential District. In his heart picture had warmed him of his bringing Lily to quiet respectable shop in a quiet decent street. He had thought out two ways of turning off her surprise and admiration when she saw so much prosperity. 'It's simple,' was one thing he was going to say, 'it's simple but the old folks knows what's comfortable.' One thing he had always feared, and that was effect his father would have on Miss Gates and now, as they walked further, and the streets were poorer and poorer streets, it was his father he suspected as having thrown his ma's prosperity away.

Ship's siren sounded, wailing, and with a great pang Miss Gates thought a factory buzzer at this time of the night, it couldn't be nightshift at this time of the night, O she did feel afraid. And that man they had asked their way of, his eyes! How dark it was getting! Well she just wouldn't look any more if it only made her shivery, she just wouldn't notice anything more. But it didn't happen often, did it, that all you thought of worst came to pass. But then she thought it wasn't quite so bad, they'd not expected to find them first go off. All the same, these streets! Well, she wouldn't look that's all.

At this time Mr Craigan and Mr Dale sat in kitchen.

'Well I'll tell you, which is more'n she did,' Mr Dale said, 'I'm going off.'

'Yes,' Mr Craigan said in low voice, 'when 'er cooked the Sunday dinner I dain't think she was goin' after. Her even doesn't wait to wash up but off she goes like that.'

'I ain't goin' to stay in this 'ouse, I'm goin'' said Mr Dale.

'What's that?'

'I'm not goin' to stay 'ere when she's gone.'

'Eh?'

'I say I'm not going to stay here, I'm off too.'

'Ah, tonight. What for?'

'I ain't goin' to stay in this 'ouse.'

'Where will you go to?'

'I don't know, I'll find a place.'

'Better you stay the night here Jim.'

'No, I'm goin' off.'

'But what's in your mind, leavin' me like this?'

Mr Dale did not answer.

'First her goes then you goes,' Mr Craigan said, looking away from him.

Mr Dale did not answer.

'Maybe her'll come back tonight,' Mr Craigan said.

'Oh ah, so she takes 'er sleeping things for the afternoon like she 'as.'

Rain kept on falling. A drip made sound like hammer striking on thick piece of iron, light tap, repeating, repeating.

'Where would you go then,' said Mr Craigan, 'if you be goin?'

'I dunno,' said Mr Dale.

'Don't you go. I might come over bad and then who'd be there to see to me.'

Someone knocked on front door.

''Tis 'er,' Mr Craigan said and got up quickly.

Trembling he went out and stopped in front of door and heart in his mouth, holding to the wall – his hands were sweating and dampness on them sucked to it – he said who

174

was it. If it was Lily he would not let her in at first, so he intended. But Mrs Eames answered him and said if Lily had bit of cheese she might borrow. Mr Craigan stood for three minutes then he said no. No.

'No cheese? Not just a little bit?'

'No,' said Mr Craigan.

'Sorry to 'ave troubled you I'm sure,' said Mrs Eames with meaning in her voice, not that she guessed Lily was away at all, only that she knew they kept cheese in their house. She went back in and said to Mr they were bad neighbours, she'd always thought it, how anybody could live with the old man, being as mean as he was, she didn't know. Mr Eames said Joe Gates was locked up for swearing and that would be on old Craigan's mind. Also Craigan had got the sack, along with Joe, for old age. Mrs said if she'd known she wouldn't 'ave gone, why hadn't he told her. 'I wanted a bit of cheese,' he said. 'What a shame on old Craigan,' said Mrs Eames 'that always kept himself so respectable and then his mate goes and gets himself locked up.' 'Well you know what I always did think about 'im,' she said, 'Well now I wouldn't like to say what I think, not now,' she said.

But Mr Dale saw in his mind when he knew it was not her knocking, he saw he could not stay in this house and not see her any more, he could not stay and not see her any more, any more. When he had told Craigan he was going he had not really meant it but waiting to know who was knocking them up had torn only one way at his heart this time. Time was when her movements, it might be her putting plates up on the rack, they had torn all ways at his heart and he hadn't known what way he felt towards her. But now, as formerly he'd wanted to be comforted by a woman for just going on and on every day, every day, now especially he wanted to be comforted for her not coming back. He saw he would get no sympathy in this house. So he went.

Now Mr Craigan raised no objections. He saw Dale really meant to go this time.

So Miss Gates did not look at anything. She just followed Mr Jones.

They went by public house. Man played on instrument, which was kind of xylophone, laid flat in the doorway. As the air sweats on metal so little balls of notes this man made hung on smell of stale beer which was like a slab outside the door. Man playing on this instrument was on his knees, and trunk of his body bent over it, head almost touched ground on other side of this flat instrument. Mr Jones saw position that man was in. He'd never seen one like it. Feeling of uneasiness grew up in him.

They were now in working class streets. Doors stood open. Miss Gates heard voices talking dialect strange to her. But she shut her ears to this, though it gave her slight feeling of comfort. She was so tired with walking. She got more and more blank.

Mr Jones took tighter grip on bag he was carrying (his own he had left at railway station). They were getting into the dockers' quarter. He did not like it. But this was Mulgrave St. And this was no. 439. He knocked on the door. Miss Gates stood, she did not look up. He knocked. Door was opened by man in his shirt sleeves. He was a stranger to Mr Jones. He told them where his parents had gone was a half-mile further on and then they'd shifted from there so he'd heard though he couldn't say where they'd gone. He'd better go there, he said, and the people there might tell him. Miss Gates heard this and did not think at all, except she thought once it would have to finish some time. Mr Jones was frightened now. Man shut door on him and he stood frightened. Street was dark.

Street was dark. Miss Gates felt something in the street looking out, looking out then it was gone. Then it was back again. Where was Bert, had he gone? She looked up quickly but of course he was there. But street was dark. She got much more frightened and was rigid with it for two moments. Again something looked and was gone. And again. She felt no, after looking up to see if Bert was there she wouldn't look up again to see what that was. There it was. She had to look. No she wouldn't. She had to, so she looked. It was searchlight from the lighthouse, it stroked over sky and was gone. With great pang she wondered what that was doing there. Then she decided that was what came from looking up. She would not look up again. They began walking again. She was blank, blank. Again it came along the sky.

Mr Jones watched, watched everything but Lil. He did not like to look at her. He thought of his parents, what could have brought them to this part? He was ashamed. What they would do now he couldn't say. What would come of it if the next address didn't know where they'd gone. What'd he do with Lil.

Once before when their relations one with the other had come to a point, he had seen it like he was setting job up on a lathe, the foreman looking on and others in the shop watching him. Job was difficult, he'd been in two minds to begin or not. Now he was alone, lathe was stopped, he was alone. Job was going wrong. If he went now, and he would never come back, chances were they could work that bit in again for now he thought this ending was like the finish of all what you might call dreams. Anything a bit out of the way and he couldn't do it. He blamed himself. What was the good in trying to better yourself when you couldn't hold a better job. Now if he went on with this bit on the lathe he would hopelessly spoil it. Now, he thought, if he went on with Lily, and his parents weren't there or in a bad way, he couldn't ask her to take on any wife's life in this town, the ordinary kind of life anywhere, when she'd come out to get on in the world. Better she went back to Mr Craigan which had money of his own.

For if he could not find father and mother who then would give them money for their passage. Besides it was like taking Lil on false pretences to take her to this. Smelling of the sea like this street did, it wasn't respectable, apart from the people that lived in it. He was afraid then she might not be able to go on, who had walked so far already this evening. He hardly dared look at her. Dragging a little behind, face turned down towards the ground, he thought she looked all one way, skint. He thought it was no wonder, but then this would be the address

He stopped. Lily stopped. Door of this house was open, man he did not know sat on chair just by it. Mr Jones said in low voice so Lily would not hear, did a man called Jones live here at one time? This man said yes but he and his wife had gone and had left no address. 'Would you be connected with the family?' he said. Mr Jones said 'Yes.' 'Well then,' this man said, he believed there'd been a bit of trouble but he couldn't say for sure and said goodnight to Mr Jones. For looking at Lily he took her for daft, and he decided he did not want to be mixed up in this, for it looked funny to his mind's eye.

Mr Jones said, 'it ain't much further to go now Lil,' and went off again. She followed a little behind. He was so ashamed he did not like to come near her to help her. He only went slower as he was afraid her strength might give up any time now. He thought her blankness he saw to look at her, was her hating him.

He had remembered great tall street which should be near to them to the west. Trams ran down it. He leads her there.

They get there. It is bright with street lamps. He was sure now was nothing but to leave her get home, if he went with her it might all begin again, he might not be able to let her alone. Here they were in this tall street. He stopped by lamp post where trams stopped. She stopped. Then he sees she is crying quietly. He comes close to her and she leans a little on him. He stood so for a bit then he said, 'Lil, here's your bag.' Without thinking, she was all blank, she reached down to pick it up. She looks up to him then. But he was running away down this street. She picked up bag and began to run after him, still not realizing and like obediently, like small children run, in steps, not strides. She put forefinger in her mouth. She could not see distinctly so did not see him turn down alley way. (When he got into dark court at end of this alley he crouches down in a corner beyond cone of light which falls in front of it.) He looks back over his shoulder but she had not seen him turn, she is still trotting. Tear drops off her chin. Then she saw a policeman and no Bert. She stopped. Tram drew up there which was another stopping place for trams. Woman that was there and had seen her face said quickly come in on the tram dear. She got on. Policeman turned away.

20

MR CRAIGAN SAT by bed at their home in Birmingham in which was Miss Gates.

'Dear heart,' he said, 'don't grieve so.'

Sobs tore her.

He put hand over her eyes, her eyes, tears would not come from them. Sobs seemed as though they would split her. 'Quiet, quiet,' he said. Her troubles stood up in her feeling like plinths to her. Sobs in spasms retched through body. Tear ran down by his nose then another, then from under his hand tears came from her eyes. Her body sank into the bed, down. Then she did not retch any more and tears came to her parched mouth and softened lips there and she opened them and sucked tears in. Her tears came more freely and she turned face into the pillow and they made wet patch on this.

Then, as after rain so the sky shines and again birds rise up into sky and turn there with still movements so her sorrow folded wings, so gently crying she sank deeper into the bed and was quieted. He still kept hand over her eyes, but she was quieted.

Sweat poured out from all her body now.

Miss Gates was still sleeping. Mr Craigan coming into room saw mass of her shapeless in the bed. Out of this her hair was like short golden rivers. When he came in she woke up and jumped round in bed.

He was carrying in his two hands – (in his two hands for his one hand would have spilt it, they trembled so, he was old) – he carried cup of tea. Sleep still lay on her, from up on her elbows she watched him. He came up to the bed and looked to see where he would put down the tea. He put the cup on floor. He brought chair up. With difficulty he bent down and put the cup of tea onto chair. She thought when she saw him do this oh not on the chair, not that way, look at him, he would spill it. When he had safely put it down she thought how kind of him, how kind, how kind he was.

Year after year, every day after every day, she had brought him cup of tea in the morning.

She made to get up. He pushed her onto her back again.

'I brought you a cup o' tea.'

'You oughtn't, no, you oughtn't.'

'Lie you back, my wench, you'll stay where you is today.'

'But what about Jim's tea?'

''E's gone.'

'Gone?' Miss Gates said. Mr Craigan did not answer. Oh dear, oh dear but she thought she better not say anything.

'There's Joe,' she said.

''E's gone too.'

'Joe gone too?' She began crying. 'Oh dear, Joe gone too. Was you about then all the time I was away?'

'You drink up that tea.'

She cried. She began drinking tea. She cried. Between catching her breaths she had sip of tea.

'You lie there all today,' he said, 'an' I'll get you a bite to eat. You must be wore out.'

He went downstairs and sat on chair in kitchen. She went to sleep again.

Later when he came up again she was still sleeping. He did not wake her.

Later she woke. He'd said for her to stay in bed, so she'd better stay. She looked at empty tea cup. Then she lay over on her back and looked at ceiling.

She thought now her father would have told everyone she'd gone when he left the house. What had he gone for? All the street would know. But they didn't make no difference to her, she'd behave like she didn't notice them. What they said didn't touch her.

Downstairs Craigan thought it was likely nobody didn't

know. She hadn't mixed much ever with the other women, only thing was Mrs Eames calling round like she had night before last. And as it was Liverpool they'd gone to, so she'd told him when she got in last night, it wasn't likely there'd be anyone knew her in Liverpool. And it was likely Mrs Eames came just by chance. Anyroad she hadn't asked after her. But what had they been up to when they got to Liverpool?

Lily was now thinking she couldn't abide their eyes on her. She couldn't stand the way they'd look at her. No she thought she'd never be able to stand face to face with them, no never, never again, it was awful. Mr Craigan came up. He came into her room. He went over to chair at side of her bed and put the cup and saucer onto mantelpiece, then he sat on the chair.

'Let's 'ave it from start to finish,' he said.

She lay on her back in bed and her face on pillow was away from him so all he could see was her cheek and one side of her nose.

'I don't know,' she said, 'we walked an' walked.'

'Begin at the beginnin',' he said.

'Well I wonder you didn't notice me makin' all those clothes and all, yes, but I didn't think you would. You were only men all of you so I didn't trouble, I just made 'em under your noses. Then goin' out with my bag like that, you'd 've thought you'd 'ave stopped me, but no not a word and there I went with all the street watching me, the eyes nearly dropping out of their 'eads I expect. But it was funny,' Miss Gates said forgetting to be defiant and now getting interested, 'it was funny but I didn't meet no one. Except at the corner of James Road and Hobmore Lane I made sure there was Mrs Ludd but no I didn't meet no one all the way to the station. And there was 'im on the station platform with a bunch of tulips in 'is right 'and, yes. but oh well, well we got into the train and it went off. It was all right for a bit but then 'e 'ad to get out at Derby and then after that I don't know but nothing seemed to go right.'

'Wasn't that train slow,' said Miss Gates continuing after gulping. Now she lay Looking up to the ceiling. She frowned a little. 'And we couldn't get anything to eat. I couldn't eat any dinner that morning only you didn't notice none of you, but I 'ad too much on me mind and we didn't like to nip out of the train to buy something, it might 'ave gone on you see and left one of us behind. O it was slow. Then we went on and on and it got like darker and darker, we was very quiet, and I got frightened. You see it was him bringing them tulips give me a turn at the start and then–' she turned face over away from him again, 'O I did wish I was back 'ere.'

She stopped. He did not say anything. He looked at his slippers. Then she went on:

'Well then, it seemed like hours and hours, and then we got to a little station and there was nine men on the platform, I counted them, and they all got in an' once the train started they began playing, it was a band. On a Sunday! One of them 'ad a green muffler on and soon as I saw it I said to myself there's a bad luck for you. Then after that there was that black that 'ad a green muffler when we was walking, that was in Liverpool. We come to a place in the road where they 'ad arc lamps up. They 'ad a crane there. There was three men right up on it doing somethin' and a great crowd of people below, I was frightened.'

Here again she stopped.

'When we got to Liverpool,' she said, 'it was night time and I knew I wouldn't like the town. But he took me to a posh place on the platform, not just a ordinary tea room and we 'ad a bite to eat there. That kind of put 'eart into me but that's what it was,' she said, 'yes, I 'ad too much heart, I didn't ought to 'ave been there at all. Then we got on a tram an' I didn't like the looks of that town, yes I thought I'll never be happy 'ere and then 'e took me off it, and we went to the first address. You see he didn't know where 'is people lived exactly, they'd changed addresses, O yes it's true, I know that by the way 'e left me. Well then we went from place to place. There was those arc lamps and the black, O it's like a dream and the ships 'ooting, I couldn't make out what that was at first. And then you see we couldn't find them. By the time it came to that I was too tired to take notice, we'd come so far. Then 'e took me to a road where the trams went and I thought we was just going on again but I was crying then and no wonder and there, he said,' said she extemporizing but she believed now he had said it, which he never had, ' "well Lil it's goodbye now" he says, "I ain't no good, you'd better go 'ome." '

Here Miss Gates cried.

'Was that all?' Mr Craigan said.

'Oh I don't know 'ow I found the train. Next thing I remember was being sick, oh dear I didn't sleep at all an' being sick gave me black eyes. And when we got to Birmingham I couldn't come back home by daylight, you see someone might spot me. So I waited about till it was dark. And then I came, when you let me in.'

Here she was so grateful to him for letting her back that she grew small again and her eyes looking at him were warm, adoring. Was silence. She drew out her arm from under bedclothes and laid it over his hands. He opened his hands and her forearm lay in over open palms. Was silence.

'Aye, he weren't much of a man,' he said.

'No grandad he was. Things is different now to what they were in your day.'

'Then you daint pass the night with 'im?'

'No grandad.'

'You would 'ave done when I was a lad.'

'Yes but things is different now you see, yes, they are really. Yes we didn't go for that.'

'What for then?'

'We went to better ourselves, and grandad I do wish we 'adn't gone.'

'You were dreamin'.'

'Yes grandad.'

'Nothin' ever come of dreams like them kind,' he said. 'Nothin' dain't ever come of dreams, I could 'ave told yer but that wouldn't be of no use, you 'ad to find out of yourselves and so you 'ave,' he said.

That morning Mr Craigan went out to buy food for both of them and Mrs Eames took it into her head to call on Miss Gates. Mrs Eames had not seen Lily about for some days. She had met Mr Craigan as he went out that morning to buy food and he had said Lily had a fever when Mrs Eames had asked after her. So Mrs Eames called in, thinking for a moment in her mind men did not know how to care for anybody when they were sick and it would be neighbourly in her to call round.

When Mrs Eames came up Lily of course was frightened with her at first. Then she began to make allusions to Liverpool. These Mrs Eames did not notice. She was too full of her child which was due any time now. She had now in her feeling contempt for this girl which had never had kids. Yet she felt kindly towards her because she thought Lily had man of her own, Mr Jones, and so was to be respected.

Both now had longing to talk of their own affairs. Mrs Eames hung back from speaking openly about herself, (she spoke now in sighs), not openly because she had in her feeling of superiority, Lily because she was frightened. Lily saw in mind Mrs Eames believing she had a kid coming in nine months time and her superiority, which Lily guessed at, was because hers would be bastard and Mrs Eames' legitimate. But she wasn't going to have a child, she'd had no chance to get one, but they'd never believe that, oh dear. When the nine months was up and she still didn't have one they'd only say she was one of the lucky ones or careful ones. But Mrs Eames was not thinking of Miss Gates, even if she were she had no call to be suspicious of her.

Is nothing wonderful in migrating birds but when we see them we become muddled in our feeling, we think it so romantic they should go so far, far. Is nothing wonderful in a woman carrying but Mrs Eames was muddled in her feeling by it. As these birds would go where so where would this child go? She thought this and Lily in her thinking now was simpler still, as she had done wrong so she had to suffer for it, thought she. Both sat intent, not saying anything now. Their relation one with the other was like two separate triangles. Till strain of that silence worked on Miss Gates till she broke it, so scattering her intentness. She said when you had done wrong you had to suffer for it. When she had gone to Liverpool it had been wrong in her to go she said. Mrs Eames said she'd gone to Liverpool? With Bert Jones then? Lily said hadn't she heard, why she'd thought all the street would know but Mrs Eames, with fine return said she'd had all day been gossiping lately but hadn't heard a word.

'Your time's coming?'

'Yes, 'e or she'll be bawling to the world in a day or two now.'

'Then you hadn't 'eard.'

'No, not a breath of it. Then you've come back,' said Mrs Eames. Lily was shocked at so little feeling in Mrs Eames. When she had expanded, had burst into admitting, so her intentness had scattered and now it crystallized in her again.

'Don't nobody know?'

Mrs Eames shook her head, looking now at Lily who was a bit disappointed at first.

'No, nobody,' Mrs Eames said, 'and I don't want to 'ear, not now anyway, I got too much on me mind with 'er coming – 'cos she'll be a gal won't you, love. I'm praying she won't sneeze every time the sun goes out like 'er dad but then,' she said, from charity perhaps, 'I certainly didn't know about you. Don't you worry your 'ead about it dear, stick by old Craigan now you're back. I suppose you 'aven't a kid coming?'

'No.'

'Certain.'

'Yes I know I 'aven't' said Miss Gates with irritation and bitterness.

'Well I'm sure I'm surprised at 'earing what you just told me,' Mrs Eames said and then said the doctors told you against going out too much, she'd better be going back and went back home.

This decided Miss Gates to get up. She felt she must get to work on the house to still her thoughts. She thought we got no one but ourselves, you learn that, yes, you do.

Some days later, when his ten days were up, Mr Gates came back. It was in morning, when Lily had gone out to buy food. Gates came into kitchen and found Mr Craigan in shirt sleeves again and his slippers.

''Ere we am,' said Gates with forced sort of joviality.

'Lil's back, but it makes I laugh to see you,' Mr Craigan

said. 'Aint you a lumpin' sort of young fool. By Christ as if that time fifteen year ago weren't enough, ah and almost to a day, but you go and 'as to get run in again.'

'I'll get back on that copper if it takes me my 'ealth. But did you say Lil was back.'

'You won't,' said Mr Craigan. He groped for something to say to him. But he was old now. He felt he should bawl him out over it. But he could not find anything to say to him except "ah 'er's come back.'

Then quickly he brought out what he had planned.

'I got a job for you.'

'At Pullins?'

'No but you'll go to Prescotts and when they come out at end of the day you'll stop Jim and bring 'im back 'ere to board like 'e used to.'

'What, did 'e go too?'

'Yes an' I'm tellin' yer if you don't bring 'im back then you mightn't come back at all, yes my lad you'll 'ave to find someone else to feed you because I'm through with you.'

'After twenty year.'

'I got no money.

'After twenty year together.'

'I'm finished.'

'Don't talk silly.'

'It's you will look silly.'

'Look 'ere' said Mr Gates – he had discovered this in prison, 'don't you be too sure of that. It'd be a pretty thing for a man like you, not too old oh no, to be living with a young wench that bears no relation to yer.' Mr Gates thought what luck she should be back for as he had thought in prison if only she had been home he would be all right. Now she was back. Things did not often happen that way. Indeed he was all right. Craigan was imprisoned by his love for Lily, he was tied down by it. Miss Gates chained him to her father and this he had never seen. So when Mr Gates spoke out Craigan seemed to shrink and now for ever, except for one time later, his old authority was gone. At last he said weakly.

'You go and get Jim.'

'I ain't got no money,' said Mr Gates with confidence.

Craigan sat silent for a long time then. At last he thought was no help for it.

''Ere's a bob then,' said he. That's what comes of talking he thought in mind, blackmail and all through a word dropped edgeways, many a man 'as lost everything by it. It's a funny kind of world, he said in mind, first you work with a man for twenty years and then he tries to blackmail you. 'And 'e's got me but what do I care,' he said in mind.

As pigeon never fly far from house which provides for them (except when they are taken off then they fly back there), as they might be tied by piece of string to that house, so Mr Craigan's eyes did not leave off from Lily where she went. We are imprisoned by that person whom we love. In the same way as pigeon have an almost irritating knack of homing so our thoughts are coming back. And as the fancier soon forgets to wonder at their sure return so we forget to notice, as we get used to it, which way our thoughts are turned. And which way our eyes.

For now, wherever Miss Gates went there Mr Craigan followed with his eyes. As her hand fell so his eyes dropped, when she got up his eyes rose up to her from where he sat in chair. He was not watching, it was like these pigeons, that flying in a circle always keep that house in sight, so we are imprisoned, with that kind of liberty tied down.

Uncertainty also gripped Mr Craigan, or rather a certainty. He thought when she wasn't many days older, strong hearty wench as her would soon find another man and they would be married this time, she would see to that, he thought. And then what would he do, would they have him? Where would he live?

That was very much, from his position, what Mr Gates was thinking. He thought if Lily didn't marry Dale and married someone else then he was nowhere. A man can't live on the old age pension, 10/- a week won't feed you and keep a roof over you. If you don't sleep under a roof then they put you in prison. He was too old to get another job, nobody would take him in but this house where he was now, he was too old to tramp. Only thing was, he thought, was to prevent her ever marrying again.

So at this first dinner after he had been let out, he made no mention of her having gone away and she did not speak to him of where he had been. He even tried to compliment her and found one to say which he thought good and which also reminded her he was her father. He said it had always gladdened him she was not cleg handed like her mother had been.

Then he thought and later he said why didn't she eat more, she didn't eat enough, not sufficient to feed a pigeon, he said.

Soon he was only thinking how he could stop Mr Dale from coming here to live when he went to ask him back this evening.

21

LATER, THAT EVENING, turned half-past five, he came into yard of Prescott's foundry. In that shop they were casting now and blast in the cupola roared and made air buzz all round him. From being used to this he took no notice but he did move away from where he had stopped from not watching his step. Because he had halted close to three great coffin shaped lumps of metal sunk in the ground. He thought Alf Igginbotham would be in one of those three, other two did it before no one could remember. With Alf the management had tried to make the men cast with molten metal Alf had suicided in, but of course the men didn't have that, they dug his coffin for him here, like had been done for those other two and poured into it the metal he was in. (The great heat there would have utterly done away with him.) There he was in that lump of metal, thirty ton to a penny, but then likely as not he'd risen in dross to top of the metal, and like dross does when you ain't casting, it'd stuck to the sides of the ladle or gone back to the bottom as they poured the metal out. So Alf had got out of it after all, though in different shape to what he'd gone in he thought and Joe chuckled. An' that's about all that man ever was, or any on 'em – dirt, he said in mind.

One or two men that had done pouring their jobs came out through open doorway of the foundry. As they went past Mr Gates they greeted him, as most ironmoulders know one another by sight in Birmingham. Joe asked them if Jim Dale were working in their shop now and they said he was and would be out directly, he was still pouring they said.

Mr Gates looked up to top of the cupola to that intermittent glare which came from it. He thought of all that heat here, where Alf had thrown himself in. He felt cold. He came in closer to that centre of the roar and buzz. More moulders came out, their work done. One asked him had he come for a job as the foreman would be out directly, they was just going to shut off the fan now. After Joe and this man shouted together in midst of the violent vibration they went on, they left Joe. He watched them. He thought all that now is over for me, coming out at night from the shop – and then at that moment the fan was stopped and that roar and buzz stopped. Mr Gates heard voices now inside the foundry. 'Yes,' he said in mind, 'and look at the way they walk, splay-footed bleeders, we always did walk slower an' more awkward than any other trade. Ah there's no more of that for me and God bless me,' he said aloud now, 'aint I glad to get shut on it.'

Then Mr Dale came out.

''Ow do Jim?' said Mr Gates.

'O it's you is it?' Mr Dale said, not stopping.

'Ah, it's I,' said Mr Gates, 'the old man sent me.'

'Well I don't want to 'ave nothing to do with you.'

Mr Dale walked so fast Gates almost trotted to keep up with him.

'Lil's come back Jim.'

Mr Dale stopped. 'Is Lil back?' he said.

'Ah 'er's back and the old man sent me to see if you wouldn't come back to lodge at our 'ouse.'

Mr Dale was silent. Then, 'where 'ave you been then?' he said to gain time.

Gates was afraid Mr Dale meant to come now, yet he was afraid to discourage him lest Craigan hear of it.

'I got pinched,' he said.

'What for?'

'For raising me eyebrow at a copper, beetlebrow.'

'What d'you mean,' said Mr Dale ominously, ''oo's beetlebrow, me or you?'

'Don't you take no notice of what I say, it's me 'ave got to take back 'ome what you says. Are you comin' or is you not?'

'I'm through with you, not on yer life I'm not coming.'

Mr Gates said nothing, delighted.

''Er's made a fool of me,' said Mr Dale. 'I ain't a'coming back and it's all along of you,' he said walking quicker.

''Ow's that Jim?' Gates said, hoping to find out so as to use it afterwards if he could.

'Dirty old waster,' Mr Dale said, having no words again. 'I aint a'coming back, no I never would, not for money.' Then he turned round suddenly. 'Get out before I 'its you,' he said, 'clear off quick, I mightn't know what I was doing in two minutes time.'

Gates almost ran away. When he was at a distance and could see Mr Dale still standing there under lamplight, when he saw Mr Dale was kicking the wall up at side of the footway he contemplated shouting – ''ave a good cry, cry your 'eart out dovvy wovvy,' but then he thought Mr Dale could run faster than him and could catch him. So he went off. But when he was quite half mile off he turned and let off one great laugh, for a gesture.

Monday night and Mr Craigan with Joe Gates went out to public house.

So they began again as they had been before Mr Craigan had fallen ill, Lily gone off, and Gates locked up. You might think they were very different now to what they had been, but they weren't, they were only quieter. Once Mr Craigan had really lost grip he never tried to get it back again, he grew remote in the memory of his young days. For the moment he had all power necessary, the money to feed them, so, once his grip was gone, he did not trouble to try any other authority over them. Gates was only too thankful anything he had said might be forgotten. Lily asked for herself that anything she had done might be forgotten, now she sat very quiet at home through evenings. She was like anyone getting better after long sickness who has taken ship. She cruised across that well charted ocean towards that land from which birds landed on her decks. She thought Mr Jones leaving her like he had done was more and more right and proper, only she was not now interested in him – she was sure she would never set eyes on him again. That land round which she steamed was every inch of it her own, her case still enchanted her as she kept watch on it. And Mr Craigan's youth, where he had to go looking through the lanes to find Lily in her aunt Ellie as they both of them had once been, enchanted him like noise of bells.

In evenings, all three were so thankful to be back together where they had been that they couldn't find two words to say of what they'd done when they were on their own. Perhaps Mr Craigan was sad, but Gates wasn't, nor his daughter. Mr Gates could never be sad. Even now, as he tapped on the bar with florin Craigan had given him, he yelled and laughed. For bar tender, with histrionic gesture, and from some earlier reason with tears of laughing running down his cheeks, snatched up a spade he had hidden there and made to cleave Mr Gates in two if he should go on tapping on the bar.

'That'll land you where I just come from,' said Mr Gates, delighted.

''Ow did you find it in there, Joe?' said bar tender.

'They didn't 'ave no beer in there,' Mr Gates said 'and I said to the superintendent I says I can't understand your not having no beer, water's what lions an' gorillas, rhinocerosses, donkeys, birds, tarts and eagles drinks, but moulders must 'ave beer I said. Two 'alves Reuben, I brought my mate along with me tonight.'

Bar tender called out good evening to Mr Craigan who nodded to him. Craigan sat by himself, his eyes on the floor. Bar tender said to Joe how his mate had aged in the last month or two, since he'd been in last, and Joe said ah, old man had been ill, he said.

Mr Connolly came in then.

'An' what about your team, Aaron,' cried Mr Gates, for Aaron was very keen on football.

'I sent me shilling last Saturday Joe, I dain't go.'

'No, you dain't like to go, that was it, not the way they're playing now. Villa supporter! You ain't no more'n a newspaper supporter shoutin' goal at the page.'

'It am a bleeder,' Mr Connolly said, 'I be frighted to go down to the Villa ground, I can't abide to see 'em beaten, not a grand team like they used to be. Why if it ain't Mr Craigan' he cried, 'and 'ow would you be feelin' now mister?' he said to him.

'It passed Aaron' said Mr Craigan.

'What ailed you?'

'It were a chill I reckon Aaron.'

'Well it am a grand sight to see you back,' Mr Connolly said. His cheerfulness was forced.

'Did they give you the sack too?' said Mr Craigan.

'Ah' Gates said, 'they give us all the sack.'

'It weren't Bridges,' said Mr Craigan, 'who was it then?'

'Why, the young chap of course,' said Mr Gates and Craigan said that he'd give something to know what went on in his mind. Then all three were silent till bar tender took it up, asking if it was true, and Mr Gates took that up, with oaths, and answered him.

Door opened and Tupe stood in doorway, holding door open.

'This way sir, come in sir,' cried he.

Who was it but Mr Bridges?

Gates, when he saw Tupe, came from where he was standing by the bar and sat down by Mr Craigan. Mr Connolly stood by the bar.

''Ow do Aaron,' Tupe said.

Mr Connolly took no notice of him.

Mr Bridges then took no notice of Connolly, remembering he'd had trouble with him and Jones. Bridges was quiet. He was poorly dressed. Then he saw Mr Craigan. He moved across through crowd of people standing about and said ''ow d'you do Craigan?' Mr Craigan nodded merely, though Gates smiled and said 'you'll 'ave a drink with me sir later in the evening.' Mr Bridges was about answering this when up came Tupe with two glasses.

''Ere you are, sir, 'ere we are then,' cried he. 'Well if it ain't Joe.'

'You got someone again as'll pay for you I see,' Mr Craigan said. He hated Tupe so, it made him feel younger. Mr Gates took hint.

'Did 'e sack you as well, strike, what's the world coming to?' said Mr Gates.

Mr Connolly came up to them then and as he passed by Tupe he jogged his arm like accidentally. 'Sorry' said he.

'That's all right mate' Tupe said to him 'accidental is as accidental does.'

'Mate' screamed Mr Gates, 'God strike, did you 'ear that. Why what is 'e but a man what snatches the bread from other people's mouths. And 'e's not content with that, oh no, 'e gets them pinched with provocating them.'

'Now then, now then what's this?' said Mr Bridges.

'Would you still be working for 'em?' said Mr Craigan to Tupe nodding his head back towards factory.

'No.'

Mr Craigan laughed.

Then Craigan looked Bridges in his eyes. Mr Bridges felt like he was being hauled up before someone and when Mr Craigan looked at him he stepped forward like he was the next now. He felt frightened even.

'An' 'ave they sacked you?' Mr Craigan said, his eyes on his eyes.

'Yes,' said Bridges 'ten years at the O.K. gas plant, fifteen years with his father, but 'e 'ad no more use for me more'n a bit of shit on 'is shoe,' he screamed and noticed Craigan was laughing at him. He stopped and drew in breath for long speech he would make now, but Joe Gates was before him.

''Tis 'im, 'tis 'im,' cried Mr Gates, crowing. 'To listen to 'im you'd think 'e was the only one in the world, but there's more'n 'im thrown out 'omeless, penniless, ah, more'n 'im by a million.' He jumped up. Then he began screaming. 'Listen to me,' shrieked he, 'listen to me.'

And Joe was about to draw attention of all the world to Mr Bridges, and bar tender was already saying with appeal Joe, Joe when Craigan got up and butted him in the stomach with his head. Both being so old this looked very silly, Mr Gates more so where he lay trying to get back his wind.

Mr Craigan turned round then and laughed and grinned at Bridges. This one put down his glass of beer and went away out of public house, with Tupe trotting after him. Mr Connolly went and talked in low voice to bar tender. Rest of those in this public house turned round now to each other as if nothing had happened.

Mr Craigan took up glass of beer which Bridges had left half drunk.

'You get this for nowt' he said to Joe who was sitting up now, 'what 'e left won't cost you nothin'. But what d'you want to go and get excited for,' he said 'you'm no better than Tupe and you knows it.'

'It weren't Tupe, it's that Bridges.'

'Well what about 'im?' said Mr Craigan. 'No it was Tupe you was after. Come along back Joe,' Mr Craigan said. When they were outside they looked older still as they walked back slowly.

'To 'ave the coppers come in an take you for disorderly be'aviour, and when you ain't even tight, it's loony, Joe. But you'm be getting quite a lad as you gets older,' said Mr Craigan, strangely pleased.

And now time is passing now.

Mr Craigan had gone to bed again. He did not get out of bed any more, and gave no reason for it.

Joe Gates was always out again now. He could not drink because he had no money. He stood about in high streets, on the corners.

So Miss Gates was alone when she sat down, with housework done, and sewed. Often she sat upstairs with Mr Craigan. After going to that public house he had altogether sunk again into himself. She did not notice he was there as she sat by his bed. She noticed him only when Mrs Eames' new baby cried next door. Walls between their houses were thin and she would wonder then if baby's crying did not worry grandad. When it was angry, which it always seemed to be at first, it raucously cried out with loud rasping shrieks, only Mr Craigan did not seem to take much notice. Then after three weeks or so it began sometimes to be amused and sound would come through the wall of its strange burbling.

When she sat sewing, always thinking of her mistake, then sometimes this baby would be amused. Sound it made then was like the fluttering of the hands, palms out, which Charleston dancers used to make, or like cymbals, in her heart. Because she was young. Because he was old, thought she, that meant nothing to him.

She never went out, why should I go out, she said in mind, who have done so wrong, so all through her days and nights she heard all the noises Mrs Eames' daughter made. Even when now and again the sun showed out she now listened to hear if it would begin to sneeze like Mr Eames did at the sun. Only what she did not like at first was Mrs Eames making noises to her baby, this was too near to her, but gradually, she had feeling of guilt about it, she came to listening for them too.

Sitting at window-sill of her grandad's window she overlooked Birmingham and the sky over it. This was filled with pigeon flocks. Thousands of pigeon wavered there in the sky, and that baby's raucous cry would come to her now and again. So day after day and slowly her feelings began to waver too and make expeditions away from herself, though like on a string. And disturbed her hands at sewing.

Friday evening and Miss Gates was sitting by Mr Craigan's bed. She was sewing. Then getting up on elbow he fetched out purse from under his pillows. He took 6d from it and said for her to go to the movies. She said what alone, and to leave him! He said she'd better go, she was in too much he said. So that night she went.

Saturday morning Gates was sitting downstairs when Mr Connolly called in. He explained he had called to ask after Mr Craigan. Lily heard their voices in kitchen so she came downstairs from where she was, she sat on chair opposite to Mr Connolly and answered his questions for Mr Craigan. She said yes he'd been to bed before, for a week or two, and now he was gone back there again and wouldn't see a doctor. Yes it was silly in him, she said, but it did seem difficult with people as they got older to move them from what they decided on. Yes he'd said so to speak in his mind to himself, yes I won't get up, I'll stay in bed. In a man of his age, she said, you couldn't go and tell him to get up, yes and there might be something the matter with him, really.

'It am a bleeder,' said Mr Connolly, 'an' when 'e went for you in the boozer that night I thought to myself well 'e am back to what 'e were when 'e was secretary of the Club.

196

D'you mind Joe the road 'e used to manage 'em meetings, 'e were a proper business man.'

'Ah,' Mr Gates said.

'Well if you'll excuse me,' said Miss Gates, 'I'll go an' do a bit more as they say.'

'Yes missus, a woman's work am never done,' said Mr Connolly and she said yes that's right and went out. She had glowing feeling over her for someone had called and had been sociable, to sympathize over Mr Craigan's illness.

Connolly and Gates sat. Mr Connolly picked his teeth.

'Would the Villa be at 'ome today Aaron?' Mr Gates said.

'They am.'

'I ain't been down to the Villa ground in years,' Mr Gates said.

Was silence.

'Cardiff they'll 'ave against them today Joe.'

'It'll be glorious football,' Mr Gates said, like he was musing. 'They am the best two teams in the League, and those two with the finest record,' said Mr Connolly.

Was silence.

'Only being out o' work –' said Mr Connolly.

'That's right,' said Mr Gates.

'Without I get a couple o' bob out of the old man,' said Mr Gates, audacious. ''E sent our wench to the movies last night.'

'I dain't mean that Joe,' said Mr Connolly, 'you knows I dain't.'

'That's all right mate, that's all right, no need to worry your 'ead about that. Why, if he 'as the doings well then it's right enough ain't it?'

'I don't like it.'

'What don't you like? Gor blimey, you a Villa supporter and won't take the loan of a bob to see 'em play. I don't know 'ow it is but some'ow today I don't feel I will rest easy till I seen the Villa play.'

Miss Gates came in then. She was thinking in mind what if Mr Connolly should stay to dinner, why she hadn't anything in, nor the money to buy it with. Yes he couldn't stay she thought.

'Lil,' said Mr Gates, 'come 'ere, there's something I wants

to ask yer. Would you reckon the old man'll lend us a couple o' bob to go an' see the Villa play?'

'Well I don't know,' said Miss Gates, serious 'you'd better go an' try 'im.'

'Will you come with me then?'

'All right, I'll come.'

They went upstairs. She went behind her father. She laughed at idea of this, like two kids, her dad and her, going to ask grandad for two shillings.

Mr Craigan gave it to Gates.

Mr Connolly did not stay to dinner and so afterwards, when Gates had gone out to meet him and she had washed up, from relief at Mr Connolly not staying and from the cinema she had been to she laughed and smiled to herself, standing by kitchen window. She thought in feeling of that band, which was playing now in her heart, in the cinema, and even without a pang now she thought of band in that railway train. And at the cinema last night, what a good band that was.

Then Miss Gates remembered words Mr Connolly had spoken this morning. He had been speaking of baby he knew, a little girl – a little wench he called her, she smiled, how nice their old way of talking was she thought in mind, yes, speaking like that made that baby grown up like in time she would be. There was some said 'it' to babies. She laughed, 'the ignorance,' she said in mind. Then she heard Mrs Eames' baby next door and she thought today she'd go and see her. She hadn't been yet but now she would go. She ran upstairs to Mr Craigan and said she was just going to pay a call on Mrs Eames, she'd be back directly she said. Mr Craigan mumbled she didn't want to sit moping indoors, nor nobody wanted her to.

So she ran round to Mrs Eames.

As Gates and Mr Connolly walked more and more men came out from other roads into street they were walking down to the Villa ground. These formed on each side of street long lines of men walking, many of them still in blue overalls. Day was dark, rain had fallen just before and the roadway was still wet with this and the sky dark, so it dully shone like iron, this time, when it has been machined. The lines of men were dark coloured.

Everyone is very quiet. They walk quickly and quietly. It is early yet. These lines of men come to big red building, they pass in quickly through turnstiles onto the stands. Numbers of policemen. Trams with FOOTBALL SPECIAL showing instead of their numbers draw up every moment and more men get out of them. Men stand about selling the Villa News, always being pushed down along the street by weight of the numbers of men coming down on them. Others sell the teams' colours in rosettes. Hawkers are selling sweets and the crowd eddies round the barrows. And here, close to the gates, everyone walks faster. Quickly, quietly they pass in onto the stands through turnstiles.

Gates and Connolly pass in and stand on the mound, they go to behind the goalposts and lean against rail there. Silver band in dark blue overcoats is playing in middle of the green, green pitch. Everything but the grass is black with smoke, only thin blue waves of smoke coming up from the dark crowds already waiting gives any colour, and the pink brick.

Band plays and always, at the gates, men are coming in, lines of them coming in are thicker and thicker. Man with a rattle lets this off suddenly, then suddenly stops. Drunk man begins shouting at this. Now as this mound is filling up you see nothing but faces, lozenges, against black shoulders. As time gets nearer so more rattles are let off, part of the crowd begins singing. The drunk man, who has a great voice, roars and shouts and near him hundreds of faces are turned to look at him. The band packs up, it moves off, then over at further corner the whole vast crowd that begins roaring, the Villa team comes out, then everyone is shouting. On face of the two mounds great swaying, like corn before wind, is made down towards the ground, frantic excitement, Gates wailed and sobbed for now his voice had left him. The Villa, the Villa, come on the Villa. Mr Connolly stood like transfixed with passion and 30,000 people waved and shrieked and swayed and clamoured at eleven men who play the best football in the world. These took no notice of the crowd, no notice.

Mr Craigan lay in bed in his house. He thought in mind. He

thought in mind how he had gone to work when he was eight. He had worked on till no one would give him work. He thought what had he got out of fifty-seven years' work? Nothing. He thought of Lily. He thought what was there now for him? Nothing, nothing. He lay.

But Miss Gates was not that way inclined. Everything, so she felt, was beginning for her again. Niece of Mrs Eames was there, girl of her own age, and they talked about this baby before its mother in rapturous voices. Then this niece had a story about the likeness to parents in their babies. Miss Gates listened with intentness and knew she would be great friends with her.

'And then I said to them,' said niece of Mrs Eames, 'I said, "well you're a wonder you are, there's a child, your own flesh and blood in the manner of speaking, and you can say that, why" I said, "Mrs Pye, how can you, the poor little lamb."'

'Yes I should think so!' said Miss Gates, while Mrs Eames said nothing, being all taken up with her daughter.

'"Well" so she said "you won't never understand dear till you've 'ad one of your own" and I said "maybe I won't but that doesn't stop me from knowing what's right from what's wrong. No," I said, "taking that road won't persuade me from thinking you love the little mite more than," – and then I couldn't think of nothing, you know the words kind of left me, well I said "more than anything, your 'usband or nothing." She 'adn't a word to say to that.'

At that moment Mr Eames came in with his son.

''Ullo mother,' he said and greeted Miss Gates and his niece. Then he said why shouldn't they take baby out between the showers, 'shall us' he said and Miss Gates and her new friend were enthusiastic over this. 'Yes and take the new-old pram for a ride,' said Mrs Eames who took gaily to this idea.

When Mrs Eames was dressed, her coat was plum coloured, and they started out she let Miss Gates push the pram. She went on ahead with husband and left her niece with Lily. Her niece was great talker, she was saying:

'So I said to him "well I declare," I said, "and would you call that a nice way to speak to anyone, with your mouth full

200

and all, what's the world coming to these days" I said, "but some boys are the dirtiest horrible things in the world." That's what I told him,' she said, and now the story was at an end.

'Yes,' Miss Gates said indistinctly. She was torn between listening to what her new friend had to say and at sight of baby blowing bubbles on her mouth. This was moment of utter bliss for her. She was like dazed by it. Then as they walked, Miss Gates exalted, friend of Mr Eames called to him out of alley way which led to his house back of the street. He invited them all in. Lily pushed the pram down alley way and they turned into small yard which was this man's, who was pigeon fancier. Mr Eames was already talking to this man about them, and both whistled to the pigeon. These were strutting on roof of outhouse in the yard. Baby now woke up and began to make waves at the pigeon with its arms and legs. 'Why the little love, look at 'er' cried Mrs Eames.

'You wait a second, missis, and we'll give 'er a closer sight of 'em,' said the pigeon fancier, and hoping to sell a few pigeon to Mr Eames he disappeared into outhouse to fetch some grain.

When he came back he put grain onto hood of the pram and one by one pigeon fluttered off the roof onto hood of this pram. As they did so they fluttered round heads of those people in the yard, who kept heads very still. Then the fancier put grain onto apron of the pram in front of the baby and one pigeon hopped from hood down onto the apron right in front of the baby. This baby made wave with its arm at the pigeon which waddled out of reach. Mrs Eames looked at its fierce red eye and said would it peck at her daughter but fancier said not on your life. Soon all were laughing at way this one pigeon, which alone dared to come onto apron, dodged the baby which laughed and crowed and grabbed at it. Soon also they were bored and went all of them into his house, only Mrs Eames did not go, nor her son who held her skirt. And Lily did not go, but stood like fascinated.

Suddenly with loud raucous cry she rushed at the baby, and with clatter of wings all the pigeon lifted and flew away, she rushed at baby to kiss it. Mrs Eames hid her son's face in her hand, laughing:

'You're too young, that's too old for you' she said.